"Can books be b ... they can—when Lee G ... Child

Monk Mysteries

Mr. Monk Is Cleaned Out

"For a lighthearted, enjoyable whodunnit with an old friend, read *Mr. Monk Is Cleaned Out*—you'll thank me later."—Christina Forsythe, *San Francisco Book Review*

"*Mr. Monk Is Cleaned Out* may well be the finest entry to date in the Mr. Monk series. Lee Goldberg has always kept a firm grasp on exactly who his characters are, and he is able to expertly play them against one another to the best dramatic and comic advantage." —Gumshoe

"Goldberg weaves a tale that is fun, entertaining as hell, and totally satisfying." —*CrimeSpree Magazine*

"Lee Goldberg has become a genius in my book! There was not a bad page in this book; each page is filled with humor, drama, and emotion. . . . Lee Goldberg has taken a serious disorder and turned it into one of the funniest dramas I have ever read—or seen."
—Love Romances & More

"What's left to say about Lee Goldberg's *Monk* books? You already know they're some of the very best TV tie-in books being published today. More than that, they're some of the very best mystery novels being published today, period." —Rough Edges

Mr. Monk in Trouble

"Once again, Goldberg expertly sails along the fine line of character quirks that make Monk so infuriating, and yet so endearing." —Bookgasm

continued . . .

"Lee Goldberg knows that the richest humor veers close to pathos, and that is one reason the novel succeeds so well. This is much more than entertainment."
— Richard S. Wheeler, author of *Snowbound*

Mr. Monk and the Dirty Cop

"Sharp character comedy combines with ingenious and fairly clued puzzle-spinning."
— *Ellery Queen Mystery Magazine*

"You'd be hard-pressed to find another recent work that provides so many hip and humorous moments. *Monk* series fans have another winner here to enjoy."
— Bookgasm

Mr. Monk Is Miserable

"Fans of the show are in for a treat. Goldberg does a stunning job capturing Natalie's voice."
— Roundtable Reviews

"Full of snippets of slapstick humor and Monk's special talents for observation."   — *Library Journal*

Mr. Monk Goes to Germany

"The story flows so smoothly, it's effortless to read."
— *CrimeSpree Magazine*

"A great escape. Lee Goldberg has written another wonderful novel."   — *Futures Mystery Anthology Magazine*

Mr. Monk and the Two Assistants

"Even if you aren't familiar with the TV series *Monk*, this book is too funny to not be read."
— The Weekly Journal (TX)

Mr. Monk in Outer Space

"You say you don't read tie-in novels? You should give the *Monk* books a try and find out what you've been missing. They're funny, they're well-written, they're carefully plotted, and they're poignant." —Bill Crider

Mr. Monk and the Blue Flu

"A must read if you enjoy Monk's mysteries on the tube." —Bookgasm

"A very funny and inventively plotted book."
—*Ellery Queen Mystery Magazine*

Mr. Monk Goes to Hawaii

"An entertaining and ruefully funny diversion that stars one of television's best-loved characters."
—*Honolulu Star-Bulletin*

Mr. Monk Goes to the Firehouse

"The first in a new series is always an occasion to celebrate, but Lee Goldberg's TV adaptations double your pleasure.... *Mr. Monk Goes to the Firehouse* brings everyone's favorite OCD detective to print. Hooray!"
—*Mystery Scene*

"It is laugh-out-loud funny from the get-go. For *Monk* fans, this is a must. Totally enjoyable. Lee Goldberg has expertly captured the nuances of what makes Monk, well, Monk."

—Robin Burcell, author of *The Bone Chamber*

"Lee has found the perfect voice for Natalie's first-person narration—sweet, exhausted, frustrated, exasperated, and sweet again. None of these feelings has to do with the mystery. They're all reactions to Monk's standard behavior as he wars with all the ways nature is trying to kill him. Lee Goldberg has managed to concoct a novel that's as good as any of the *Monk* episodes I've seen on the tube." —Ed Gorman

The Monk Series

MR. MONK
ON THE ROAD

A Novel by
Lee Goldberg

Based on the USA Network television series created by
Andy Breckman

AN OBSIDIAN MYSTERY

OBSIDIAN
Published by New American Library, a division of
Penguin Group (USA) Inc., 375 Hudson Street,
New York, New York 10014, USA
Penguin Group (Canada), 90 Eglinton Avenue East, Suite 700, Toronto,
Ontario M4P 2Y3, Canada (a division of Pearson Penguin Canada Inc.)
Penguin Books Ltd., 80 Strand, London WC2R 0RL, England
Penguin Ireland, 25 St. Stephen's Green, Dublin 2,
Ireland (a division of Penguin Books Ltd.)
Penguin Group (Australia), 250 Camberwell Road, Camberwell, Victoria 3124,
Australia (a division of Pearson Australia Group Pty. Ltd.)
Penguin Books India Pvt. Ltd., 11 Community Centre, Panchsheel Park,
New Delhi - 110 017, India
Penguin Group (NZ), 67 Apollo Drive, Rosedale, North Shore 0632,
New Zealand (a division of Pearson New Zealand Ltd.)
Penguin Books (South Africa) (Pty.) Ltd., 24 Sturdee Avenue,
Rosebank, Johannesburg 2196, South Africa

Penguin Books Ltd., Registered Offices:
80 Strand, London WC2R 0RL, England

Published by Obsidian, an imprint of New American Library, a division of Penguin Group (USA) Inc. Previously published in an Obsidian hardcover edition.

First Obsidian Mass Market Printing, May 2011

AUTHOR'S NOTE AND ACKNOWLEDGMENTS

If you haven't watched the final episode of the TV series *Monk*, and you don't want the solution to the murder of Adrian's wife, Trudy, ruined for you, don't read this book yet, because I am going to give it all away in the first few pages.

This story picks up a few months after the events in my book *Mr. Monk Is Cleaned Out* and the final episodes of *Monk*. But don't worry, you won't be lost if you haven't read the previous Monk books or missed the TV show.

I have invented all of the campgrounds described in this book and took several geographic liberties to serve my creative needs, so any attempt to replicate Monk's road trip, or to see what Ambrose saw out of the window of their motor home, will be frustrating.

I want to thank Martin Onken at Expedition Motor Homes in Calabasas, California, and Jim Royal at Niel's Motor Homes in North Hills, California, for their help.

I also found several books extremely useful, including

The Complete Idiot's Guide to RVing by Brent Peterson, *RVing Basics* by Bill and Jan Moeller, *RV Vacations for Dummies* by Shirley Slater and Harry Basch, *Road Trip USA: Pacific Coast Highway* by Jamie Jensen, *Frommer's Exploring America by RV*, and *Frommer's Best RV & Tent Campgrounds in the U.S.A.* But I am especially indebted to the late William C. Anderson for a key clue, which was inspired by a memorable anecdote he related in his very funny and entertaining book *Please . . . Don't Tailgate the Real Estate.*

And I owe Sean Vitousek a nod for the mathematical equation regarding the stresses on the Bixby Creek Bridge.

As usual, I have to thank my good friend and cardiologist Dr. D. P. Lyle for his advice on all things medical, which I have undoubtedly screwed up, much to his shame and disappointment. And, finally, this book would not have been possible without the continued support of Andy Breckman, Gina Maccoby, Kim Niemi, and Kerry Donovan.

But most of all I thank you for continuing to read these books and letting me know what you think of them. You have truly been my inspiration. I look forward to hearing from you at www.leegoldberg.com.

For Jan Curran, on the road to a better place.

1

Mr. Monk and the Big Changes

Adrian Monk thinks change is fine as long as everything stays the same. That may sound like a contradiction to you, but it's not one in the parallel universe that Monk lives in.

He wants everything in his life to be orderly, consistent, symmetrical, and even numbered. But now he's closer than he's ever been to achieving that balance and he owes it all to change.

It's an irony he'll never appreciate.

That's because irony is a humorous contradiction and Monk doesn't have a sense of humor and can't accept incongruity. I think it has something to do with his obsessive-compulsive disorder, which got so bad after the murder of his wife a decade ago that he was thrown off the San Francisco police force as psychologically unfit. But it's his OCD and his almost supernatural ability to see details the rest of us take for granted that make him such a brilliant detective, so the police ended up hiring him as a homicide consultant.

That's another irony that's lost on him.

Irony seems to go hand in hand with the changes in Monk's life and he had a lot of them happen all at once.

California had been hit hard by the bad economy, and as a result his consultancy job—and with it my employment as his long-suffering assistant—was constantly at risk because of budget cutbacks. Twice he'd been fired because the city couldn't afford, financially or politically, to keep him on the payroll at the same time they were making draconian cuts in jobs and services. It made us both very nervous. Luckily, I was able to use Monk's ability to solve a particularly puzzling, high-profile homicide as leverage to get him a three-year, pay-or-play contract, giving us both some job stability.

Uncertainty is a kind of imbalance, so giving Monk that job security was an important change, even if all I did was keep everything the same for three more years. Sameness was a change he could embrace.

But as much as he wanted everything to remain the same, there was one ever-present thing in his life he was yearning to change.

And it finally happened.

For more than a decade, he'd been haunted by his inability to solve the murder of his wife, Trudy, a reporter killed by a car bomb a few days before Christmas. The solution to her murder eluded him even though he solved every other homicide case that came his way, no matter how puzzling or complex.

He was painfully aware of the cruel contradiction. It was a constant, nagging imbalance at the center of his being that didn't change no matter how even, symmetrical, and orderly he managed to make everything else in his life.

But the cruelest twist was still to come. It turned out

that the solution to Trudy's murder had been right in front of him all along.

On the day of her death, Trudy videotaped a message for him, put the tape in a box, and wrapped it as a Christmas gift, which, after her murder, he couldn't bring himself to open.

It wasn't until he'd been poisoned by an assassin and his own death seemed certain (a false alarm, fortunately) that he finally opened the gift and watched her final message.

In the tape, Trudy revealed that she'd had an affair with a married law professor a few years before she'd met Monk. She'd gotten pregnant, and the baby died in childbirth in the midwife's arms. Now the professor was being appointed as a judge and insisted on meeting Trudy, who agreed to see him even though she felt very uneasy about it. She recorded the video so Monk would know the truth if something terrible happened to her.

Armed with this knowledge, Monk was able to find the evidence that proved that the judge killed both Trudy and the midwife who helped deliver the baby, to keep his adultery and the pregnancy from ever becoming a public scandal. The judge ultimately took his own life rather than face prosecution.

Solving the mystery of Trudy's murder gave Monk the peace and internal sense of balance that he'd lost. It didn't cure his OCD, but it lessened the sadness that he'd carried with him every day since her murder.

Trudy was still gone, but he no longer felt as if he'd failed her, too.

A few days later, he learned that Trudy's baby didn't actually die as she'd been told but had been secretly given up for adoption by the midwife.

Captain Leland Stottlemeyer, Monk's oldest friend and his boss on the SFPD, found the now-adult child.

Her name was Molly Evans and she worked as a movie critic for the *San Francisco Chronicle*.

She was a sweet young lady and gladly welcomed Monk into her life. It gave them both something they were desperate for: a lasting connection with Trudy.

Those weren't the only changes that happened in Monk's world. The people around him also saw their lives change in significant ways.

Captain Stottlemeyer had a whirlwind romance with a magazine reporter and married her, all in the space of a few weeks.

Her name was Trudy. Honestly. I'm not kidding.

And if you think *that's* strange, get this: Lieutenant Randy Disher, Stottlemeyer's right-hand man, abruptly quit the force to become the chief of police in Summit, New Jersey. He didn't take the job just because it was a wonderful opportunity to be the boss and run his own department.

He did it to be close to his girlfriend, a recently divorced woman.

Her name?

Sharona Fleming.

That's right, Randy fell for Monk's former nurse and the woman who preceded me as his assistant.

As for me, some big changes were going on in my life at the same time, too. My daughter, Julie, left home to live in the dorms at UC Berkeley, and I got into a pretty serious relationship with navy lieutenant Steve Albright, who'd been a friend of my late husband, Mitch, a navy pilot who was shot down over Kosovo.

I knew that Steve spent a lot of time at sea in a submarine. But what I *didn't* know was that he had a girl in every port and that he wasn't going to drop them just because he had a girl in this one. So I gave him the heave-ho and was back to being single, and I was feeling it more than ever before now that Julie was gone and I had the house to myself for the first time.

After that flurry of change, though, things settled down and Monk and I went back, more or less, to our old lives. And yet I detected a difference. Monk seemed content in a way that I'd never seen before.

One day in his apartment, as he was cleaning his cans of disinfectant spray with disinfectant wipes, he actually admitted it.

"Have you noticed that things seem a lot more even lately?"

"You're saying that you're happy."

"I'm saying that I don't see as many things that don't match, or that are out of place, or that are oddly numbered."

"Maybe that's because you aren't looking for them as much," I said. "You're easing up."

Monk shook his head. "No, that can't be it. The world is just more even."

"And why do you suppose that is?"

"Because my years of hard work are finally paying off," Monk said.

"With your shrink," I said.

"With humanity," Monk said. "People around here are finally seeing reason."

"And that makes you happy?" I said.

He rolled his shoulders. "It makes me slightly less miserable."

An essential part of Monk's even life was routine. And for us, it was routine to start a day looking at a corpse. A few minutes after that conversation, we got invited to see one.

It's going to sound odd to say this, and I mean no disrespect to the dead, but it felt like all was right with the world.

2

Mr. Monk and the
Seventeen Steps

We weren't going to a murder. We were going to a suicide.

That didn't mean there was anything suspicious about the case. It was standard procedure for the police to investigate unattended deaths, especially those involving a gun.

But Monk wasn't usually called for suicides unless there was a connection to another case he was investigating, or the victim was really high profile, or the situation was just plain weird, like someone killing himself by gorging on Ding Dongs.

None of those scenarios applied this time. In fact, it was so routine that it wasn't even Captain Stottlemeyer who called us. We got the call from an officer at the scene who didn't know any of the details except the victim's name and address in Dogpatch, the industrial flatlands between Potrero Hill and the decaying shipyards of the city's eastern waterfront.

Nelson Derrick, the dead man, lived on Tennessee Street in one of a handful of surviving Victorian-style single-family cottages built on narrow strips of land in the 1880s for the workers who toiled in the factories and shipyards.

Derrick's cottage was built over a garage that would be a tight fit even for a Corolla. The front of the house was covered in gray scalloped shingles, with a heavy, protruding cornice arched like a raised eyebrow over the single front window, as if the cottage disapproved of having to look at the weedy asphalt parking lot across the street. A long, steep staircase spilled from the front door to the ground next to an inconveniently placed electrical pole that bore the scars of numerous violent encounters with car bumpers.

There was a warehouse on one side of the house and a once-identical cottage on the other that some moron had contemporized into blandness by removing the cornices, adding a huge picture window, and smearing every surface with stucco. There was a "For Sale" sign stuck in the neighbor's flower box.

We climbed up the front steps, Monk counting each one as we went, until we reached the young police officer who was manning Derrick's door. He looked barely older than my daughter.

"Seventeen," Monk said.

"I'm twenty-three," the officer said, clearly self-conscious about his boyish appearance.

"I was talking about the number of steps."

"Oh," he said, his cheeks reddening slightly. "Is that significant?"

"Very," Monk said, stopping to examine the door, which had obviously been broken open.

"What does the number of front steps have to do with the man committing suicide?" the officer asked.

"That's like asking me if going completely broke, being diagnosed with inoperable brain cancer, or being dumped by his wife for his best friend might have contributed to a suicidal depression."

Monk studied the doorknob, the dead bolt, and then the splintered doorframe and the chain-bolt assembly that had been torn, screws and all, from its mounting by the force of someone's well-placed boot.

The officer looked totally baffled. "But we're only talking about steps."

"Odd numbered and treacherous, a glaring flaw indicating not only shoddy construction but profound moral decay," Monk said. "Ask yourself this: What kind of man would live in a home like that? Only someone totally beaten down by life, unable to escape from his own bottomless financial and spiritual squalor, would trudge up and down those stairs of despair each day, continually reminding himself of his pitiful, worthless, doomed existence. Putting a gun to his head must have been sweet release."

The officer stared at him. "Because he had seventeen steps?"

"It's a cruel world. And that's on a good day." Monk lowered his head and stepped inside, examining the hardwood floor and colliding with a man in the narrow entry hall who was doing the same thing.

"Oh, pardon me," the man said, flustered and backing out of Monk's way.

The man appeared to be in his forties, with a frosting of gray hair at his temples and the first etching of age around his eyes. He was tall, square jawed, and wearing an impeccably tailored navy blue suit, a white shirt, and a red and white striped tie that made him appear positively presidential, if not for the three bandaged fingertips on his right hand.

That's when Captain Stottlemeyer stepped out of the book-lined study to our left, which was crowded with half a dozen crime scene technicians who blocked our view of the body. Since his marriage, the captain had started to pay attention to his personal appearance. His bushy mustache was neatly trimmed, his hair was combed, and his clothes didn't look as if he'd slept in them.

"Thanks for coming down, Monk," the captain said. "I see you've already met David Hale."

"Actually, we haven't met," Monk said. "We bumped into each other."

It would have been hard not to, even if they weren't both looking at the floor. The entry was very cramped. The three of us were standing so close together that we were practically having a group hug.

"I'm sorry," Hale said. "I guess I'm still dazed from the shock. I can't believe that Nelson did this to himself."

"Didn't you see the steps?" Monk asked.

"Steps?" Hale said. "Are you saying I could have prevented this?"

"No one is blaming you, Mr. Hale," the captain said, then turned to Monk. "Nelson Derrick was a writer, Monk. Mr. Hale was his agent. He's the one who discovered the body."

"Nelson was my client for over ten years. He was a deeply troubled man, frequently depressed, occasionally suicidal, but I really thought he'd gotten past that."

"You just didn't want to see it," Monk said. "Nobody wants to look at seventeen steps. It's probably what drove his neighbor away."

"I just don't get it," Hale said. "Everything was going so well for Nelson lately. In fact, we were supposed to meet this morning for a very important breakfast with an editor to discuss a new book contract. But Nelson didn't show. I called him repeatedly, but there was no answer, so I came right over. I banged on the door for a while, then tried to peek in the window. The curtains were closed, but there was a tiny gap, and I saw him slumped over in his desk chair. I immediately called the paramedics."

Hale gestured down the short hall to the kitchen, where two paramedics sat at the table, sipping coffee out of white disposable foam cups. One of them picked at the rim of his cup and wiggled his leg impatiently.

"They broke down the door," Hale continued. "But it was too late. There was nothing they could do for him."

Monk started toward the kitchen, but Stottlemeyer grabbed him by the arm.

"Let it go, Monk."

"We have to stop him," Monk said, almost pleading.

"There's no law against picking at a cup," Stottlemeyer said.

"There's something called basic human decency," Monk said. "Look, the entire rim is ragged."

"It's only a cup, Monk. No one is getting hurt."

"Would you be saying the same thing if he was clubbing a baby seal?"

"No, I wouldn't, because clubbing baby seals is actually illegal."

"Oh God, now he's poking a hole in the side," Monk said. "He's putting his finger right through."

"He's just impatient and eager to leave," I said. "Look at the way he's wiggling his foot. The faster we're out of here, the sooner he'll get going and stop picking at his cup."

I turned Monk back toward the study.

Stottlemeyer glanced at Hale. "Would you mind sticking around in case we have some more questions?"

"Of course not," Hale said, and shifted his gaze back to the floor.

"You can go outside if you like," Stottlemeyer said. "Just don't stray too far."

Monk looked once more over his shoulder at the paramedic, cocked his head with curiosity, then faced the study. He tugged at his sleeves.

"Okay, let's do this," he said.

Stottlemeyer addressed the forensic techs who crowded the study. "Okay, everybody out, the detectives need the room."

The forensic techs filed past us out the front door, leaving only a female detective and the body.

Nelson Derrick sat with his back to us in a leather desk chair that had been patched with duct tape. He wore a bathrobe, sweatpants, and untied running shoes. His body was draped over an armrest, and the top of his head was blown off. The gun was on the floor, just out of reach of his dangling arm.

There was an old IBM Selectric typewriter with a sheet in the carriage, a neat stack of manuscript pages splattered with blood, an ashtray overflowing with cigarette butts, two cans of Coke, and an open bag of Cheetos.

Monk cocked his head from side to side, held his hands up in front of him, and framed the scene like a movie director as he ventured slowly and deliberately into the room, weaving and dipping and swaying as if he were doing some kind of tai chi.

He went from the body to the bookcases, stopping briefly to examine a few framed photos. The pictures showed a younger Derrick, sitting at his typewriter, his index fingers poised over the keys, a cigarette dangling from his lips, and a bottle of scotch within close reach.

There was something self-conscious about him, as if he knew everything about the staging and his pose was a cliché.

The female detective watched Monk warily as he circled the desk. She wore faded jeans, a V-neck sweater with a white T-shirt underneath, and a leather jacket that looked as if she'd owned it, and abused it, for years. A badge and a holstered gun were clipped to her belt, and she wore them comfortably, like a construction worker carries his tools.

I figured her to be in her mid-thirties. She was pretty, but I could see every one of those years in the hard look in her eyes. She was tall and thin, with short black hair and a lean runner's body. She was probably drop-dead gorgeous when she wanted to be, but I had a feeling that wasn't often. I was willing to bet that she owned one dress, a dozen pairs of jeans, and no skirts at all.

She caught me studying her and met my gaze with a cold stare as Monk worked his way back to the desk.

"This is Lieutenant Amy Devlin," Stottlemeyer said. "She's transferred into homicide from vice, where she spent years doing undercover work, mostly infiltrating the drug trade."

"I'd still be doing it if the judge in my last case had let me testify without showing my face," she said, "but he didn't. That bad decision burned me for good as an undercover agent."

"Vice's loss is our gain. Not many homicide detectives have her experience on the street." Stottlemeyer gestured to Monk, who squatted beside Derrick's body. "This is Adrian Monk, our special consultant, and his assistant, Natalie Teeger."

We shook hands. She had a very firm grip.

"Nice to meet you," I said.

She gave me a cursory nod and directed her attention to Monk, who was under the desk. "I've heard a lot about you."

"I need a pair of gloves," Monk said.

Stottlemeyer reached into his pocket and handed him a pair. We all gathered around Monk as he slipped the gloves on and waited to see what evidence he'd found.

He began tying Derrick's shoelaces.

"Why are you doing that?" Devlin asked.

"Because they are untied."

"But he's not going anywhere."

"What does that have to do with anything?" he replied, tying one set of laces into a perfect bow.

"He's dead," she said, "so there's no point."

"They're untied," Monk said.

"So what?" she said.

"I thought that you said that you spent years working in vice."

"I did."

"Don't you recognize a vice when you see one?"

"The untied laces or you getting freaky with a corpse's feet?"

Monk finished tying the other shoe and looked up at Stottlemeyer. "She has a lot to learn about police work."

The captain stifled a smile. He actually seemed to be enjoying this, even though this was usually the kind of Monkish behavior that gave him a headache. It was certainly giving me one. Marriage obviously had a calming influence on him. I debated whether I should get hitched just so I could be as easygoing as Stottlemeyer appeared to be.

Devlin turned to the captain. "I thought you only called Monk in on the tough cases."

"We haven't had any lately, so I figured this might be a good opportunity for you two to meet and get a feel for how each of you works."

She shrugged. "Seems like a waste of his time to me. It's an obvious suicide."

Monk stood up and tugged at his sleeves again. "What makes it obvious?"

"Well, there's the suicide note in his typewriter, for starters," she said in a patronizing tone of voice as she tipped her head toward the paper in the carriage. "And there's the gun on the floor, just beneath his hand. And there's the fact that the doors and windows were all locked from the inside."

"You left out the front steps," Monk said.

"What about the front steps?" she asked.

"There are seventeen of them. It says a lot about his state of mind."

"It does?"

"Ask the rookie officer out front later and he'll explain it to you," Monk said. "You're going to need to be more observant if you're going to last in this job."

He leaned in to read the suicide note and missed the cold look that she gave him. I peered over his shoulder. The note said:

> *I wrote one good novel ten years ago and I've been ripping it off again and again ever since. I'm not fooling anybody anymore, least of all myself. I should have done this a long time ago and saved everybody a lot of misery.*

"What was the time of death?" Monk asked.

"The ME figures it was around three or four in the morning."

"Nobody heard the gunshot?" I asked.

She looked at me as if I'd belched loudly in the middle of a wedding ceremony.

"There's a parking lot across the street. It's empty

at night. The warehouse next door was unoccupied at that hour, and the neighbor's house is vacant and on the market. There was nobody around to hear it."

"How do you know Derrick wrote the suicide note?" Monk asked.

Devlin sighed with weariness. "Forensics positively matched his fingers to the prints they lifted from the typewriter keys."

"Which fingers?"

"All of them," she said. "We're very thorough. There were no other fingerprints on the typewriter or anywhere else in the room. The victim lived alone."

Monk looked at the note and at the typed manuscript pages, and then turned to Hale, who was circling the entry hall, staring at the floor. And then Monk tilted his head from side to side, as if trying to work out a kink in his neck.

I knew what that meant and so did Stottlemeyer, but when I tried to catch his eye, he pretended not to notice me. I think he was really enjoying himself, which made me wonder what he had against Lieutenant Devlin.

"Satisfied?" Devlin asked Monk.

"Totally."

"I told you it was a simple case."

"It certainly is," Monk said. "A simple case of murder."

3

Mr. Monk Gets Hooked

I noticed that David Hale, out in the entry hall, looked up from the floor at the mention of murder. I didn't blame him. The word is always an attention getter.

Devlin glared at Monk. Apparently, she was not someone who liked being challenged on her conclusions. "Didn't you listen to anything that I just said?"

Monk nodded. "You said the doors and windows were locked from the inside, there was a suicide note, and Derrick's fingerprints were all over the typewriter keys."

"So how can you say it's murder?"

"Because the doors and windows were locked from the inside, there was a suicide note, and Derrick's fingerprints were all over the keys."

Devlin looked like she might pull out her gun and shoot him.

Once again, I noticed Stottlemeyer fighting a grin. I finally realized now the point of the whole exercise. He was exposing her to Monk's unconventional methods on a relatively small case so she'd be prepared when an unusually perplexing murder came along.

Monk dealt with her like he did with everyone. In other words, he was doing things his way without caring about the impact of his actions on others. That was never going to change. So if they were going to have any kind of working relationship together, it would be up to her to learn how to adapt to him. But it wasn't going to be easy. I knew that from long, and painful, personal experience.

She turned to the captain. "He's not making any sense."

"He's saying that everything that points to suicide actually points to murder," Stottlemeyer said, but this time he didn't quite succeed in hiding his amusement, which only irritated her more.

"Yes, I know that, Captain," she said, her voice and face tight. "But I don't see how that's possible."

"Neither do I, Lieutenant. But Monk is going to tell us, and then you and I can feel stupid together."

I didn't think that feeling stupid was something Devlin was going to appreciate.

"Let's take it from the bottom," Monk said. "You told me that Derrick's fingerprints were all over the keyboard. But Derrick was a two-fingered typist."

"How do you know that?" she asked.

"You can see it in the photo on the wall, but, more important, you can tell from the calluses on the tips of his index fingers. Those are the only prints you should have found. Someone wiped the keyboard, typed the note, then put Derrick's fingers on the keys."

"Or maybe Derrick learned over the years how to type with more than just his two fingers," Devlin said.

"Perhaps, but then there's the suicide note itself."

"What's wrong with it?"

"The paragraph indent in the note is two spaces, but if you look at his manuscript, all of the indents are five." Monk pressed the indent key, and it jumped forward five spaces. "Whoever wrote the note used the space bar instead of the indent key."

"That proves nothing," she said. "It still could have been Derrick who wrote it."

"It's obvious that he didn't. There's no mention whatsoever of the seventeen steps."

"What steps?"

"The ones out front," Monk said. "He wouldn't have overlooked mentioning them if he killed himself."

"If that's your reasoning, and I use that term very lightly," she said, "then I'm confident in declaring this case a suicide."

"You forgot about the doors and windows that were locked from the inside," Monk said.

"No, I haven't, but I'm glad you brought it up. It proves that it couldn't have been murder."

"It conclusively proves that it is," Monk said. "If, as you believe, Derrick shot himself in the head at three a.m. and nobody was around to hear the shot, why bother locking all the doors and windows? Who was going to come running inside to save him?"

"He didn't want to take any chances," she said.

"Let me show you something," Monk said and marched out to the entry hall, where David Hale was waiting.

We huddled around Monk as he pointed to the door.

"The doorknob and the sliding chain bolt were locked, you can tell because when the door was kicked open they splintered the door frame or were torn off completely."

"That's not news," Devlin said.

"But the dead bolt wasn't locked. There's no damage to the socket in the doorframe."

We all squinted at the doorframe. He was right.

"I don't see the significance," Devlin said.

"The reason the dead bolt wasn't used was because it was the one lock that the killer couldn't set and still walk out the door," Monk said.

"Neither is the sliding chain bolt," Devlin said.

"He used a hook and a fishing line to lift the chain bolt and slide it into place before closing the door," Monk said. "The only problem was that the line broke when he was dragging the hook back out again."

"If that's true," she said, "where's the hook?"

Monk turned and gestured to Hale. "That's the same question he's been asking himself."

Hale shook as if someone had just thrown a big bucket of ice water on him. "It isn't true. I have no idea what you're talking about."

"Nelson Derrick's head was blown off," Monk said. "It's an incredibly gruesome sight, particularly if the victim is a friend or loved one. Most people wouldn't want to be anywhere near the corpse, but you haven't left the entry hall since the paramedics arrived."

"I was asked to stay," he stammered.

"Nobody told you to remain in the entry hall," Monk said. "You could have stood outside, or waited in the kitchen. But no, you didn't, you remained here, your head down."

"So I didn't have to look at Derrick," Hale said. "Surely you understand. You said yourself that it's extremely difficult for the people who knew him to see him like that. I can see his brain, for God's sake."

"That's not why you've been staring at the floor. You've been desperately looking for the hook."

"That's not true," Hale said. "This whole theory of yours is absurd. There is no hook."

"We'll find it," I said.

"I already have," Monk said, and then abruptly pointed down the hall at the paramedic, who, by this time, had picked his cup into pieces that he'd gathered into a pile on the table. "I expect you to clean up that mess and seek professional help for your problem."

The paramedic looked up, startled. "Are you talking to me?"

"Do you see anyone else in this house desecrating cups?"

"This?" The paramedic gestured to the pile. "It's a disposable cup, not the freakin' Holy Grail."

"Monk," Stottlemeyer said. "Forget the cup. Where's the hook?"

Monk pointed to the paramedic again. "It's right there, dangling from the bottom of the defiler's left shoe. He snagged it as he came through the door."

"You can see that from here?" Devlin asked.

"I saw it earlier when he was wiggling his foot."

Devlin marched down the hall to the kitchen and stood in front of the paramedic. "Let me see your shoes."

The paramedic lifted his feet and she examined the soles.

"I'll be damned," she said and came back toward us.

Stottlemeyer smiled at her. "I think this would be a good time to read Mr. Hale his rights."

"And the paramedic, too," Monk said.

"So there was a hook," Hale said. "That doesn't prove I had anything to do with Nelson's murder."

"The cuts on your fingertips do," Monk said, motioning to his three bandaged fingers. "You sliced yourself with the fishing line trying to free the hook."

Devlin pulled out a pair of handcuffs from behind her back and approached Hale. "Assume the position."

Hale did. And while Devlin read him his rights, Monk went to the kitchen to lecture the paramedic about his responsibility to respect the sanctity of disposable cups, especially while in uniform. I won't inflict the rant on you.

Stottlemeyer glanced at me. "Have you noticed that whenever Monk solves a murder on the spot, half of the time the killer is whoever discovered the body?"

I thought about it for a moment. "Maybe from now on you should arrest that person the moment you arrive at the scene. Half the time you'll be right, your workload will plummet, and your case closure rate will skyrocket."

"And the other half of the time the department and I will be sued for millions of dollars for false arrest," he said.

Devlin led Hale out of the house and down to a squad car. We watched her go.

"I miss Randy," I said.

"So do I," he said.

There was one person in Monk's tiny social circle whose life hadn't changed over the last few months or even in the last few decades. I'm talking about Ambrose Monk, his older brother.

Ambrose still lived in their childhood home in Marin County and had been outside only twice in thirty years, once because his place was set on fire by a neighbor and later because he'd been poisoned by tainted Halloween candy (Monk was somewhat responsible for both of those incidents, but that's another story).

The brothers weren't close, but I had made it my mission to change that. I dragged Monk over the Golden

Gate Bridge to Tewksbury to see Ambrose every couple of months, on major holidays, and on their birthdays, whether Monk liked it or not.

Mostly it was not.

I don't know why. Maybe going back to the house where he grew up brought back memories of all his childhood torments, although they were pretty much the same as his adult torments. Or perhaps Monk was frustrated by his inability to talk Ambrose out of his agoraphobia. Or maybe Monk felt guilty for leaving Ambrose behind to pursue his own life.

It could have been anything. But if Ambrose resented Monk for keeping his distance, he rarely showed it. Ambrose had, after all, intentionally distanced himself from people, so he could hardly blame others for not rushing to see him.

Ambrose supported himself as a writer of technical manuals, encyclopedias, and textbooks, which made him an expert on a myriad of subjects and products, knowledge that he enjoyed demonstrating whenever he talked to people.

He was socially awkward, especially around women, but he was more technologically adept and plugged into what was going on in the world than Monk was.

That's because Ambrose spent so much time on his computer, surfing the Web and getting involved in sites and discussions relating to his many, and often arcane, interests. He had pals all over the world whom he kept in touch with via e-mails and video chatting. Julie and I were among them.

He was also something of a pack rat. He'd saved every piece of mail and every issue of the *San Francisco Chronicle* that had come to the house since the day their father abandoned them when they were children. Ambrose used to say that he was saving it all for their dad.

But even after their father finally returned a few years ago, Ambrose continued to collect the stuff. The mail was carefully organized in dozens of identical file cabinets, and the newspapers were kept in neat stacks lining the living room in rows that Julie used to run through as if she were in one of those garden-hedge mazes.

Ambrose called me as we were leaving Nelson Derrick's house and invited us over for breakfast the next day. Monk wanted to put off the visit until Ambrose's birthday, which was coming that weekend, but Ambrose was insistent.

So early the next morning, as a heavy fog hung over the city, we drove across the Golden Gate to Tewksbury.

4

Mr. Monk Has Breakfast

Tewksbury is known for its small-town feel, the meticulously preserved Victorian- and Craftsman-style homes, and the hundreds of backyard hot tubs (or, as Monk called them, "boiling cauldrons of pestilence") left over from the swinging '70s.

Of course, Monk's childhood home didn't have a hot tub, but Ambrose kept the property in excellent repair inside and out, as if he feared their controlling and pathologically overprotective mother might claw her way out of the grave just to run her white-gloved finger over all the smooth, disinfected, spotless surfaces.

I didn't blame their father for walking out on Mrs. Monk, with her twisted sense of order and cleanliness, but I did resent him for being too gutless to take the boys with him. I held her responsible for their deep psychological problems, all of which she wouldn't have seen as problems at all. From what I could tell, they were perfect reflections of her bizarre worldview.

Ambrose greeted us at the door wearing his usual long-sleeve flannel shirt, sweater vest, and corduroy slacks. He gripped the doorframe as if he was afraid he might get sucked out into the street by explosive decompression if he let go.

"Greetings. It's delightful to see you, Natalie," he said. "And you, too, Adrian. Won't you please come in?"

He stepped back in the entry hall, giving us plenty of leeway and putting lots of distance between himself and the door.

I kissed him on the cheek as I came in and he instantly blushed. "You're looking great, Ambrose."

"He looks exactly the same as the last time we were here," Monk said.

Ambrose ignored Monk and kept his eyes on me. "Thank you, Natalie. This is the newest of my brown sweaters, and it's just back from the dry cleaners. I was very sorry to hear that you broke up with your boyfriend and that you're available again for new romantic opportunities."

"Is that what we are here for?" Monk asked. "So you could slobber all over my assistant?"

Ambrose turned an even darker shade of red. "Do not be grotesque, Adrian. I was merely expressing my sympathies. It's what people do. It's called being considerate. Could you please close the door?"

Monk slammed the door shut.

"Out of curiosity," I said to Ambrose, "who told you about Steven?"

"Julie mentioned it," Ambrose said. "We were IMing the other day."

"You were doing *what*?" Monk said. "She's only nineteen."

"We were instant messaging, Adrian," he said. "It's a technology that people in our modern society use to communicate with one another, using text messages over the telephone or with your computer. I really don't know how you function in the world."

"But I do," Monk said.

"With lots of very attractive help," Ambrose said, smiling at me. "Adrian, could you please lock the door?"

Monk locked, bolted, and chained the door. "What's the big emergency?"

"There isn't one," Ambrose said. "I just wanted to see you."

"Why?"

"Because you are my brother, Adrian."

"I have been for forty years."

"But I haven't seen you in months. You didn't even bother to tell me that you'd solved Trudy's murder. I had to read about that in the newspaper."

Monk lowered his head. "I'm sorry. It was a hectic time."

"Trudy was my sister-in-law, Adrian. And you know I felt somehow responsible for what happened to her because she was running an errand for me the same day that she was killed."

"Her murder wasn't your fault at all."

"Yes, I know that now, but it would have been nice to have heard it from you," he said. "And I wouldn't have known about Molly if it wasn't for Natalie calling me to share the joyous news."

"I didn't think you'd care," Monk said.

"Of course I care. I hope you'll bring her to meet me sometime."

"Why?"

I glared at Monk. How could he be so insensitive? Of course, I knew how, but it didn't make it any easier to take.

"Because she is Trudy's daughter and I loved Trudy,"

Ambrose said. "Maybe not as much as you, but I loved her."

"I'm sorry," Monk said. "Of course you did."

Ambrose waved away the whole subject with his hand. "You can make amends by telling me all about her over waffles."

Monk brightened up immediately. "You made waffles?"

"Mom's recipe. Six squares on every side."

Monk practically swooned. So we went to the kitchen, where breakfast was already laid out. We sat down, and Ambrose supplied each of us with an individual cup of maple syrup and an eyedropper. I had no idea what the eyedroppers were for until I saw the Monks use them. They carefully extracted the syrup from the bowls with their droppers as if they were handling nitroglycerin, and then precisely squirted it out again in equal amounts into each individual waffle square.

While we ate, Monk told Ambrose all about Molly, including such pertinent details as her favorite foods, the exact floor plan of her apartment, her vital stats (age, height, weight, width, eye color, number of fingers and toes, length of her hair, number of freckles on her face, overall symmetry of her features, Social Security number, blood type, location and number of teeth with fillings, length of fingernails), and the make, color, and license plate number of her car.

"She sounds wonderful," Ambrose said.

"She is," Monk said. "And I am still getting to know her. She could be even more wonderful than I already know."

"I am sure she is." Ambrose opened the cupboard, took out a bright red box of cereal, and shook it. "Can I tempt you with a delicious bowl of Major Munch Peanut Crunch?"

Monk looked horrified. "How can you eat *that*?"

"Breakfast is not complete without it," Ambrose said. "I've had it every morning since I was four years old."

I understood Monk's concern. I felt it, too, and not just because Major Munch Peanut Crunch was nothing but a bowl full of candy, sugary yellow squares with a mushy peanut butter center. The big selling point of the cereal was that it "never gets soggy in milk!" Neither would sugar-coated foam pellets, but you wouldn't want to eat them.

The front of the cereal box featured a cartoon illustration of square-jawed Major Munch, flying his spaceship through a universe filled with cosmic peanuts. Big letters inside a starburst promised that each box contained one of four plastic toys based on the cartoon dogs wearing trench coats in the movie *Spy Dogs*.

"You keep up on the news, Ambrose," I said. "Surely you've heard about the salmonella outbreak. It was traced back to tainted peanut paste, and your cereal was among the four hundred products on the recall list."

"Of course I know that," Ambrose said.

"And you're still eating it?" Monk asked in disbelief. He doesn't generally follow the news, unless it involves plagues, epidemics, and natural disasters. He loves those stories because they scare the crap out of him and confirm his general worldview that living is too dangerous to attempt.

In this case, a single peanut processor in Texas that supplied peanut butter and paste for cookies, cereals, candy bars, and ice cream had a leaky roof in its warehouse. As a result, the paste ended up being contaminated by bird and rat feces, causing a salmonella outbreak that had sickened more than five hundred people nationwide and killed two dozen others, most of whom were elderly, were very young, or had weakened immune systems.

The contaminated products had been found in school and hospital cafeterias, retirement homes, grocery stores, and prisons.

As soon as Monk heard the news, he threw out his peanut butter, as well as everything else that was in the pantry. He treated the peanut butter as if it were radio-active without even bothering to check if it was actually on the list of tainted products.

He'd probably never eat anything with peanuts in it again for the rest of his life.

Ambrose shook the box of Major Munch Peanut Crunch. "This is not one of the tainted boxes."

"How can you be sure?" Monk asked.

"This one was produced after the peanut paste was recalled. You can tell from the lot number."

"What if you're wrong?" I said.

"I'm not," Ambrose said. "The cereal produced after the recall includes toys from *Spy Dogs*, a movie that just came out. The tainted boxes contained Peanut Cars, Peanut Rockets, and Peanut Boats from the Major Munch Peanutiverse."

He motioned to a row of plastic toys in a glass china cabinet at the far end of the kitchen. At the end of the bottom row, there were a car, a rocket, and a boat shaped like peanuts.

"Those toys came from the boxes of tainted cereal," Monk said.

"Yes, they did," Ambrose said. "I kept the toys but I threw out the cereal."

"But the cereal was virulent with plague," Monk said.

That wasn't entirely accurate. Salmonella isn't a plague, but he had a good point, so I kept my mouth shut.

"I had to have them, Adrian. I have all the Major Munch toys, going back for decades. I even have an extra set in case of an emergency."

"Like what?" Monk said, practically yelling, his voice cracking with exasperation.

It was odd hearing him ask that. It was the kind of rational question I usually asked him about his irrational behavior. And yet now he was doing the asking. Granted, he was asking another Monk, but it was still gratifying to hear. Maybe Monk was getting a better grip on himself after all.

"I have a list," Ambrose said.

Of course he did. Monk had lists, too. And lists of his lists. He'd promised to will all the lists to me when he died, which I found kind of ironic, since it was those insane lists, and his insistence on living by them, that would provoke me into strangling him one day.

"I can show the list of emergencies to you if you like," Ambrose said.

"Don't bother," Monk said.

"Both sets of toys are perfectly safe."

"You dug them out of a box of sugar-coated plague!"

"Each of the toys was sealed in a plastic bag and I thoroughly disinfected them after I took them out," Ambrose said.

"But you opened the box in the house, releasing plague into the air. We're probably breathing it right now," Monk said. "We'll know because within minutes we'll experience fever, chills, sweats, headaches, weakness, nausea, vomiting, fall into a coma, and die, though I would prefer if death preceded the vomiting."

"You don't have to worry, Adrian. I took the cereal box into the basement. I cleared the room, covered it entirely with plastic sheeting, sealed all the vents, and wore a hazmat suit while I performed the extraction procedure. The room was virtually airtight the entire time."

"You're joking," I said.

Ambrose gave me a look. "I wanted the toys, but I'm not insane. Afterward, I had the tainted cereal and the plastic removed from the house by a hazardous waste company."

I shook my head. "All of that just for three lousy peanut-shaped plastic toys?"

"Yes," Ambrose said and shook the box again. "So now that I've reassured you, how about savoring the delights of Major Munch with me?"

"I'll pass," I said.

"Me, too," Monk said.

"We're stuffed," I said. It was one of the few times Monk and I had ever agreed on anything.

"Very well," Ambrose said, setting the box down. "I'll have my bowl later. So I guess that brings breakfast to a close, and we might as well get to it."

"Get to what?" Monk asked.

"There's a reason I invited you over today."

"You wanted to show me where to find your will in case the Major Munch Peanut Crunch ends up being your last meal."

"I have something special for you." Ambrose led us into the living room.

"I really don't need any more instruction manuals for products that I don't own," Monk said.

"There are many discerning readers who enjoy them for the breezy writing style, the sly wit, and the opportunity to enhance their knowledge of the world," Ambrose said, casting an appreciative glance my way. I think he expected me to raise my hand so Monk was certain whom he was talking about.

But Monk already knew it was me. I was probably

the only person on earth with a collection of signed first-edition owner's manuals.

"Your guide to the Heiko 61B678 Blu-ray DVD Player was positively sublime," I said to Ambrose. "It blew away the instruction manual for my old DVD player."

"The Kinyosonic 47GGT DVD-VHS Combo, correct?" Ambrose said with a nod. "A manual totally devoid of artistry, texture, pacing, and theme. Pure Ed Bevnick, the miserable hack. He's an embarrassment to the industry. But don't get me started."

"Too late now," Monk mumbled.

Ambrose stopped beside a four-foot-high wall of copies of the *San Francisco Chronicle* that stretched to the back of the room and into the last decade.

"Molly has been writing movie reviews for the *Chronicle* for a few years now," Ambrose said. "Two or three a week."

"Her writing is glorious," Monk said. "Did you read her review on Monday of *Bloodbath Daycamp for Girls, Part 7?*"

Ambrose nodded. "She has the potential for a bright future in the technical manual field if she's willing to apply herself. I would gladly be her mentor. I've been waiting for a promising apprentice that I could mold into greatness."

"Is *that* what this is about?" Monk asked.

"No, my profession is a calling, and the desire to follow it has to come from within. This is about you, Adrian. I know how much you'd like to catch up on all of Molly's reviews and that you don't know how to operate a computer. So I want you to have these."

Ambrose placed his hand on the top of the nearest stack of newspapers.

Monk cocked his head. "You're giving me your newspapers?"

"I've been saving them for something special," Ambrose said. "And I think this is it."

Monk cleared his throat and shifted his weight between his feet. "I'm honored, Ambrose. But I think you should keep them."

"But you need them, Adrian. I have every review that Molly has ever written."

"I'll come here to read them."

"It's a long way for you to go," Ambrose said. "You would have to spend a lot of time here."

"That's okay with me," Monk said.

Ambrose smiled. "Maybe we could read them together."

"That would be nice." Monk glanced at his watch. "Oh gosh, would you look at the time. We really should be going. We have work today."

Nobody from the police station had called us to a crime scene, but I wasn't going to argue with him. Monk wasn't very good at handling emotional moments, and this had been a big one.

We thanked Ambrose for a wonderful breakfast and promised him that we'd be back on Saturday to celebrate his birthday.

"That was a very nice gesture on Ambrose's part," I said as we walked out and headed for my car.

Monk nodded. "I wish I could do something for him."

"You just did," I said.

But I could see from the expression on Monk's face that he wasn't satisfied yet.

5

Mr. Monk Meets Lieutenant Devlin Again

As we drove back over the Golden Gate Bridge, I made a call to Captain Stottlemeyer using the Bluetooth unit in my ear, a device that made me look like Lieutenant Uhura did on the bridge of the *Enterprise* in the original *Star Trek*.

When I was a kid, I thought that Lieutenant Uhura's ear thingie, which resembled the end of a honey dipper (and probably was), looked ridiculous and extremely uncomfortable. But now everybody had a device sticking out of their ears. It had become stylish, cool, and even required by law if you wanted to use your phone in your car. Frankly, I was surprised that nobody had come out with a Bluetooth replica of Lieutenant Uhura's *Star Trek* earpiece to bring it all full circle.

It's not the twenty-third century yet, and already it seems to me that almost everything in *Star Trek* has come true, except for starships, dilithium crystals, transporter beams, photon torpedoes, and Klingons, of course.

Every time I used my Bluetooth I was tempted to open the hailing frequencies with the Romulans, or contact the landing party on the planet below, or send an important message back to Star Fleet Command. Calling Stottlemeyer, whom I almost always addressed as "Captain," only added to my Trekker fantasy.

He answered on the first ring.

"Hello, Captain, this is Natalie," I said. "I'm just checking in for Mr. Monk."

"You can let him know that we nailed David Hale."

"He knows that. He was the one who did it."

"Yeah, but now we have irrefutable evidence to back up Monk's deductions. Some of Hale's blood was on the piece of fishing line that was still attached to the hook in the paramedic's shoe. We've made a positive DNA match."

"Have you figured out why Hale killed Derrick?"

"He won't say, but Devlin found out that Derrick was leaving Hale for another agent who'd managed to sell the movie rights to his first novel for six figures. Hale had represented Derrick for decades and felt betrayed."

"That's what Hale gets for being a lousy agent. If the money was out there, Hale should have found it for him."

"I didn't say that Hale was right," the captain said.

Monk leaned toward me. "Ask the captain what's being done about the paramedic."

"We're having him executed this afternoon," Stottlemeyer said, but only I heard him. The mike picked up what Monk was saying, but Monk couldn't hear the captain's replies.

I turned to Monk. "He says that the fire department is taking harsh disciplinary action."

Monk nodded with approval. "I hope the paramedic learns to respect the sanctity of a cup."

"I didn't know that coffee cups were sacred," Stottle-meyer said. "Did you?"

"No, I didn't."

"We have a responsibility to keep things intact," Monk said. "This is especially true for things that can't be reassembled, like foam cups. What the paramedic did was an act of wanton destruction."

"Did you hear that?" I asked Stottlemeyer.

"Consider me enlightened."

"Do you need us for anything, Captain?"

"Nope. It's real slow around here. I just sent Devlin out to pick up a box of Major Munch Peanut Crunch."

"I hope you're not planning on eating the cereal," I said. "You heard about the recall, right?"

"That's why we're picking it up."

"I didn't know the FDA uses cops now to confiscate tainted food."

That got Monk's attention. He sat up real straight and stared at me.

"They do when the Justice Department is preparing to file criminal charges against the company responsible for the salmonella contamination," Captain Stottle-meyer said. "A lot of people have gotten sick and died."

"Tell him I want to help," Monk said.

"The latest victim is a thirty-three-year-old woman, a recovering cancer patient here in San Francisco," Stottlemeyer continued. "She ate a bowl of Major Munch a couple of days ago and died this morning from septice-mia."

"So you're charging the peanut paste maker with ho-micide," I said.

"That's not enough," Monk said. "Anyone who vio-lates basic sanitary standards in food preparation and storage should be prosecuted in The Hague for crimes against humanity."

"I don't think they'll go quite that far," Stottlemeyer said. "Maybe multiple charges of involuntary manslaughter."

"I want in on the investigation," Monk said, yelling into my ear.

"You don't have to yell, Mr. Monk, he can hear you just fine," I said.

"Tell him there is no investigation," Stottlemeyer said. "We're not doing anything but picking up the box as a courtesy to the Justice Department to maintain the chain of evidence."

"What's the local connection?" Monk asked. "Why is Captain Stottlemeyer involved?"

"A woman here died from eating Major Munch Peanut Crunch," I said to him. "Lieutenant Devlin has gone to her house to pick up the cereal box because the Justice Department is prosecuting the manufacturer of the contaminated peanut paste."

"I want in on this," Monk said.

"Tell him there's no mystery here," Stottlemeyer said. "We know who died, we know *how* she died, and we know *who* killed her."

I translated for Monk. "The captain says there's no case for you to investigate."

"Ask him for the address," Monk said. "I want to see the crime scene."

"There's nothing to see," Stottlemeyer yelled.

"You don't have to yell, Captain. You're already talking right into my ear."

"Tell him it's a heinous, disgusting crime that's the direct result of unsanitary conduct," Monk said into my ear. "It's an affront to everything that I believe in and my entire way of life. I need to be part of bringing them down."

Monk had a good point. The company's actions, regardless of whether it was the result of avarice or incompetence, violated every principle he had about order and cleanliness.

"You heard the man," I said to the captain.

He sighed and gave us the address.

Brenda Monroe's home was in the Castro District at the top of Collingwood Street, which was on a hill so steep that the sidewalks were concrete steps.

Her house looked as if it had been built one room at a time, the contractor improvising as he went along rather than working from blueprints. The final result, a mix of architectural styles and materials, reminded me of the Swiss Family Robinson tree house without the tree.

Amy Devlin was leaning against the front grille of her unmarked Mercury Marauder Interceptor as we pulled up behind her car. I'm not sure why the detectives called their cars "unmarked," because they aren't fooling anyone. Her car might as well have had placards on all sides that read "POLICE" in huge letters.

Monk and I got out of my Buick Lucerne, a gift from my parents that also might as well have had placards on all sides, but mine would have read "SENIOR CITIZEN."

Devlin scowled when she saw us. "What the hell are you two doing here?"

"Nice to see you, too, Lieutenant," I said.

"I wanted to see the crime scene," Monk said.

"There is no crime scene," she said. "There's just a box of cereal."

"Stuffed with plague," Monk said. "And the victim ate it in that house."

"This isn't our case. I'm not investigating anything here," Devlin said. "But if I was, I wouldn't need two civilians looking over my shoulder."

"You did yesterday," I said. I couldn't resist the jab. I might have made more effort, though, if she hadn't been so impolite when we arrived.

"I just got off a yearlong undercover assignment. It's been a while since I've had to process a crime scene," she said. "But I would have analyzed the photos, the forensic evidence, the autopsy report, and reached the same conclusions that Monk did in a day or two."

"You're pretty sure of yourself," I said.

"You have to be to survive undercover. Out there, I'm on my own. I'm the only person I can trust."

"I used to think that way," Monk said. "Then I got an assistant. You should get one. They're great."

"I don't need one," she said. "I don't need anybody."

"That lone-wolf attitude won't get you far in homicide," I said.

"I don't need advice on being a cop from a secretary," she said.

I felt my face flush with anger. I didn't have a badge, but I'd been an active part of more than seventy homicide investigations. I had more experience at it than she did. But I decided not to challenge her, mainly because she was already irritable and I was afraid she might beat the crap out of me.

"The point I am trying to make, Lieutenant, is that we're all on the same side trying to accomplish the same goal. We can help one another."

"I heard that you, Monk, and Disher were all pretty chummy," she said. "I'm not chummy."

"Neither am I," Monk said.

"Then we'll get along fine," Devlin said.

I doubted that.

A dented Ford pickup truck with a large rusted camper shell parked behind my car, and a shaggy-haired man in his forties, with a gray-flecked goatee and wire-rimmed glasses, got out and approached us. The man and his car were like a married couple who had grown to resemble each other. They both had a lot of miles on them.

He was wearing a baggy, hooded black fleece, corduroy pants, leather loafers, and a befuddled expression that had probably become permanent years ago.

"I'm Aaron Monroe, Brenda's older brother," he said, offering me his hand since I was the nearest to him. We shook, and I saw that his watch was twenty minutes slow and that the crystal was cracked. "Sorry I'm late. I was at the mortuary making arrangements."

"We understand," I said.

Devlin glowered at me. "I'm Lieutenant Amy Devlin. These two are Adrian Monk and Natalie Teeger. They're civilian consultants to the department. We are very sorry for your loss."

She stressed the word *civilian*, though the emphasis seemed lost on Aaron, who offered his hand to Monk, who pretended not to notice, so he moved on to Devlin, who was next in line.

"Not as sorry as Graylick Foods is going to be," he said, shaking Devlin's hand. "I hope you'll see to that."

"I'm afraid we're just here to pick up the box of cereal," she said. "The Justice Department is handling the case."

"Has the crime scene been secured?" Monk asked.

"I've left everything as it was, if that's what you're asking." Aaron reached into his pocket, took out a key chain festooned with supermarket discount club cards, and led us up the winding brick path to the door. "I haven't been back since the paramedics took my sister to the hospital."

"Tell us what happened," Monk said.

"You really don't have to, Mr. Monroe," Devlin said. "We only need the box."

"I want to. Brenda beat her cancer after months of grueling chemotherapy and radiation, only to be killed by a bowl of Major Munch. It was a cruel joke, and I want the bastards responsible for it to pay dearly."

"Was this the first time your sister ate Major Munch Peanut Crunch?" Monk said.

Devlin glared at Monk, silently mouthing the words *shut up* behind Aaron's back.

"Oh no, it was like comfort food for her. It made her feel better," he said. "But with her weakened immune system, she might as well have been eating rat poison. Some comfort."

"Didn't she know about the nationwide recall of peanut products?" I asked.

The question earned me a nasty glance from Devlin, too.

"I wasn't around, but I'm sure that all of her attention was focused on fighting the Big C and not the current events of the day." Aaron unlocked the front door, and I saw his tongue moving against the inside of his cheek. "But even if she did know about it, the chemo brain really messed with her head."

"Chemo brain?" Monk said.

"You're on a lot of meds when you're on chemo, on top of whatever meds you're taking for your other problems. It scrambles your brain. You don't know up from down."

He ushered us into the house. The interior was every bit as eclectic and disorganized as the exterior. There was no logic to how the house was laid out. Hallways went in every direction, taking us through rooms of all shapes, sizes, and heights, as if the occupants included both giants and leprechauns. There were stairs going up that seemed only to lead to another set of stairs going down. Some floors were carpeted, some were hardwood, others tiled. If Aaron hadn't been there to lead us, it might have taken us hours to find our way to the kitchen on our own.

"I grew up in this house. My parents built it themselves. It was their passion, and they didn't stop until they died."

"It is going to have to be demolished," Monk said.

"Why?" Aaron asked.

"It's an architectural nightmare," Monk said. "Nothing is balanced, nothing is square."

"That was intentional," Aaron said.

"Were your parents insane?" Monk asked as we followed Aaron up and down stairs and along twisted hallways.

"They had eclectic sensibilities."

"In other words, they were delirious," Monk said.

"They saw the house as an ever-changing, residential piece of performance art."

"It's an encyclopedia of building code violations," Monk said.

"I didn't realize you were a building inspector," Devlin said to Monk.

"Building codes are laws," he said. "And that's what we're expected to enforce."

"You aren't a cop," Devlin said. "You aren't expected to enforce anything."

"Maybe tearing the place down is a good idea," Aaron said. "Brenda couldn't bear the idea of anyone else living in the house anyway. She's lived here her whole life and refused to sell after my parents died. But I walked out the door when I turned eighteen, and I've been living on the road ever since, supporting myself as an artist. My home is the highway, my backyard is America."

Monk cocked his head, telegraphing that he was processing some tidbit of information. "So you're saying you live in your car."

"It's a camper," Aaron said. "My home goes where I go, like a turtle in his shell."

"Was it Brenda's illness that brought you back?" I asked.

He shook his head. "Brenda was very independent. She wanted to fight this battle alone. I wasn't invited. But once she beat the cancer, she finally relented and let me come down to see her. I guess she figured the worst was over. Three days ago I walked in and found her on the floor in the bathroom. I could tell that she'd been very sick. I'll spare you the ugly details."

"You can spare us all the details and save them for the Justice Department investigator," Devlin said, putting on a pair of gloves. "We don't want to waste your time or cause you any more pain. We'll just take the cereal and go."

The kitchen smelled like death even though there was no corpse in the room. The stench came from the carton of milk that had been left on the kitchen table, along with a bowl of cereal that looked like a Chia Pet, a glass of orange juice that resembled a large urine sample, a toasted bagel slathered with a layer of fungus, and a salt-shaker-size, molded-plastic toy dog wearing a trench coat and fedora.

The sink was full of dirty dishes and cutlery, flies buzzing over everything, giving the kitchen an almost electric hum.

"It looks like she got sick immediately after she had breakfast," I said.

"I might get sick right now," Monk said, surveying the scene.

Monk covered his nose and mouth with a handkerchief and stepped closer to the table, cocking his head as he viewed it from different angles. I didn't want to get near the table, so I stayed where I was, a few steps away from the sink, where Aaron stood behind me.

"The incubation period for *Salmonella* bacilli is six to thirty-six hours," Monk said. "She might have been eating her second or third breakfast of contaminated cereal before she was stricken with severe abdominal distress. She probably didn't realize it was the cereal that was making her sick, so she kept eating it. It was her comfort food, after all."

"I'm sorry about the mess," Aaron said. "Like I said before, I haven't been back to clean up since Brenda got sick. I've been spending all my time at the hospital."

"That's totally understandable." Devlin took a large evidence bag from her jacket pocket and placed the cereal box inside of it.

"But there's so much that isn't," Monk said, rolling his shoulders.

"We're done here," she said, ignoring his comment.

"Have you confirmed the lot number on the box matches the list of recalled cereals?" Monk asked.

Devlin sighed, took her notebook out of her pocket, glanced at a page, then looked at the box top of the cereal. "Yes, it does. But the FDA lab will compare the DNA of the bacteria in the cereal to the DNA of the bacteria that invaded her bloodstream to confirm the connection to her death."

"It was murder," Monk said.

Aaron nodded. "That's exactly how I feel."

"You should," Monk said. "You killed her."

6

Mr. Monk and the Dirty Knife

Monk's comment did not go over well with Lieutenant Amy Devlin and Aaron Monroe. It didn't bother me any. I was used to Monk accusing people of murder seemingly without any basis at all for his charges. I also had the benefit of knowing that he didn't make the accusation unless he knew he was right.

And he always was, at least about homicides.

So I wasn't shocked or offended, and I could afford to be patient, knowing from experience that he'd eventually get around to regaling us with the evidence.

But Devlin was new to this and Aaron was a murderer, so, as I said, neither of them was happy with Monk.

Aaron stared at him in disbelief. "What did you just say to me?"

"I said you murdered your sister," Monk said.

Aaron shifted his gaze to Devlin. "Who is this crazy son of a bitch? The cereal killed her. The doctors will tell you that."

"I apologize for Monk, Mr. Monroe," Devlin said. "He shouldn't even be here."

Monk addressed himself to Aaron, as if Devlin hadn't even spoken.

"Here's what happened. You were counting on your sister dying of cancer but, much to your disappointment, she survived. But then you heard about the Major Munch recall and managed to snag a box of the tainted cereal before it was pulled off the shelves. You came down to San Francisco, snuck into the house, and found her half-eaten box of Major Munch, which wasn't one of the recalled lots. You emptied her box and replaced the contents with contaminated cereal. You knew she'd eat the cereal because it was her comfort food and, thanks to her weakened immune system, it would be fatal. Sure enough, she got sick. As soon as she was taken away, you replaced her box with the one that was recalled and that was still half-filled with contaminated cereal. It was nearly the perfect murder. Her death would have been just one more blamed on salmonella-infected peanut paste."

"I'll give you this, Monk, it does sound like a clever way to kill somebody," Devlin said. "You've got imagination. What you don't have is any evidence for your wild accusation."

"Thank you," Aaron said, sighing with relief. "I'm glad that somebody is seeing reason and that it's a police officer."

"The evidence is right here," Monk said, picking up the little plastic dog in the overcoat and fedora. "This is Spy Dog, a toy being given away in new boxes of Major Munch. But it's not the toy being given away in that box." Monk pointed to the cereal box in Devlin's evidence bag. "So Brenda must've been eating from a new box, and it's not here."

"So maybe she had a new box and an old box," Aaron said. "And she ate the new box before the old one."

Devlin set the evidence bag down on the table and regarded Aaron warily. "So where's the old toy?"

I'll give this to Devlin—neither her animosity toward Monk, nor her pride, prevented her from recognizing that something didn't fit.

Aaron shrugged. "Maybe she didn't like the other toy and threw it out. Who knows? She had chemo brain. She hadn't been thinking straight for weeks."

Monk shook his head. "You made a mistake. You had the wrong toy in the wrong box. That was your undoing."

"I can't believe we're even having this conversation," Aaron said. "Why would I want to kill my sister?"

"My guess is money. It's obvious you're broke. Your jacket is frayed, your glasses are held together with the wrong-size screws, your watch crystal is cracked, the registration on your truck is expired, the soles of your shoes have been repaired twice, and you've been rolling your tongue over a bad tooth because you can't afford to see a dentist to have it fixed."

"So my cash flow is a little crimped," Aaron said. "That doesn't make me a killer. That makes me just like everybody else in America right now."

I spoke up. "But now that your sister is dead, you're next in line to inherit the house, one that she wouldn't give up."

To my surprise, my remark didn't earn me a nasty look from Devlin. She was standing very still, expressionless, her eyes on Aaron, her arms loose at her sides. She reminded me of a sheriff waiting to draw on a bad guy on a dusty western street.

"I don't know, maybe I do inherit the house now," Aaron said. "I haven't thought about that. I don't really care about material things. Isn't that obvious from the

way I live? But even if you're right, and she was murdered the way you say she was, you can't prove I had
anything to do with it."

"I don't have to," Monk said. "You've already proved
it for me."

"I may not be a fancy dresser or have perfect teeth,
but that doesn't make me a murderer."

"Your key chain does," Monk said. "You belong to
a bunch of supermarket discount clubs, and you're too
cheap not to use them. They track all of your purchases.
It shouldn't be hard to find out when and where you
bought that box of tainted cereal."

What happened next happened very, very fast.

In hindsight, I wonder whether Devlin wasn't expecting something to happen from the instant she set
down the evidence bag with the cereal box in it. She in-
stinctively wanted her hands free in case Aaron made a
move.

And he did.

Aaron grabbed me from behind with his left arm,
snatched a butcher knife from the sink with his right
hand, and held the blade to my throat as he pulled me
tight against him.

Devlin whipped out perhaps the largest gun I'd ever
seen from somewhere underneath her jacket and aimed
it right at me. She might have shot me if Monk wasn't
standing directly in the line of fire.

"Back off or I will slit her throat," Aaron said to them.
His arm was across my chest and his knife was pressed
so close to my neck that I was afraid to swallow for fear
it would cut me. I wasn't the only one who was afraid. I
could feel his heart pounding against my back.

Devlin's stare was cold and steady. I'm not even sure
she heard what he'd just said.

"You don't want to do this," I said to Aaron.

"I didn't want to kill Brenda, either," he said. "But you've got to do what you've got to do to survive."

"You won't survive. I can guarantee that," Devlin said. "I always shoot to kill, and I don't miss."

"Did you hear what I just said?" Aaron yelled. "I will slice her head clean off."

"It won't be clean," Monk said. "That's a dirty knife. It's been sitting in the sink for three days."

"Who cares?" I said. "Getting an infection is the least of my problems right now."

"Be reasonable," Monk said to Aaron. "Put the knife down."

"The hell I will." Aaron looked past Monk to Devlin, who was in a firing stance, her aim steady, her gaze unwavering.

"Your death will be instantaneous," she said. "But you can forget about an open casket, Aaron. The top of your head will be gone."

"Put the gun on the floor and step away from it now, or I will kill this woman," Aaron said. "I have nothing left to lose. You don't want to mess with me."

But she didn't move.

"For God's sake, drop the knife," Monk said, "and take this clean one instead."

Monk grabbed a knife from the knife rack on the counter and took a big step toward us.

"Get away from me." Aaron took a step back, dragging me with him. "Do you want her to die?"

"We can switch knives," Monk said.

"No, we can't," Aaron said.

"Of course we can. It'll be quick and easy," Monk said. "You'll thank me later."

I couldn't believe what I was hearing. "What difference does it make if I get my throat cut with a clean knife or a dirty one? I'm dead either way."

"Shut up!" Aaron said.

"It makes a huge difference, Natalie," Monk said. "Why do you think they disinfect scalpels before surgery? If he even nicks you with that disgusting knife, you could die from a staph infection or something even worse whether he slits your throat or not."

"I told you to shut up!" Aaron said.

"He'll kill me if you don't step back," I said. "So I'll take my chances with the infection."

Monk took two more tentative steps toward us, his arms open in front of him.

"Think about it, Aaron. Do you really want her oozing, feverish, drooling death on your conscience? Because that's what will happen if you don't use a clean knife."

"You're insane!" Aaron screamed at Monk.

"Me? I'm not the one holding a filthy knife to a woman's throat. My knife is not only cleaner, it's sharper. Here, use this." Monk thrust his knife at Aaron.

"Back off!" Aaron jabbed his knife at Monk. And that was the instant that Devlin fired, shooting the knife right out of Aaron's hand.

Aaron shrieked in pain and surprise, pulling me down to the floor with him as he fell back.

Devlin shoved Monk aside, kicked the knife away, and pressed the barrel of her gun against Aaron's forehead.

"Release her or die," she hissed.

He let go of me. I rolled off him and scrambled to my feet, my heart racing.

Monk took a deep breath and let it out slowly.

"That was close," he said. "Did you see the food caked on that knife?"

"Oh yeah," I said, taking deep breaths and trying not to have a post-near-death-experience panic attack. "It was all I could think about. The thought of bleeding out from a severed jugular vein never even crossed my mind."

Devlin holstered her gun, pulled out her handcuffs, rolled Aaron facedown, and cuffed his arms behind him.

"You're under arrest," she said and read Aaron his rights. When she was done, she got up and gave Monk an appreciative nod.

"That crazy routine about the dirty knife was a great distraction. You provoked him into giving me the opening I needed to take my shot. You're a ballsy guy, Monk. I may have misjudged you."

She took a dish towel and wrapped it around Aaron's hand as a crude bandage.

"I thought you'd decided to kill him," Monk said to her.

"So did I. But I started to think about all the paperwork I'd have to do, and then you gave me a clear shot at his hand, which I never thought I'd get, so I changed my plans." She glanced at me. "You backed Monk's play perfectly. That arguing-couple act really threw him. I don't know how you two worked that out on the fly like that."

I shrugged and fought the urge to throw up from the anxiety.

"What can I tell you?" I said. "We're pros."

"Watch him," Devlin said, motioning to Aaron. "Make sure he doesn't bleed out while I call this in and request an ambulance."

I nodded and gave her a thumbs-up. She stepped out of the kitchen and left Aaron moaning facedown on the floor, bleeding on himself.

"She's dangerous," Monk said.

"So are you. That's the second time someone has held a knife to my throat and you didn't listen to their demands."

"And both times it worked out fine. What does that tell you?"

"That my luck is running out," I said. "I can't believe you offered to trade knives with him."

"I was only thinking of your safety," he said. "No need to thank me."

Monk put on a pair of gloves, found an apron, and began to do the dishes.

"I need a vacation," I said.

I was sitting on the hood of my Buick, eating Oreos and sipping a carton of apple juice that the paramedics had given me, when Devlin walked up and took a seat next to me.

I held the Oreos out to her. "Want a cookie?"

She nodded and took one. "Oreos are my weakness."

The paramedics gave me the food to deal with my light-headedness, which was a symptom of the high anxiety I'd experienced with the knife to my throat. I wondered whether Devlin knew that, and I decided that she probably did. Even so, I wasn't going to admit anything.

"They are everybody's weakness," I said. "That's why I make a beeline to the paramedic unit as soon as they show up. They usually have some Lorna Doones around, too."

Devlin took a bite of the cookie and chewed on it thoughtfully as we silently surveyed the activity going on in front of us.

The street was clogged with patrol cars, an ambulance, and a forensic unit. Brenda's neighbors were standing on the other side of the crime scene tape, talking and pointing and taking videos with their phones, as Aaron was wheeled on a gurney into the ambulance.

"I don't get along well with people when I am myself," she said. "I'm much better when I'm undercover, when everyone is an enemy, and I'm just playing a role. I haven't been a regular cop in a long time."

I nodded. "You could pretend you're undercover as a homicide cop."

"It doesn't work that way," she said. "The adrenaline isn't there."

"It's there," I said. "It's just a different kind of fear."

She turned and looked at me as if seeing me for the first time.

"Are you some kind of shrink?"

I shook my head. "I spend a lot of time with Mr. Monk, which forces me to think about fear, relationships, and what it takes to fit in. You two are more alike than you think."

"Where is he?"

I gestured toward the house. "He's still cleaning the kitchen."

"He doesn't have to do that."

"Yes, he does," I said.

Captain Stottlemeyer drove up and got out of his car. He acknowledged us with a nod and conferred with the crime scene guys for a moment.

"That doesn't make any sense," she said.

"It makes sense to him, and part of your job now, whether you like it or not, is going to be learning how he sees the world," I said. "For instance, that stuff with the dirty knife? That wasn't a distraction and it wasn't an act. It was Mr. Monk being Mr. Monk."

"I was afraid of that," she said.

"I guess that changes your opinion of us."

She shook her head. "Not really. I mean, yeah, I think Monk is crazy, but he's got guts. He stood his ground even though a killer had a knife to your throat. Aaron saw Monk's fearlessness. It unnerved him. And I got my shot. I also saw something in your eyes."

"Tears?"

"Sure, you were afraid, but you were in control of

yourself, weighing the options, looking for an opportunity to make your own move."

"I don't think so," I said.

"I know what I saw," she said. "Reading people is what has kept me alive undercover. I could see that it wasn't the first time your life was in danger. You can take care of yourself. That's probably what makes you so good at taking care of him."

"Mr. Monk is irritating, and he will drive you crazy, but he's a brilliant detective."

"I don't need help doing my job."

"Everybody needs help," I said. "If Mr. Monk wasn't here today, would you have realized that Aaron killed his sister?"

"Probably not," she said.

"Definitely not. Nobody would have. It was the perfect murder. But he saw right through it and you didn't. That's what really pisses you off."

She nodded. "You're right, I don't like it."

"Join the club," I said, gesturing to Captain Stottlemeyer as he approached us. "How do you think he's felt about it all of these years? But he's made peace with it."

"The hell he has," she said.

Stottlemeyer stopped in front of us. "I heard you had some excitement today. How are you girls holding up?"

"Girls?" I said.

"I meant ladies," Stottlemeyer said.

"Ladies?" Devlin said.

"Women," Stottlemeyer said.

"Women?" Devlin and I said in unison.

"Okay, fine," he said. "Forget I asked."

Stottlemeyer turned and walked away.

Devlin waited until the captain was out of sight and then grinned at me.

"We're gonna get along fine," she said.

7

Mr. Monk Has a Plan

I think it's entirely reasonable to want a few hours off after your life has been placed in jeopardy.

Monk didn't agree. He believed that risking my life was part of my job as his assistant and that I should have been used to it by now.

"I don't recall you ever saying when you hired me that risking my life was part of the job," I said as we stood outside of Brenda's house.

"I don't see why you are complaining," Monk said, examining Aaron's camper truck. "You didn't get killed."

"If I did, then you'd have to give me some time off."

"Let's cross that bridge when we come to it."

"I'm done for the day, Mr. Monk. Either I can drop you off at home or you can ask the captain to do it on his way back to the station."

I turned my back on him and walked up to my car. Monk hurried after me.

"You can't be serious. You weren't even nicked."

"I had a knife held to my throat by a murderer until it was shot out of his hand by a cop."

"So what? I washed the dishes. You don't see me asking for the rest of the day off."

"It's not the same thing," I said. "Your life wasn't in danger."

"You obviously didn't get a good look at the dishes."

"Good-bye, Mr. Monk." I unlocked the car and opened the driver's-side door.

"Fine. We'll go home." He walked around the front of the car and got into the passenger seat. I started the car and was pulling away from the curb when he spoke up again. "But I am only paying you for half a day."

"You do that and I'll quit."

"If you aren't working a full day, why should I pay you for one?"

"Because I was nearly killed," I said. "Consider yourself lucky that I don't demand hazard pay."

"You aren't being reasonable or rational about this."

"See? That's what happens when I have a near-death experience. Clearly I need some rest."

He sulked all the way to his place. I dropped him off and went straight home.

But I was only in the house for a few minutes before I started to feel anxious. It wasn't that I was afraid. I just didn't like being alone after nearly getting killed. I needed companionship, the comfort of another person's company. I needed to be with somebody. And no, that's not a euphemism for getting into bed with someone, though that certainly would have been nice if I'd happened to be in an intimate relationship. But I wasn't.

It would have been enough just to sit at the kitchen table with Julie while she did her homework or ate her dinner. But she was off at Berkeley now, starting her own life. Even so, I called her to see whether she was interested in having dinner with me, but she was busy, studying with friends for a test.

So now what?

Before Stottlemeyer got married, I could have called him and we'd get together for a casual coffee. But now it would have felt inappropriate, even though there was never anything romantic between us. His free time belonged to his wife, Trudy, now.

I didn't have any other friends to call. Being a single mother and working for Monk took up nearly all my time, so I didn't have an opportunity to make friends or maintain the friendships I once had. The truth was that, except for times like this, my life was so chaotic that I didn't really miss not having friends.

There were some old boyfriends and some wannabe boyfriends I could call, and I knew that they'd be glad to see me, but I didn't want them to get the wrong idea. More important, I knew how easy it would be for me to fall into bed with one of them and then regret it in the morning, leaving both of us feeling lousy.

I felt adrift.

I was so desperate that I almost regretted dropping Monk off. I was about to make the big mistake of calling him when I realized that there was someone else I could call, someone I could relax with and who could give me the simple companionship I needed.

I picked up my phone and dialed.

He answered on the second ring. He always answered on the second ring. Or the fourth. Any ring as long as it was an even number.

"How would you feel about me coming by tonight with a pizza and a movie?"

"That would be wonderful," Ambrose said.

*   *   *

I brought over a plain cheese pizza and the latest James Bond movie. I figured Ambrose would enjoy the exotic locales and I could enjoy Daniel Craig.

While we ate on the living room couch, I told Ambrose about the Major Munch Peanut Crunch case and how Aaron nearly got away with the perfect murder. I left out the part about me nearly getting killed and Devlin shooting Aaron. That bit would have freaked Ambrose out and it would have jacked up my anxiety all over again.

Ambrose had an interesting take on the events.

"Adrian couldn't have solved it without me."

"I don't know about that," I said. "Mr. Monk has a very good eye for detail."

"But he knows nothing about the rich history of Major Munch toys," Ambrose said. "It was Adrian's knowledge of my collection that brought a felon to justice."

"I suppose it was."

"It just goes to show that you never know how things are interconnected. Maybe the reason why I've been collecting those toys for all these years was just so Adrian could catch a murderer today."

"I didn't know you were such a strong believer in fate," I said.

"I'm not," Ambrose said. "But I believe in balance and that everything fits together somehow."

"That's not fate?"

Ambrose shook his head. "It's order."

"If you say so. Ready for the movie?"

"Okay," he said.

I got up, put the movie into the DVD player, and then returned to my place on the couch beside him, though there was enough room between us to fit a family of four. That was his idea of intimacy.

"This is nice," he said.

"Yes, it is."

"You're still coming for my birthday on Saturday, aren't you?"

"Of course I am," I said. "Why wouldn't I?"

Ambrose shrugged. "This feels like a birthday party."

"It's not. At a birthday party, there are friends, and family, and cake, and gifts. That's what you will have on Saturday."

"You don't have to bring me a gift."

"I want to," I said.

"This was enough."

"I came here because I wanted to spend time with you," I said. "It's not a gift."

"You're wrong," Ambrose said.

He was right. But he wasn't the one getting the gift that night. It was me.

Monk was waiting at the curb in front of his apartment the next morning as I drove up, which was odd, since we weren't in a hurry to go anywhere, at least not as far as I knew.

"What's up?" I asked as he got into the car. "Did Stottlemeyer call you about a murder?"

"Nope," he said. "I figured out what I want to get Ambrose for his birthday."

"That's great. But what's the hurry?"

"We don't have much time."

"His birthday is the day after tomorrow," I said. "That still leaves us plenty of time to get him a level, or Q-tips, or a duster, or a first aid kit and get it wrapped."

"I'm getting him something else this year and it's not going to be wrapped."

"What are you getting him?"

"Freedom," he said.

"I don't understand."

"He hasn't left the house in thirty years. There's a whole world out there he has never seen because he's afraid to step out the front door. I want to show him what he's missing."

"He has a TV. He's seen pictures. He knows what the world looks like."

"It's not the same as experiencing it," Monk said. "That's what I want to give him. I want to take him on a trip."

"He's not going to step out of the house."

"He doesn't have to," Monk said. "We'll bring the house with us."

I had no idea what he meant by that, but I was stuck on something else that he said.

"We?" I said. "What makes you think I want to take a trip with you?"

"Yesterday you said that you needed a vacation."

"From you, Mr. Monk. From murder."

"You didn't say that," he said.

I took a deep breath and let it out slowly. "At what point yesterday did I say that I needed a vacation?"

"Right after Lieutenant Devlin shot the knife out of Aaron Monroe's hand."

"The knife that he held to my throat after you exposed him as a murderer."

"Yes, the filthy knife."

"Given the context of my statement, isn't it obvious that what I want is a vacation from my work?"

"This wouldn't be work."

"What happens every time we go out of town together?"

"You don't bring enough cleaning supplies."

"You inevitably get involved in a homicide investigation," I said. "That is not a vacation for me."

"You just don't know how to relax."

"This may shock you, but I don't find stumbling across corpses and hunting down killers relaxing."

"That's my point."

"I am not going on a trip with you."

"And Ambrose," he said.

"He's not going on a trip with you, either. So this whole ridiculous conversation is moot."

Monk turned in his seat to face me. "Ambrose has been imprisoned in that house for thirty years. His life has been the same day in and day out. Nothing ever changes."

"He's living your dream."

"You've got it backward, Natalie. My life has been his dream. I left home. I lived on my own. I fell in love. I saw the world. And while I was doing all that adventurous living, he has been stuck in that house, living vicariously through me. The only solace I have is that at least he was spared the sorrow of losing the love of his life the way you and I lost ours."

"The pain was worth it," I said.

"And you have Julie," he said. "And I have Molly. My life is even now in a way it hasn't been since Trudy was killed. Everything is balanced. I have it all. I want Ambrose to have it, too. So, for his birthday, I would like to give Ambrose the same balance. I would like to give him something new to see out of his window. I would like to give him a chance to experience life beyond his front door. But I can't do it without your help. The truth is, there's very little in my life that I can do without you."

I was boxed in. I'd tried so hard to bring Monk and Ambrose closer together. Now that Monk wanted to do something special for his brother, to express how much he loved him, how could I possibly refuse to help?

Monk's intentions were good, and I was sure that Ambrose would be touched just knowing that his brother wanted to do something special for him, but I didn't see how he was going to accomplish it.

Then again, I never knew during our investigations how Monk would solve the seemingly impossible cases that he tackled—and yet he always did. And I knew he would. I went along on loyalty, faith, and confidence in his abilities. So why should this be any different?

"Okay," I said. "I'm in."

8

Mr. Monk and the
Happy Birthday

Monk soon realized that my help wasn't going to be enough, at least not in the initial stages. So he drafted two more people to give us a hand. And once I fully understood what form his gift to Ambrose was going to take, and what would be required of us to pull it off, I was convinced that in the history of bad ideas, this was the worst one ever.

I tried to back out of it almost immediately, but Monk refused to listen to my objections. I pointed out the many ways it could all go wrong, and what an ordeal it would be for him and for his brother, but he waved off my concerns. He was willing to take those risks.

That left me with only one remaining objection: the big, personal reason I wanted him to call it off.

But I couldn't bring myself to tell him what it was.

I knew I had to, but every time I tried, I couldn't summon the words. It was just too embarrassing.

And before I knew it, the day had come to celebrate

Ambrose's birthday and the plan was too far along for me to stop it.

It was a bright, sunny, beautiful day. We arrived at Ambrose's house promptly at noon. I carried the chocolate cake, and Monk carried the presents. Of course, they weren't the real presents. They were a ruse, a way to convince Ambrose we weren't deviating from our usual birthday ritual.

Ambrose opened the door and beckoned us in before we even reached the front porch. I wondered how long he'd been standing by the window, waiting for us and wearing the red sweater vest he saved just for his birthdays.

"Greetings and felicitations," he said.

"Happy birthday, Ambrose." I kissed him on the cheek as I came in.

"It is now," Ambrose said, blushing.

I walked past him and set the cake on the dining room table.

"Why did I even bother to come?" Monk asked.

"I'm happy to see you, too, Adrian. But that goes without saying."

"Why does it?"

"Because it would only go to your head, and it's big enough as it is." Ambrose closed the door and locked it.

"What did I do to deserve that remark?" Monk set the gifts down at the far end of the dining room table.

"It's been three days since you solved the Brenda Monroe murder and you haven't called to thank me."

"For what?"

"For solving it," Ambrose said, going into the kitchen. Monk trailed after him, but I stayed in the dining room, within earshot, and took the cake out of the box.

"I don't recall bumping into you at the crime scene," Monk said.

"I was there in spirit. Without me, and the knowledge I gave you of Major Munch cereal toys, you wouldn't have even realized that she was murdered."

Ambrose returned to the dining room with plates and silverware, and Monk carried four bottles of Fiji water, the brand they'd turned to when Summit Creek went out of business.

"I would have," Monk said.

"How?"

"I don't know," Monk said. "But I would have. It's what I am world-famous for."

"And his modesty," I said.

"Why can't you just acknowledge my contribution and thank me for it?" Ambrose said. "You can still take credit for combining the information that I gave you with your powers of observation to determine that her brother was her killer."

"Wait a minute," Monk said. "My involvement in the case wasn't reported in the newspaper or anywhere else. How did you find out I had anything to do with it?"

Ambrose involuntarily glanced at me and tried to cover it by quickly looking the other way, but he was too late. Monk saw it and glared at me.

I pretended to be intensely interested in the cake. "Are we going to use birthday candles or go *au naturel* this year?"

"That's an interesting question," Ambrose said, eager to change the subject and save my hide.

"No, it's not," Monk said. "The interesting question remains unanswered."

"And isn't that what adds spice to life?" I said. "The unanswered questions?"

"No, those missing pieces create an imbalance that must be fixed because, if enough of them pile up, the entire universe will collapse."

"Is that all?" I said.

Ambrose sighed. "Adrian has a good point, Natalie."

"No, he doesn't. The universe is not going to collapse over this."

"It might," Monk said. "This could be the unanswered question that's the cosmic breaking point."

"It was her," Ambrose said, pointing at me. "She told me."

Before Monk could unleash his wrath, there was a knock at the door. I hurried over to answer it, thankful for the reprieve.

I opened the door and my daughter, Julie, stepped inside, carrying a big present. She was wearing her black Uggs, skinny blue jeans, and a UC Berkeley hooded pullover.

"Are you Ambrose's butler now, too?" Julie asked with a sly grin.

"Just for today," I said, giving her a kiss.

Ambrose joined us and I closed the door before he could get a peek outside.

"What a lovely surprise," Ambrose said. "I didn't expect to see you."

"I haven't missed your birthday yet," she said.

He gave her his version of a hug, bending forward at the waist and managing to keep most of his body from making any contact with hers.

"I always assumed your mother dragged you along against your will."

"Not true," she said, setting her present down with the others on the dining room table. "I've always loved coming here. You're like an eccentric, colorful uncle."

"What does that make me?" Monk asked.

"My mom's weird boss," she said.

Monk frowned and Julie gave him a kiss on the cheek.

"Can't you take a joke?" she said.

"No," Monk said, motioning to me for a wipe. "You should know that by now."

"I am not giving you a wipe for my daughter," I said.

"Didn't you see what she just did to me?"

"Consider yourself lucky."

"There are thousands of students at UC Berkeley," Monk said. "Who knows how many diseases they are carrying?"

"I don't know," I said. "You can keep count if you're stricken by them."

Someone knocked at the door.

"Who could that be?" Ambrose asked.

"I hope you don't mind," Julie said, opening the front door, "but I invited one of my friends."

And in stepped Molly, absolutely adorable in her pumps, gray pencil skirt, white blouse, and blue cardigan sweater. The sight of her brought tears to Ambrose's eyes.

"Hello, Molly," he said. "It's a pleasure to meet you."

"How did you know it was me?" she asked. "Did Adrian show you some pictures?"

"No, he wasn't that considerate," Ambrose said. "But you look just the way I imagined you would."

Of course she did. Monk had described her to Ambrose in intimate and minute detail.

"She has 128 freckles on her face, Adrian, not 122, and you were an eighth of an inch off on her height. I thought you were supposed to be remarkably observant."

Julie was stunned. "You saw all that in just a glance?"

"I'm a year older," Ambrose said. "I'm not dead."

He was also a Monk. I had no doubt that he was accurate in his appraisal.

"You didn't factor in her heels," Monk said.

"Of course I did," Ambrose said.

"And those are new freckles," Monk said.

"Yeah, right," Ambrose said in a patronizing tone of voice.

"Adrian has told me so much about you," Molly said. "But even before I met him, I already felt like I knew you."

"How is that possible?" Ambrose asked.

"You wrote the manuals for my TV, my DVD player, my refrigerator, and my microwave."

"How did you know that?"

"Your style, your unique voice, are unmistakable, at least to anyone who appreciates writing," Molly said. "You make it seem as if a knowledgeable friend is explaining how even the most needlessly complicated devices are really very simple. I had to find out who the writer was. Most of the time, your name was hidden in the acknowledgments or on the copyright page. Other times, I had to call the manufacturer to confirm my suspicions."

Oh, she was good. I had no idea whether what she was saying was true or a calculated attempt to win Ambrose over, but it didn't matter. It was his birthday and the whole idea was to make him feel special.

Ambrose was clearly overwhelmed. He shook his head and turned to his brother. "She's amazing."

"I told you so," Monk said proudly.

"At least you got that part right," Ambrose said, then faced Molly again. "May I give you a hug?"

"Of course you can." She opened her arms. "We're family."

He gave her the same awkward hug that he'd given Julie.

Molly's arrival was an important part of Monk's carefully orchestrated plan. He figured that after she showed up, Ambrose would assume that there were no more surprises in store for him and let his guard down—not that there was any reason he should be wary of his family and friends. She also had a role to play in what was to come.

"This is going to be the best birthday ever," Ambrose said.

Or it would be a disaster of unparalleled proportions. I sincerely hoped he was right and I was wrong.

It didn't take long for the sleeping pills in Ambrose's slice of birthday cake to knock him out cold.

As soon as he slumped forward onto the table, we jumped into action with the precision of the Impossible Missions Force. We didn't have much time.

Monk and Molly carried Ambrose to the couch while Julie went out to her car and brought in some cardboard boxes left over from her move to Berkeley. Ambrose never left the house so he didn't own any suitcases.

I grabbed some boxes, rushed into the kitchen, and gathered dishes, utensils, and cookware, while Monk took some boxes upstairs and got Ambrose's clothes, shoes, linens, and toiletries together. Julie got Ambrose's laptop computer, some books, and his reading glasses.

Molly went outside, ran around the corner, and drove up in the Jamboree, a loaded class-C motor home that Monk had rented for the week and that I was supposed to drive. But we'll get to that part later.

The Jamboree was an automotive Frankenstein, a typical Ford van chassis with a cab-over, thirty-two-foot trailer grafted inelegantly onto it. A swish of vibrant color, meant to create an illusion of constant motion, ran along both sides and onto the cab in a halfhearted attempt to join the two disparate pieces into one unified whole. Viewed from the side, the deception almost worked. But from the front, it looked like a trailer was in the midst of consuming the van that was pulling it.

The motor home also had two side sections, called slide-outs, that at the flick of a switch expanded the living space dramatically once the vehicle was parked.

Molly deftly backed the Jamboree into the driveway and got out. I carried the box of kitchenware from the house to the motor home, and she helped me unload everything into the cabinets in the galley.

Notice that I didn't call it the kitchen. The rental guy described everything about the motor home in nautical terms, as if it were a yacht and we were going on a cruise, and insisted that I do so, too.

The entrance to the motor home was on the starboard side. As you entered, the L-shaped galley was to your immediate left, the dinette area was in front of you, and the built-in leather sleeper couch and the cab were to the right.

The dinette area was one of the two slide-outs, as was the private stateroom that was at the rear of the motor home. Excuse me, I meant to say the stateroom was *aft*.

The bathroom was separated from the living area and the stateroom by a short corridor on the driver's side—I mean the *port* side—of the motor home.

There was a cab-over bunk that had been converted into a built-in entertainment center with a nineteen-inch flat-screen TV, DVD player, and surround-sound speakers.

The cabinetry throughout was a pleasing natural cherrywood. The floors were imitation travertine vinyl tile in the kitchen and bathroom and beige shag carpet everywhere else. The upholstery was rust colored, with a subtle checked pattern that complemented the off-white blinds. Everything was lit with pinpoint halogens and fiber-optic accent lighting.

I hate to admit it, but the interior was more upscale than my house.

The day before, after the rental place had thoroughly cleaned the unit, Monk did his own cleaning, which took him almost all night. That morning, we'd loaded our clothes, Monk's linens, and several cases of Fiji bottled water, filled the refrigerator with food in labeled Tupperware containers and Ziploc bags, and then left the keys with the rental office so Molly could pick up the motor home and bring it to Ambrose's house.

"You backed that motor home into the driveway as if it was your little Miata," I said to Molly.

"My adoptive parents owned one a lot like this when I was a kid," she said. "We mostly used it for weekend getaways. I loved it."

"Maybe you'd like to come along as our driver."

"I wish I could," she said, "but I don't have any vacation time left."

Monk brought out Ambrose's clothes and linens. We made up the bed in the stateroom with Ambrose's pillows and sheets while Molly and Julie unpacked his clothes and toiletries and stowed his laptop and books.

Then, while Molly and Julie kept watch for witnesses, Monk and I carried Ambrose out of the house and laid him down on the queen-size bed.

We put the leftover birthday cake in the refrigerator, and then we were ready to go.

Well, Monk was ready to go. I was not.

The three of us women stood outside the motor home while Monk locked up the house.

"Are you sure you want to do this, Mom?" Julie asked. "It seems insane to me."

"Me, too," I said.

"I think it's sweet," Molly said.

"That's because you're not going to be stuck on the road with the Monk brothers from San Francisco, down the California coast, to Los Angeles, the Grand Canyon, Yosemite, and back," I said.

But that wasn't the real reason for my apprehension. Not even Julie knew what that was. I'd managed to keep it a secret, which was easy, since I'd never had an opportunity to travel in a motor home until that moment.

"It shows how much you love them," Molly said. "That's going to mean a lot to Ambrose."

"If he doesn't have me and Monk arrested for kidnapping," I said.

"Then you better make sure he enjoys the trip," Julie said. "But if he doesn't, I left before you abducted him."

"Me, too," Molly said.

"Thanks for the support," I said.

"We're too young, pretty, and vulnerable to go to jail," Julie said.

"We have our whole lives in front of us," Molly said.

"What does that make me?" I said. "Old, ugly, and hopeless?"

"No, of course not," Julie said. "Just insane. But don't worry, I'll visit you every week in prison, or the nuthouse, whichever the case may be."

"That's comforting," I said and gave her a kiss.

Monk came out and joined us. "The house is all locked up and the oven is off. I checked twice."

"We never turned the oven on," Molly said.

"It never hurts to be sure," Monk said. "In fact, I should check again."

He went back to the house. I sighed and gave Julie and Molly each a hug.

"Thank you both for your help," I said. "We couldn't have done this without you."

"My pleasure, unless you are arrested," Julie said. "And then you did it all by yourselves."

Monk came back out. "Everything is locked up. We're ready to introduce Ambrose to the outside world."

"Have a great trip," Molly said, and gave Monk a hug. "You're doing a great thing for him. He'll appreciate it for the rest of his life."

"Or you're committing a felony that he'll never forgive you for," Julie said. "Remember that as you're crossing state lines."

Julie led Molly to her car and they drove off. After they went, I turned to Monk.

"She has a good point," I said. "It's not too late to rethink this."

"We aren't committing a crime," Monk said. "We're going on a vacation."

"You drugged him," I said.

"You've never given your daughter medication?"

"This is different."

"No, it's not," Monk said.

"He would never have left the house if we hadn't knocked him out," I said.

"See?" Monk said. "We're helping him."

"We're removing him from his home against his will," I said. "It's an abduction."

"It's a family vacation."

"You have a strange family," I said.

"Yes, I do. I'm glad we got that settled." Monk climbed inside the motor home and I could see him getting into the passenger seat in the cab. He waved for me to get in.

I took a deep breath and joined him, settling into the driver's seat. From where I sat, it seemed like a normal Ford van. But I knew that it wasn't. I knew that it was a motor home and that we would be on the open road, sleeping in RV parks and off-road locations for the next week.

I broke into a cold sweat.

"I can't do this," I said.

"Trust me, even if Ambrose is angry with us, he won't press charges."

"That's not it," I said.

"Then what is it?"

"I'm scared."

"No, you're not."

I showed him my hands. They were shaking. "I'm terrified, Mr. Monk."

"It's no big deal," Monk said. "The rental guy told you it's just like driving a car. You just have to approach driveways at an angle to avoid scraping the bottom of the RV and take special care backing up since you've only got side-view mirrors. Otherwise, it's no different than being in your Buick."

"It's not that."

"So what are you afraid of?"

"Devil worshippers," I said and tried not to whimper. "If we go out there in this, they'll get us."

"You're kidding," he said.

I shook my head. "We're going to die."

9

Mr. Monk and the Devil

One Saturday night, when I was nine years old, my father succumbed to my incessant nagging and took me and two of my girlfriends to a drive-in movie theater.

The three of us girls got into our pajamas, took our sleeping bags, and crammed into the "way-back" of my dad's Ford Country Squire station wagon.

When we got to the drive-in, he backed up so the rear of the station wagon was facing the screen. He got us a huge bucket of popcorn, a bunch of candy, and some drinks, then settled into the backseat, where he had to watch the movie with his head turned to one side the whole time.

The movie was *Race with the Devil* and was about these two couples who go on a trip in their motor home, witness a Satanic sacrifice one night, and are then chased all over the place by evil devil worshippers. Everywhere they went, wide-eyed, unblinking Satanists were waiting for them. There was nowhere they could run, no one they could trust, and no way to escape their doom.

It was the scariest movie I'd ever seen, made even more frightening because my dad leaped out from behind us in the backseat and roared like a monster at the most frightening moments. We screamed until our throats were raw. He thought we were having fun. Maybe my friends were, but I certainly wasn't.

Race with the Devil scarred me for life.

Ever since that Saturday night, I'd been terrified of motor homes. Whenever I saw one on the road, I was sure that it was being chased by devil worshippers, or driven by devil worshippers, or would soon attract devil worshippers.

I always got away from RVs as fast as I could. Even parked RVs made me uneasy.

So clearly there was no way I could drive a motor home around the western United States and become chum for whatever devil worshippers might be around, just waiting for a woman to sacrifice to Beelzebub.

And that's what I told Monk.

I expected sympathy and understanding. What I got was a look of disbelief.

"That's the dumbest thing I have ever heard," he said.

"It's the truth," I said.

"It's ridiculous."

"I know," I said.

"It was a movie," he said. "It wasn't real."

"I know," I said.

"So there we have it. Problem solved. Let's go."

He slapped the dashboard as if it was the flank of a horse, not that he'd ever ride a horse, much less touch one.

"My heart is racing. My throat is dry. It's not that simple, Mr. Monk."

"Of course it is. Your fear is irrational and absurd. All you have to do is tell yourself that and you'll see reason."

"I wasn't this scared when I had a knife to my throat. Knowing my fear is irrational and making it go away are two entirely different things."

He glanced at his watch. The sleeping pill we gave Ambrose would begin wearing off soon and Monk wanted to be well on our way before that happened.

"Oh, for God's sake, Natalie, you're a grown woman. Suck it up and let's go."

I gave him a look. "Phobias can't just be rationalized away."

"Of course they can."

"So how come you're terrified of tumbleweeds?"

"That's not a phobia," Monk said. "That's common sense. They can mow you right down."

"What about milk?"

"It's a health and safety issue."

"Trees?"

"They're a haven for killer insects and rabid animals."

"Dust bunnies?"

"Carriers of death."

"Well, I feel the same way about motor homes."

"That's just stupid."

"No stupider than dust bunnies."

"You can't compare dust bunnies to motor homes. Balls of dust and pestilence are dangerous. Motor homes are completely safe, unless you're run over by one, but since you're driving this one, not crossing in front of it, that's not an issue."

"You're not helping, Mr. Monk."

"We aren't going to encounter any devil worshippers."

"How can you be sure?"

"Because I'm a sane, rational person," Monk said.

That was supposed to be my role in our relationship. I couldn't help feeling that I was letting us both down. But my fear was real.

"Devil worshippers don't announce themselves, Mr. Monk. You don't know someone is one until he's got you on the sacrificial altar. Anybody could be one of them."

"Including me?"

"You're too fussy to be a Satanist."

"What about Captain Stottlemeyer?"

"You're not taking me seriously."

"No, I'm not," Monk said. "Think of this vacation as an opportunity for you and Ambrose to finally overcome your irrational fears."

"What about yours?"

"I don't have any," he said. "I'll be your rock. But not like a rock you find on the ground, caked in dirt. I'll be the disinfected rock that's all clean and shiny."

"I can't do this," I said as I pulled the key out of the ignition and started to take off my seat belt.

"Fine, back out of this," Monk said. "But you will have to explain to Julie, Captain Stottlemeyer, and Lieutenant Devlin that we canceled our vacation at the last second because you're afraid of motor homes and devil worshippers."

"Why would I have to do that?"

"Because they will ask and I'm a lousy liar."

"But I'll be humiliated," I said.

"Oh, it will be much worse than that," Monk said. "You'll be a disappointment to your daughter, who'll never take your authority as a parent or your advice seriously again, and you'll be a joke to the entire police department, which would be tragic considering how many years it took you to earn their respect."

I stared at him, my anger almost outweighing my fear. "You'd really do that to me?"

"Of course," Monk said. "It would be for your own good."

"It would be selfish, insensitive, and cruel."

"You'll thank me later."

"No, I'll kill you."

"I'd catch you," he said.

"That's going to be hard to do from the grave."

"I'd catch you anyway," he said. "I'm that good."

"I can't believe we are having this stupid discussion."

"Now you're talking sense," he said. "So what are you more afraid of? The unlikely possibility of running into devil worshippers or the absolute certainty of being ridiculed for the rest of your life?"

I took a deep breath, swallowed hard, started the RV, and shifted it into drive.

Satan, here I come.

As I drove the motor home out of Tewksbury toward San Francisco, my heart was beating so fast that I figured at least I'd succumb to cardiac arrest before the Satanists ever caught up with me.

I knew I was being silly. I knew Monk was right. And that's why I drove on, not so much because of his threats, but because it was time to confront my fears. Mine weren't nearly as crippling as what Ambrose was facing. Of course, it helped that a person doesn't run into many RVs living in the heart of San Francisco.

We were on the freeway and nearly at the Golden Gate Bridge when there was a loud yelp from the back of the motor home.

"Earthquake!" Ambrose, disoriented and in a dazed

panic, came staggering out of the stateroom, clutching the walls for support. "It's the Big One!"

I quickly steered the RV toward the turnoff leading to the scenic outlook, a popular tourist spot for taking postcard-perfect pictures of the bridge and the city. It was like trying to turn an aircraft carrier, but somehow I managed.

"It's okay," Monk said, climbing out of his seat and heading into the back. "It's not an earthquake."

"Then why is the house moving?" Ambrose said. "Wait a minute, this isn't my house. And why is there a car in the living room?"

"Sit down and I'll explain everything," Monk said, leading Ambrose to the couch.

I found a parking spot with a fantastic view of the bridge and angled the motor home so Ambrose could see the bay from the window across from him.

"I'm having a nightmare," Ambrose said, closing his eyes. "I am going to wake up now." He opened his eyes. "Oh God, I'm still dreaming. Wake up! Wake up!"

He dropped onto the couch and shook his head.

I glanced around quickly to make sure there were no Satanists in the cars next to us or lurking in the bushes on the periphery of the parking lot.

"You're in a motor home," Monk said to Ambrose. "Also known as a recreational vehicle or an RV."

"Oh God, does that mean I am outside?"

"You're inside but outside at the same time," Monk said. "That's the brilliance of it. Since you won't leave the house, I decided to move the house instead. For the next week this is your home on wheels."

"How did I get in here?" Ambrose asked.

"I drugged your slice of birthday cake and then we carried you inside," Monk said.

"You abducted me," Ambrose said.

My gaze fell on a middle-aged, very prim lady in the Honda Civic parked right beside us. She was sitting ramrod straight, staring out at the bay. She turned mechanically toward me and smiled. A chill ran down my spine.

"Don't panic," I said. "But I think they are onto us already."

"Who?" Monk asked.

"The Satanists," I said.

"Why do you say that?" Monk said.

I tipped my head toward the driver's-side window. "Look at that lady. She hasn't blinked in at least thirty seconds."

"So?"

"Devil worshippers don't blink. They stare at you like wide-eyed zombies," I said. "Just like her."

"There are no devil worshippers in Marin County," Monk said. "Only swingers, nudists, poets, and NPR subscribers."

"I am none of those things," Ambrose said.

"Only because you never leave the house," Monk said.

"That's *why* I don't leave the house," Ambrose said.

"We are setting you free," Monk said.

"I don't want to be free," Ambrose said. "I want to go home."

"You heard the man," I said, starting the RV up again and stealing another glance at the Devil Woman. "Let's get going before she takes out her pitchfork."

"We're not going back," Monk said. "We're going through with this."

"With what?" Ambrose said. "Why are you doing this to me?"

"Because I'm even. I have a balance in my life that I haven't had in years, and it feels really good. You deserve to have that, too. So that's what I'm giving you for your birthday, something that you've been missing, that's made your life unbalanced." Monk motioned to the view. "The world. Something new to see outside your window besides the same old street you've been looking at for decades."

Ambrose leaned forward a little bit and looked out the window, staring wide-eyed at the Golden Gate just as a massive cruise ship passed beneath it. He sat back quickly and took a few deep breaths.

I looked at the woman in the car beside us. She was texting on her cell phone, probably alerting the entire Satanic network to be on the lookout for us.

"This is madness," Ambrose said. "Where did you get such a crazy idea?"

"From a murderer," Monk said. "The guy who killed his sister with Major Munch Peanut Crunch."

"Of course you did. Sociopaths always give the best advice. What are you going to do next? Kill me?"

"We're taking you on a road trip."

"I'd rather be killed," Ambrose said.

"It's a vacation," Monk said. "You need one."

"Is that what the sociopath told you?"

"You'll thank me later."

"Like his sister thanked him," Ambrose said, then shifted his angry gaze to me. "I can't believe you went along with this insidious plan. I trusted you, Natalie. I thought you were a true friend."

"I am, Ambrose."

He shook his head. "No, you're a black widow, wooing men to their doom with your feminine wiles."

"You wooed? With your wiles?" Monk said. "What are you doing waving your wiles around?"

"I didn't woo, with wiles or anything else," I said to Monk and then turned to his brother. "I helped Mr.

Monk because he loves you and wants to make you happy."

"Do I look happy to you?"

"Not yet, but give it some time. This is going to be a lot of fun," I said, trying to convince him as much as myself. "It will be an experience that you will treasure."

"That's what they told the passengers on the *Titanic*," he said. "And look what happened to them."

10

Mr. Monk Hits the Road

Monk began showing Ambrose the world by taking him on a tour of San Francisco's major landmarks—Monk's apartment, Monk's shrink's office, and police headquarters.

As we passed Dr. Bell's office, Ambrose urged me to pull over and invite Monk's psychiatrist to come out and join us.

"I'd love to get his professional opinion of what you're doing to me," Ambrose said.

"Dr. Bell doesn't practice drive-through psychiatry," Monk said.

I didn't blame Monk for not wanting to bring Dr. Bell into this. I didn't want to, either. I doubted that Dr. Bell would endorse Monk's plan and I didn't want him to find out about my *Race with the Devil* fears.

As we passed the police station, Ambrose banged on the windows of the RV and tried to attract the attention of the cops outside. Monk closed the blinds, perhaps afraid that the police would take a dim view of us drugging, abducting, and imprisoning his brother. I didn't blame him for that, either. I didn't relish the idea of being interrogated over my part in the scheme.

But Dr. Bell and the police weren't my big worries. I was more concerned that we were showing all the devil worshippers in San Francisco precisely where Monk lived and I worked so they could catch us later if we managed to elude them on the open road.

Yes, I knew those were crazy thoughts, but the scariest thing of all was my realization that Monk was probably the most rational person among the three of us. That fact shocked some sense back into me and gave me a modicum of control over my phobia. I forced myself to concentrate on my driving and to make Ambrose feel safe and secure, even if I didn't.

As we drove through the city, and then south through San Mateo, I could see that Ambrose was conflicted. He wanted to be angry with us, but he couldn't stop staring in fascination out the window at all the activity. He reminded me of a child watching a monster movie, scared and captivated at the same time.

We were silent for the next two hours and, since we had no predetermined destination in mind, we were in no hurry to get anywhere.

Monk, being Monk, had wanted to plan out the entire week in detail, to keep to a strict timetable, and to know exactly where we would be going, what we would be seeing, and when we would be seeing it. He had to know where we'd be parking the RV each night and what time we'd get there.

But I reminded him that we were doing this trip for Ambrose and that we should be guided not by some arbitrary schedule but rather by his brother's interest and curiosity, assuming he ever got past his anger and fear.

I also reminded him that since we were in an RV, we were virtually self-sufficient. We didn't have to worry about finding a place to stay, and if we couldn't find a suitable campground or trailer park, we could simply pull off the road somewhere for the night.

That level of uncertainty unnerved Monk, but I made it clear that if he wanted me along, that was the way it was going to be.

Much to my surprise, he gave in. He didn't have much choice, not if he wanted me to be his driver.

Our only plan, if you could call it that, was to do a loop, going south down the California coast to Los Angeles, then perhaps east as far as the Grand Canyon, then northwest, maybe passing through Las Vegas and Yosemite on the way back to the San Francisco Bay Area. Of course, all of that was open to change depending on what caught our fancy along the way.

We had some maps and a travel guide to the western United States, but that was all the advance preparation we had done.

The longer we drove, the more relaxed I became, and I supposed it was the same for Ambrose. He was safely indoors and, since the cab is the same as any Ford van, I actually forgot I was in a motor home.

It also helped that I was entering familiar territory. We were heading down the coast along Highway 1 toward Monterey Bay, where I grew up. There's something undeniably comforting in being around places where you have some history and lots of good memories. I'm sure that was one reason Ambrose never left the house.

Ambrose seemed utterly enthralled by the high cliffs and the crashing surf, gripping the back of the couch for dear life and rearing back to avoid getting wet as each wave hit the shore far below us. But he couldn't tear his eyes away from the natural spectacle.

"Do you have to drive so close to the edge?" he said. "Are you trying to send us hurtling to our deaths?"

Monk turned to me. "See, I'm not the only one who thinks you're a reckless driver."

"Ambrose has been in a motor vehicle twice in thirty years," I said. "He's hardly in a position to be critical about my driving."

"I'll have you know I've won the Mushroom Cup, Flower Cup, Special Cup, Shell Cup, Banana Cup, and Leaf Cup multiple times in Super Mario Kart," Ambrose said. "I've experienced things on the international racing circuit that would curdle your toothpaste. I've survived the blood-soaked sands of Shy Guy Beach, the hairpin turns of Toad's Turnpike, and the quicksand pits of the Dry Dry Desert, all while dodging pirate cannon fire, piranha plants, and the pincers of mighty crabs."

"That's very impressive, Ambrose," I said. "But one thing you will discover on this trip is that the real world is infinitely more complex and exciting than what you can experience in a video game."

"Show me something that can beat Yoshi Falls or Mushroom Gorge, and then we'll talk," Ambrose said.

"Just look out the window," I said.

He did. And that shut him up again.

Santa Cruz is Berkeley by the beach. Like Berkeley, the city is home to a university, which means the entire place has a student vibe. But it's also inexplicably caught in a time warp, still evoking the 1960s, the counterculture, and the laid-back, hippie lifestyle. Berkeley has gentrified, sanitized, and marketed its hippie history to the point that the city feels like a theme park re-creation of itself. But in Santa Cruz, it doesn't feel self-conscious, prefabricated, and franchised. It feels authentic.

There wouldn't be a lot of Satanists here, and if there

were, they were probably too busy studying for finals or getting high to bother with us.

I found a parking spot on West Cliff Drive facing the beach, the bay, the pier, and the boardwalk, which was dominated by the massive, and iconic, wooden roller coaster. The view was spectacular.

"What happens now?" Ambrose asked nervously.

"We eat," I said.

I got up from the driver's seat to open the window beside Ambrose. The light breeze outside filled the RV with fresh air. I found it revitalizing.

I went outside and unlocked a compartment on the side of the motor home that contained the propane tanks that supplied gas to the stove. I opened the valves on the tanks, then went back inside to the galley to begin making my first motor home meal.

My culinary ambitions were modest. I was going to prepare three *croque monsieurs*, which is basically the French version of a grilled cheese sandwich. The difference in the French version is better bread, a few slices of ham, and Gruyère cheese instead of one of those Kraft American cheese slices. The French use some kind of fancy sandwich press to make their *croque monsieurs*. I made do with a frying pan and a spatula. I also tweaked the recipe by using Boudin San Francisco sourdough instead of regular French bread.

"That's my frying pan," Ambrose said.

"All the cookware and dishes are from your kitchen," I said. "We want you to feel at home."

"If you really wanted me to feel at home, you would have left me there."

Monk opened the refrigerator, took out two cold bottles of Fiji water, and handed one to his brother before settling into the dinette area with his California guidebook.

"What are you making?" Monk asked me.

"*Croque monsieurs*," I said, "served with Wheat Thins on the side."

Monk smiled, something he rarely did. He fell in love with *croque monsieurs* during our trip to Paris. I figured if Monk liked them, then Ambrose would, too.

Ambrose sniffed the air from outside and furrowed his brow. "What is that salty smell?"

"It's called the ocean," I said.

"The ocean smells?" Ambrose said.

"Of course it does," Monk said. "It's filled with stinky fish."

"I don't think fish stink until you take them out of the water," I said.

"Just because you can't smell underwater doesn't mean there aren't smells," Monk said, flipping through the guidebook. "What do you think, Ambrose?"

But Ambrose wasn't paying attention. He was staring out the window.

I was comfortable with silence and so were the Monks. Ambrose probably appreciated it most of all. The poor guy was probably on sensory overload as it was.

I finished up the sandwiches and set them down on the dinette table along with knives, forks, napkins, and the box of Wheat Thins.

"Lunch is served," I said. "Come over and join us."

Ambrose slid in beside Monk at the dinette. There was no way he'd sit that close to me, not with the likelihood that our bodies might touch.

"Isn't this terrific?" Monk said, carefully counting out six Wheat Thins and setting them on his plate beside his *croque monsieur*. "There's nothing like a square meal."

He meant that literally, of course, referring to the shape of his sandwich and his Wheat Thins and not their combined nutritional value.

Ambrose eyed his sandwich suspiciously.

"It's not drugged," I said, "if that's what you're worried about."

"I can't be too sure anymore," he said and cut into it with a knife and fork, carving out a perfectly square piece. I watched him as he ate his first bite, chewing carefully, squinting as his palate did a forensic chemical analysis of my cooking. Finally, he looked at me with surprise. "This is delicious."

"Thank you," I said.

"It's gourmet French cuisine," Monk said. "One of the new meals I had in France. That's what you discover when you're willing to be adventurous."

"What else did you eat in France?" Ambrose asked.

"Just that," Monk said.

"You said it was one of the new meals."

"That's the new one I had for every meal."

"That's adventurous," I said and put six Wheat Thins on Ambrose's plate. "Speaking of which, what's it like being somewhere new for the first time in thirty years?"

Ambrose rolled his shoulders, immediately reminding me of his brother, who exhibited the same mannerism when he was considering something.

"Unsettling," he said.

"In a good way?" I asked.

"There's no such thing," Ambrose said.

"Falling in love is unsettling," I said, "in a good way."

"I wouldn't know," he said.

"You've never been in love?"

"Not lately," he said.

"Define lately," Monk said.

"Forty years," Ambrose said.

"You were still in kindergarten," Monk said.

"Suzy Mills took my heart out and stomped on it. Those scars run deep. But thank you for reminding me,

Adrian, the pain was nearly gone. Now it's fresh again. What a wonderful birthday this is turning out to be."

"So, where would you like to go next?" I asked, just to change the subject.

"Home," Ambrose said.

"Besides there," I said.

Monk tapped a page in the guidebook. "Here."

"What is it?" I asked.

"The Mystery Spot," Monk said. "They say it's a place where the laws of physics and gravity don't apply."

"That's impossible," Ambrose said. "The laws of physics and gravity always apply. That's why they are called laws."

"I agree," Monk said. "But they say that at this place balls roll uphill, people walk on walls, and other unexplained phenomena consistently occur."

Ambrose pushed his plate away and read aloud from the book. "Tens of thousands of people have come from all over the world to witness these strange events. Scientists speculate the cause could be dielectric biocosmic radiation or radiesthesia."

"What are those?" Monk asked.

"Radiesthesia is energy created by paranormal powers in the human body," Ambrose said. "It's never been empirically proven to exist."

"And dielectric biocosmic radiation?" Monk asked.

"Meaningless babble," Ambrose said. "Nevertheless, the book says that these anomalies have perplexed scientists and defied explanation for more than seventy years."

"Not anymore," Monk said. "Start the car, Natalie. It's time that this mystery is finally solved."

"Nobody wants it to be," I said. "People enjoy the mystery."

"No, they don't. It confuses and perplexes them, creating uncertainty and anxiety."

"And that can be thrilling," I said.

"If you are mentally ill," Monk said.

"Or on dope," Ambrose said.

"I went to the Mystery Spot when I was a kid and it was a lot of fun," I said. "That's why people keep buying tickets year after year."

"They are *charging* people to see this?" Monk said. "And the police have done nothing about it?"

"Why should they?" I asked.

"Because people are making money off of flagrant lawbreaking."

"The laws of physics and gravity," I said. "It's not like bank robbery or murder."

"It's worse," Monk said. "They are crimes against the universe."

"So let the Federation handle it," I said.

Monk stared blankly at me.

"It's a cultural reference to the Federation of Planets, the governmental body in *Star Trek*," Ambrose said. "It was a science fiction television series set in outer space that was broadcast in the late 1960s and subsequently developed a strong following in reruns, becoming the basis for several sequel series and theatrical films."

"What does that have to do with anything?" Monk asked me.

"The point I was making is that it's none of our business," I said. "Besides, we're supposed to be taking Ambrose sightseeing, not indulging your need to solve mysteries."

"I agree with Adrian," Ambrose said. "These are important laws that govern the universe. We can't stand idly by while they are being violated and people are profiting from it. It's a crime."

"It's unsettling," Monk said, "in a very bad way."

11

Mr. Monk and the Mystery Spot

Everybody who grew up in the Monterey Bay area had been to the Mystery Spot at least once. It was deep in the redwood and eucalyptus forests above Santa Cruz and was the stuff of legend. Rumor had it that all the weird anomalies were caused by the crash landing of an alien spacecraft. There was even talk, especially around Girl Scout troop campfires, that the ghosts of the dead aliens still roamed among the trees at night.

The folks at the Mystery Spot don't bother trying to explain the reasons for the strange goings-on, they just state the facts, if you can call them that. In the late 1930s, a guy built a summer cabin atop the gentle slope. But the cabin toppled downhill, coming to rest at an odd angle. He rebuilt again and again, but the same thing always happened—the cabins slid downhill and landed in the exact same spot as the others, as if pulled inexorably by some powerful magnetic force. So the guy finally gave up the fight and started offering paid tours of the place instead.

His last cabin still sits at the bottom of the slope, dead center atop the Mystery Spot, the seventeen hundred square feet of strangeness surrounded by a tall wood-plank fence to protect people, as well as birds and other wildlife, from accidentally wandering in and becoming disoriented by the "unknown vortex."

However, under proper supervision, the experience could be entertaining, educational, and awe-inspiring.

We drove up the winding, narrow road through the forest to the Mystery Spot, which resembled a children's summer camp with its wooden cabins, well-marked trails, and vans parked in the gravel lot out front.

Ambrose leaned close to the open window and took a deep breath of air, redolent with redwood and eucalyptus.

"It smells like air freshener," he said.

"No, air freshener smells like this," I said.

"Only without all that nature," Monk said. "You don't want nature all over your house."

Monk took his trusty level from the kitchen cabinet, opened the door, and hopped out of the motor home.

Ambrose took a huge step back and grabbed desperately onto the dinette table to avoid being sucked out of the RV by the Mystery Spot vortices.

"Don't ever open the door without warning," Ambrose said. "Terrible things could happen."

"Like what?" Monk asked from the parking lot.

"Someone could fall out and get lost forever in the miasma of humanity."

I paused at the door before going out and looked back at Ambrose. "Are you sure you don't want to come with us and witness the awe and wonder of the Mystery Spot for yourself?"

"I've never been more certain of anything in my life."

I stepped out, firmly closed the door behind me, and ventured into the miasma. As we walked to the ticket booth, I glanced back at the RV and saw Ambrose watching us, his forlorn face pressed against the window.

I insisted that Monk pay the fifteen dollars to cover our admittance and the parking for our RV, since I knew I'd never get paid back if I did it myself, and then we joined the group of adults and children being led up the path to the cabin by the bored young guide.

Her name was Mitzi, and she was wearing khaki slacks and a tan short-sleeve shirt with a badgelike Mystery Spot logo on its chest. The whole ensemble made her look like a junior forest ranger. Mitzi was a local UC Santa Cruz student and this was a part-time job that she found extraordinarily tedious but that gave her time to study.

I deduced that she was a student because of the textbooks, highlighter, UC Santa Cruz thermos, and lipstick tube that I saw on a table in the back of the ticket booth. She was wearing the same color lipstick as was in the tube on the table, and she had a touch of yellow ink on her fingertips from the highlighter.

I deduced that she didn't like her job by the listless way that she performed the lines from her tour script, so I sort of tuned it out, which is why you don't see it reproduced verbatim here.

I was quite pleased with myself for my deductions. But while I was analyzing our guide, Monk was studying the area like it was a crime scene, cocking his head from side to side and holding his hands up in front of him, framing what he was seeing, his level pinned against his side by his arm.

Mitzi took out a board that she demonstrated was flat by laying a level on it. Then she set the board at an angle, placed a billiard ball at the bottom of it, and it rolled up the board, defying gravity. She demonstrated the same trick with a kid's bottle of water, which she laid on its side. The bottle also rolled up.

I was as amazed at that moment as I was when I first saw it as a kid. I felt a rush of nostalgia tinged with joyful bewilderment. The simple, no-frills demonstration was as awesome as any $100 million 3-D effect in *Avatar.*

After the crowd moved on to the next demonstration, Monk took out his own level and set it on the board.

"It's level," I said.

"Of course it is," Monk said.

He didn't seem amazed at all.

The rest of the group was in front of the cabin, which was at a slight angle against the tall fence. Monk stared at the fence while everyone else stared at two six-foot-tall adults who, once they stood on a particular board, seemed to shrink in size when standing beside their much smaller children.

How was that possible?

Mitzi set her level down on the board at their feet to prove it was flat. And it was. There were gasps of disbelief, and everybody whipped out their cameras, cell phones, and camcorders to record the unbelievable event.

Mitzi pointed out that the trees behind us were growing at an angle, pushed by the unseen forces at work in the Mystery Spot. The crowded oohed and aahed, but Monk yawned.

She then led the group into the cabin, where the really amazing things were going on. It was like a carnival funhouse inside, everything slightly askew but without the strange mirrors to distort your perceptions. It was just drab, ordinary wood. And yet people were able to step onto shelves on the wall and stand at forty-five-degree angles without falling. It was creepy. There was a pendulum hanging from a straight ceiling beam that swung only one way instead of in a full arc. Nobody could make it swing in the other direction. It made no sense.

"Did you see that, Rhoda?" said a man with a heavy Southern accent and a huge camera around his neck. "It just won't swing."

"I think I'm gonna puke," said Rhoda, his beanpole of a wife, who was wearing a flowered dress so colorful, it created its own unexplainable vortex. "This place is making me dizzy."

"It will pass and is totally harmless," Mitzi said. "People who are very attuned to nature can be sensitive to dielectric biocosmic radiation."

"That's true, I am a very attuned person," Rhoda said.

"You might want to step outside where the forces aren't quite so powerful and give your personal energy a chance to counterbalance."

Rhoda went outside, but her husband stayed behind to take pictures of his kids standing on the walls at bizarre angles and hanging sideways in midair from handles on the doorframes.

After a few minutes of bending the laws of physics, everyone went back outside, where Mitzi was about to begin another demonstration of the powerful forces at work at the Mystery Spot.

"Who'd like to stand on this picnic table?" she asked.

Half a dozen children raised their hands. Mitzi picked a little Chinese girl who must have been about ten years old and invited her to climb up on the tabletop. The girl did and stood rigidly at a forty-five-degree angle even though she was on a flat surface. Everyone gasped in wonderment and used whatever electronic devices they possessed to share the moment on their Flickr, MySpace, Facebook, YouTube, LiveJournal, Blogger, and Twitter pages.

Monk cocked his head from side to side and rolled his shoulders. He seemed impatient.

"The answers to these mysteries lie well beyond science," Mitzi said by rote, "and continue to defy explanation."

"I can explain them," Monk said.

Everyone turned to him.

"Is it buried wreckage from a flying saucer?" one man asked.

"Is it aberrant magnetic fields?" one woman asked.

"Is it playful ghosts?" a child asked.

"It's none of those things," Monk said. "It's a trick."

Mitzi quickly spoke up. "You are welcome to use your own level or testing equipment anywhere you like, and you will get the same results."

"Undoubtedly," Monk said.

"Then how can it be a trick?" a Chinese man asked, pointing to the little girl on the picnic table. "My daughter is really standing there. She's never been here before. And look at her!"

"It's our eyes and our minds that are deceiving us, helped along by the intentional distortion of the cabin and the fence, which create a false sense of context for everything we see."

"I saw the ball roll upward," a woman said. "And a bottle, too."

"Actually, you saw them rolling down," Monk said.

"I did not," she said.

"Neither did I," said another person.

Soon everyone was voicing their disagreement with Monk's statement.

"You must be a very attuned person, like me," Rhoda said, "because you are seeing things."

"We have a natural need to keep things straight and balanced, and the trickery here plays on that," Monk said. "Here's how it works. The curving trail that led us here, and the fence alongside, were designed to distract us from the angle at which we were walking. The house is tilted far more than it appears to be because part of it is buried in the hillside. The fences are not a uniform height. They are actually taller, narrower, slanted, and shorter in key places to confuse your depth of field. More important, the top of the fence creates a false horizon and, therefore, an inaccurate context from which to determine whether something is actually straight. The truth is, we are all standing at an angle right now. Your daughter is the only one of us who is standing straight relative to the actual landscape."

"You're saying that we're faking ourselves out?" one teenage boy asked.

"Don't take it personally. It's how our brains are wired. That's why all airline cockpits have a gauge called an 'artificial horizon' for pilots to use when the real horizon isn't visible or the context might be deceiving. That fence, this path, and the roofline of the house are artificial horizons, only unlike the gauge in an airplane, these are intentionally designed to fool you." Monk turned to Mitzi and wagged a finger at her. "Shame on you."

"I didn't know," she said. "Honest to God."

I believed her. Everyone was silent for a long, awkward moment while Monk beamed with pride, waiting for the accolades that usually followed one of his summations. But they didn't come. The Chinese girl climbed down from the table and started to cry, her special moment ruined.

I didn't feel so good, either. And it wasn't because I was sensitive to dielectric biocosmic forces. It was a sense of loss. We were all grieving.

Monk was oblivious, of course, because as smart as he was about some things, he was completely clueless when it came to understanding people, unless they'd killed someone. He was the murderer this time, but the victim wasn't a human being.

"I've been coming to the Mystery Spot since I was a kid," one old man said with a heavy sadness in his voice. "It hasn't changed in sixty-five years. I brought my children and my grandchildren here."

"And now you can tell them it's not the Mystery Spot anymore," Monk said. "It's the Solved Spot."

"Where is the wonder in that?" the old man asked.

"Now you don't have to wonder anymore," Monk said. "Your lifetime of confusion and frustration is over."

"Did it ever occur to you, young man, that there isn't enough wonder left in the world?"

"No, it didn't. Wondering is what you do until you find the solution to what you're wondering about, and then order, the natural balance of things, is restored. Wonder is wrong, so I fixed it."

A young woman stepped out of the crowd, her face red with anger. "What you've done is the same thing as standing up in a theater while a magician is performing and telling everybody the secret behind the magic trick. How would you like it if somebody did that?"

"I wish more people would," Monk said. "Then I wouldn't have to do it anymore and all those so-called magicians would be forced to find honest work."

"A magician came to my birthday party and he was great," a little boy said. "Why would you want to ruin his show? Isn't that being rude?"

"Because there's no such thing as magic, only deception, lies, and trickery," Monk said, squatting down to his eye level. "Like Santa Claus."

The boy's faced turned ashen. "Santa Claus isn't real?"

"Obviously not," Monk said. "No more than the Tooth Fairy is."

"She's not real either?" the boy said in horror.

His mother picked up her mortified son and glared furiously at Monk. "You're a monster."

"I'm not the one who is swindling you out of your money with blatant lies and cunning spatial trickery," Monk said and pointed at Mitzi. "It's them."

"I didn't do anything," she said. "I really thought it was a buried meteor or something like that. I feel so stupid."

"No one is angry with you, dear, you're sweet," Rhoda said to her and then glowered at Monk. "But you're not."

Her husband, the big man with the camera, stepped up to Monk and got an inch from his face. "Get out of here, you insensitive bastard, before I beat the crap out of you."

Monk took a step back. "I'm telling the truth."

"You have five seconds," the man said and started counting slowly.

"Could you make it four or six?" Monk asked.

I took Monk by the arm and led him away. "Let's go, Mr. Monk."

He didn't resist and came along with me. He seemed genuinely stunned by everyone's reaction.

"I tried to warn you that this wouldn't go over well," I said as we hurried down the path to the parking lot. "But you wouldn't listen."

"Everything about this place is a lie," he said. "How can they be angry at me for revealing it?"

"To be honest, Mr. Monk, I'm as hurt as they are. The only reason I'm not furious with you is because I know you, and I understand why you were compelled to do what you did." I looked over my shoulder and was relieved to see that nobody was pursuing us yet. "Even if you were wrong to do it."

He looked at me in disbelief. "How can you say that?"

"Because this isn't a mean-spirited ruse. It's harmless entertainment."

"What's entertaining about being deceived?"

"Everyone wants to believe in magic. It's exhilarating to think that on this one tiny patch of land the impossible might just be possible. It's called the willing suspension of disbelief."

"It's called ignorance and self-delusion."

"We do it every time we step into a theater to see a movie or watch a magician. We know it's all fake, that we're watching actors and sleight-of-hand trickery, but we allow ourselves to believe in it anyway because it's fun, it's an escape from our everyday lives."

"You people need psychiatric help, and this place needs to be shut down. I'm calling the police as soon as I get back to the motor home," Monk said. "Save your ticket, Natalie. The detectives will want that as evidence."

But Monk didn't have to call the police. They were already waiting for us.

12

Mr. Monk and the Police

The two police officers were emerging from their patrol car just as we walked up. They'd parked right behind our motor home.

Monk gave me a look of smug satisfaction. "Apparently someone in the tour group realized the seriousness of the crime and called the police. I'm disappointed that it wasn't you."

One of the uniformed officers was a big man with a fat neck that had absorbed his chin so that he appeared to have a very long face. His partner was considerably younger and seemed to be having trouble getting used to wearing his equipment belt.

"I'm so glad to see you two," Monk said. "You got here fast."

Perhaps too fast, as if they'd known that we'd be there. "Are you Mr. Monk?" the chinless cop asked. His name tag identified him as Sergeant Mitchell Brozinsky.

"Yes, I am. Do you need me to brief you on the details of the crime or are you ready to make an arrest?"

"You don't look to me like you're being held against your will," Brozinsky said.

"Maybe he just escaped," the young officer said, hiking up his belt. His name was Santos.

"Wrong Monk," Ambrose said from the open window of the motor home. "I'm the prisoner."

"You called the police?" Monk said. "How could you?"

"I've been abducted from my home, taken captive, and spirited away into the unknown. I'd be a fool not to take advantage of my first opportunity to escape."

"So why are you still in there?" Brozinsky asked. "Are you tied up?"

"No, I'm not," he replied.

"Can you open the door?"

"Yes, but I would prefer not to."

"It's okay, we're here." Brozinsky glanced at the two of us, giving us each the once-over, then turned his gaze back to Ambrose. "They aren't going to hurt you."

"Of course we're not," Monk said. "My name is Adrian Monk, that is my brother, Ambrose, and this is my assistant, Natalie Teeger. We're from San Francisco and we're on a road trip."

"Against my will," Ambrose said. "They put sleeping pills in my birthday cake and I woke up in here."

The sergeant looked at us. "You drugged his cake?"

"It's not as bad as it sounds," I said. "It wasn't malicious or a prank."

"Then what was it?" Santos asked.

"A birthday present," I said, feeling like an idiot. "It's complicated."

Brozinsky sighed and looked back at Ambrose. "You aren't drugged now, are you?"

"No, sir."

"Are you afraid of these two?" Brozinsky asked, gesturing to us.

"No, sir."

"So why won't you come out of that RV?"

"Because I can't," Ambrose said.

Brozinsky rubbed his brow. "You called 911, told the operator that you've been kidnapped and that you're being held prisoner."

"I am."

"But you can walk out of there anytime you want," Brozinsky said.

"No, I can't."

"Are you paralyzed or disabled in some way?" Santos asked.

"Not physically," Ambrose said. "So I would appreciate it if you'd knock me out with tranquilizers and take me back to my house in Tewksbury before I wake up."

Brozinsky turned his back to Ambrose and lowered his voice so only we could hear him. "Is your brother mentally ill?"

"Yes," Monk said.

"No," I said.

"He's only left his house three times in thirty years," Monk said. "And even then only for a few hours."

"That sounds pretty crazy to me," Brozinsky said. "On the other hand, it explains a lot."

"Good," Monk said. "Now that we've settled that, we can focus on the real crime."

"Which is what?" Santos asked.

"That place." Monk pointed at the entrance to the Mystery Spot, where I noticed most of the tour group had gathered to watch us. "The proprietors of the Mystery Spot have been swindling people for seventy years and I can prove it."

"I hope you're arresting him, officers," Rhoda yelled from the crowd. "That man is a lunatic and a danger to the community."

"You are an ignorant rube. You'll thank me later for this," Monk yelled back, then turned again to Brozinsky. "You need to shut this place down immediately and arrest the owners."

"We're not going to arrest them because you didn't enjoy your tour," Brozinsky said.

"You don't understand, Sergeant. I am a detective, I consult with the San Francisco police on their most difficult cases, and I have solved the mystery of the spot."

"No way. It defies explanation," Santos said and pointed at the sign. "It says so right there."

"It's a fraud that has bilked hundreds of thousands of people out of millions of dollars. The only thing that 'defies explanation' is how the Santa Cruz Police Department let it go on for so long. It's either corruption or incompetence, but either way, it's time for justice to finally prevail."

"You stay there, Mr. Monk." Brozinsky motioned me over to one side, out of Monk's earshot, and spoke to me in a low voice. "You seem like a rational person, at least compared to those two."

"Thank you," I said.

"So tell me straight," Brozinsky said. "Is he crazy?"

"Mr. Monk really is a police consultant and a brilliant detective. You can call Captain Leland Stottlemeyer at the SFPD and he'll vouch for him."

"That doesn't explain his rant about the Mystery Spot or why he drugged and abducted his agoraphobic brother."

"Mr. Monk can't resist solving a mystery, and this one was too in-his-face to ignore," I said. "As for his brother,

Ambrose has led a very sheltered life, and all Mr. Monk wants to do is show him the outside world."

"It sounds like a kidnapping to me," he said.

"It's a private, domestic dispute," I said. "It's not a crime like, say, abducting nubile women and sacrificing them to Satan would be."

"Who said anything about Satan or sacrifices?"

"Nobody," I said. "I was just using that as an example. I guess that's not something you see a lot around here."

"Sorting this mess out is beyond my pay grade." He turned back to Santos and raised his voice again. "Watch this bunch for me while I make a call."

Brozinsky went back to the patrol car and got on his radio. Santos hiked up his belt.

"You're in big trouble now, Adrian," Ambrose said through the window. "If you apologize, I won't press charges."

"How kind of you. But I'm not the one who is going to be arrested. *They are.*" Monk pointed to the Mystery Spot ticket booth. "From now on, this will be known as the Solved Spot."

"I don't think it will be as popular," Santos said, fiddling with his belt some more.

"You ought to tighten that belt up a notch," I said.

"I ran out of notches," Santos said.

"Add another one."

"We aren't allowed to modify our equipment. I'll just have to eat a lot of donuts and hope that I fill out some."

"Sounds like hell," I said. "Speaking of which, have you noticed any goats disappearing in the area?"

Before Santos could answer, Brozinsky got out of the squad car. "Captain Simcoe wants to see you, so you're going to have to follow us."

This couldn't be good, but I was in no position to argue.

"What about the Mystery Spot?" Monk said. "It's a crime scene. It should be secured."

"It's been here for seventy years," Brozinsky said. "I'm pretty sure it will be here when we get back."

"But the felons might flee," Monk said.

"We're prepared to take that risk," Brozinsky said.

We got into the motor home. Monk glared at Ambrose, who glared right back. I wasn't worried about the Monk brothers being angry at each other. I had concerns of my own.

"Buckle up, everyone," I said as I got into the driver's seat. "If I see any goats where we're going, we're making a run for it."

We followed the patrol car to a beach in a rocky cove. A jetty of boulders reached out into the bay to protect the little strip of sand from eroding away.

The parking lot was filled with official police vehicles, one of which was a morgue wagon. It was a familiar sight for me, and I didn't like the implications for our vacation. But at least we weren't headed for a sacrificial altar.

I parked horizontally, so I wouldn't have to back up, but it meant that our windows looked right out at the ocean, which ordinarily would have been perfect. Unfortunately, it gave Ambrose an unobstructed view of the young woman's corpse on the sand. It wasn't one of the splendors of the outside world that we'd hoped to show him, especially not on his first day on the road.

"Is she dead?" Ambrose asked.

"They don't call the morgue otherwise," Monk said, peering out the window. There was a lone beach chair, towel, and paperback book on the sand, and the forensic techs were taking pictures of them.

"That's a cold thing to say, Adrian."

"I'm just stating a fact."

"From here," Ambrose said, "she looks like she's sleeping."

"I wish she was," I said.

Brozinsky knocked on the door. I opened it.

"Come with me, please," Brozinsky said, and we stepped out, closing the door behind us.

"What about me?" Ambrose asked from the window.

"Stay there," Brozinsky said.

"No problem," Ambrose replied.

Brozinsky led us down to the beach, where forensic technicians wearing white jumpsuits and plastic booties over their shoes were erecting a tent over the woman's body to preserve the scene and the evidence it contained from the elements.

The woman was attractive, with red hair, and was dressed in sandals, short shorts, and a sleeveless T-shirt. Her freckled skin was chalk white and bloated from being in the water. She looked to me to be in her mid-twenties.

Monk cocked his head, looking at her for a moment before we were greeted by a potbellied detective wearing dark sunglasses and a toupee that looked like a carpet sample. The sleeves of his blue shirt were rolled up, and his red tie was loose at the collar. His badge hung from a chain around his neck in case somebody couldn't tell that he was a cop from the handcuffs and holstered gun clipped to his belt.

"Thank you for coming down, Mr. Monk," he said, offering him his hand. "I'm Captain Russell Simcoe. I saw you speak a few years back at a police conference in San Francisco."

Monk shook his hand, then motioned to me for a disinfectant wipe, which I already had ready for him. "So you know me to be a man of sterling character and you realize that my brother's charges against me are preposterous."

"Of course," he said, watching Monk clean his hands and drop the wipe in the Ziploc baggie that I held open for him. "I know how complex family relationships can be. Don't worry about any of that."

"Thank you, Captain, we both appreciate it," I said. "I'm Natalie Teeger, by the way, Mr. Monk's assistant."

"It's a pleasure to meet you, too," Simcoe said.

"What are you going to do about the Mystery Spot?" Monk asked.

"I'm assigning a special task force to look into it immediately."

Simcoe was being facetious, but Monk's eye for detail didn't extend to the subtleties of human interaction, especially when it came to the nuances of speech. But I got it, and Simcoe knew that I did.

"That's good news," Monk said. "So why are we here?"

"Please forgive me, but once I heard you were in town, I couldn't resist seeing you in action," Simcoe said, gesturing to the body. "A swimmer found her floating in the water and brought her ashore. The ME figures she's been in the water since early this morning. She doesn't have any ID, a phone, nothing. She's the second woman to get swept off the rocks by waves this month. I thought you might be able to tell me whether it was an accident or suicide."

Before I could say that we couldn't help him, that we were on vacation and would have to go, Monk spoke up.

"It's neither," he said. "It was murder."

Simcoe couldn't have been more stunned if Monk had slapped him across the face.

And I felt like slapping Monk. He'd spoken without thinking of the consequences of what he was about to say and what they would mean to Ambrose and me.

"How can you say that?" Simcoe said. "You've been here two minutes and you haven't even examined the body yet."

"It's obvious," Monk said.

"Not to me," Simcoe said.

"No wonder the Mystery Spot was able to thrive here for seventy years," Monk said. "She's wearing sandals with half-inch heels. She couldn't have walked on the rocks with those. Her heels would have gotten stuck and she would have fallen."

"That's probably exactly what happened. She's got a wound where her head hit the rocks," Simcoe said, crouching down and turning the victim's head so we could see the contusion on the left side of her skull. "The ME says it definitely would have knocked her out."

"I'm sure it did," Monk said. "But she didn't get it losing her footing on the rocks. She's too familiar with the water to make a mistake like going out there with those sandals on."

"You don't know that," Simcoe said. "You don't even know who she is."

"I know that she's in her mid-twenties and has been rowing boats and swimming for most of her life."

"How do you know that?"

Monk crouched beside him and pointed to her arms. "She's got an inch-long, hairline scar behind the elbow on the inside of both of her arms."

I crouched down so I could see the scars, too, getting sucked into the situation despite myself. It was amazing to me that Monk had spotted those scars in a single glance. Then again, he had an uncanny knack for picking up things that were out of the ordinary.

"What's that have to do with rowing?" Simcoe asked.

"The scar is from a medial epicondylectomy and ulnar nerve decompression. It's done to relieve a condition that's commonly known as 'tennis elbow' because so many players in the sport are afflicted with it, typically between the ages of thirty and fifty. The condition is characterized by elbow pain and numbness in their forearms, pinkies, and ring fingers caused by damaged tendons and pinched ulnar nerves, the result of hitting hundreds of thousands of tennis balls, year after year. One of the few sports that would inflict that kind of repetitive stress injury on *both* elbows is rowing or swimming."

"Couldn't it be weight lifting?"

"Perhaps," Monk said. "But she doesn't have the upper-body muscle definition that would come from that kind of bodybuilding."

Simcoe nodded and looked at me. "Damn, he's good."

"There's more," Monk said.

"There is?" Simcoe said.

"There always is," I said wearily. I could see what this was going to lead to.

"She's fair skinned and burns easily. She wouldn't go in the sun without strong sunscreen. But there isn't a bottle of sunscreen on her towel."

"Maybe that's why she was here so early," Simcoe said, "to enjoy the beach before the sun got too intense."

"That could be, but the novel on her chair belies that theory."

"It does?" Simcoe looked over at the chair. "What's so special about the book?"

"It's *Moby Dick*," Monk said.

"You can see that from here?"

"I saw it when we walked over. She'd never read that book. She's a whale lover."

"Is there a scar on her body that tells you that?"

"No, there's a bumper sticker on her car," Monk said.

"How do you know which car is hers?"

Monk pointed to the parking lot. "There's only one car in the lot with a roof rack for a kayak, and it has a Greenpeace sticker on the rear bumper."

I'd noticed the car. It was an old Volvo sedan. Based on the car, I could make a few stereotypical deductions about her myself.

"Why did you even notice the sticker?" Simcoe said.

"I couldn't help it," Monk said. "It's off center."

"My God," Simcoe said. "You're saying this was all staged by her killer. She was clobbered and thrown in the water."

Monk nodded. "Do you have any suspects?"

"How could I? Until now, I didn't even know she'd been murdered."

"So where should we start?" Monk asked.

"By leaving here as fast as we can," I said, taking Monk by the arm and leading him back toward the RV. "We're on vacation."

"But we don't know who killed her."

"Captain Simcoe can send us a postcard with the solution," I said.

"I can't walk away from a murder investigation."

"Our trip began today, but if you get involved in this investigation, it ends right now because I will leave you here alone."

"You wouldn't do that."

"Try me," I said, staring him right in the eye. I meant it and I wanted him to know it. "I remember what happened to our vacations in Hawaii, Germany, and France. If you're serious about the gift you want to give Ambrose, then you will get in that motor home with me right now, continue on with our road trip, and let the police handle this case on their own."

"I don't think I can do that," Monk said. "I've never left a case unsolved."

"How can you expect Ambrose to find the courage to leave his house, to overcome his greatest fear, when you can't even summon the will to walk away from an investigation?"

I turned my back on him and walked across the beach toward the parking lot, leaving him standing indecisively on the sand, halfway between the crime scene and the motor home.

13

Mr. Monk Drives Through

I picked up a couple of sand dollars off the beach to keep as souvenirs and got into the motor home.

Ambrose sat at the dinette, sipping a bottle of Fiji water and watching his brother, who was standing still, looking back and forth between the corpse and the RV.

I slid into the booth beside Ambrose and showed him the sand dollars, setting them down in front of him. This was probably the first time in at least thirty years, if not his whole life, that he'd been this close to a seashell.

"These are for you," I said. "Your first souvenirs of the trip."

"What are they?"

"Seashells. These particular ones are called sand dollars because of their shape, but they are actually a type of sea urchin."

Ambrose nodded and leaned back. "In other words, you've just dropped the skeletons of two dead sea creatures on the table where we eat."

"I thought you might like them, especially with that leaflike pattern in the center. I used to spend hours collecting them when I was a kid. You can keep them like this, or we can paint them, or we can coat them with shellac, which will make them smooth and shiny."

"What a good idea. Why don't you go out, pick up the woman's decomposing corpse, and drop her on the kitchen table while you're at it? Maybe we can preserve her in shellac, too."

"Go to hell." I got up, stuck the sand dollars in a drawer, and slammed it shut.

"What's the matter with you?"

"You and your brother, that's what. I've had it. Both of you are selfish, insensitive slaves to your individual routines and rituals. Neither one of you will compromise for anyone else, even if doing so would make you both infinitely happier and your lives a lot easier. There's a reason why both of you are alone."

"Adrian has you."

"Because he pays me."

"That's not why you're with him," Ambrose said, "or why you're here right now."

I gave him a hard, angry stare and he wilted under it, shifting his gaze around so it was anywhere but on me.

"If you realize that, Ambrose, then you understood exactly what motivated us to bring you here. You should be ashamed of yourself for calling the police." I glanced out the window at Monk, who was still standing in place, his hands balled into fists, shifting his weight between his feet. "And if Mr. Monk comes back here instead of returning to that crime scene, then you'd better appreciate the sacrifice he's making and dedicate yourself to making this trip work. Otherwise, you don't deserve to have people like us in your life, and I'll gladly take you back right now to that big empty house where you belong."

I didn't wait for him to say anything. I went to the driver's seat, buckled up, and started the engine.

Suddenly the door to the motor home flew open and Monk flung himself inside as if he were leaping onto a speeding train, which was odd, since the RV wasn't moving yet.

"Floor it, woman," Monk yelled, "before I can jump out again!"

I shifted the RV into drive and sped off as fast as I could without getting a ticket from the cops all around us.

Monk sat down across from Ambrose and gripped the edges of the table.

"Someone killed a woman and tried to disguise it as an accident," Monk said. "And I don't know who did it and I'm not going to do anything to find out."

"Is that hard for you?" Ambrose asked.

"No harder than deciding not to breathe."

"Now you know how I feel leaving the house."

"Then I guess we're in this together now," Monk said.

I drove as if we were being pursued by Satanists. I wanted to put as much distance between us and Santa Cruz as I could before we stopped for the night, which I figured would be somewhere around Carmel, since I wanted to make the trip through Big Sur in the daylight so Ambrose wouldn't miss the stunning coastline and one of the best drives in the nation.

I briefly entertained the notion of parking in the driveway of my parents' house in Monterey, sleeping in my old bedroom, and leaving the Monks on their own in the motor home for the first night, but that felt like cheating. Besides, I didn't really want to deal with my parents and their bound-to-be negative, and heavily judgmental, reaction to the Monks, the road trip in the motor home, my job, and my continuing singlehood.

While I drove, Monk and Ambrose thoroughly washed and scrubbed the tabletop so we wouldn't be poisoned by the deadly germs left by the sand dollars.

It also distracted Monk for a short time from the murder investigation he'd left behind. He was beginning to shake like an addict going through withdrawal.

"It couldn't hurt to call Captain Simcoe just to see how things are going," Monk said.

"There is only one cell phone in this motor home, and it's in the pocket of my pants. I've also removed the battery and Sim card and put them in the suitcase with my underwear."

I might as well have put the components of the phone in canisters of nuclear waste. Monk would never reach into my pocket or go near my underwear.

But I'd told him a lie. The phone was still in my purse. I hadn't had a chance yet to dismantle my phone. I would do it as soon as we stopped for the night.

"What if they need to reach me?" Monk asked.

"They've solved crimes before you got there and they will continue to do so long after you've left."

"Tell that to the millions of people conned by the Mystery Spot."

"You can contact Captain Simcoe when we get back to San Francisco," I said. "If they still need your help, they can hire you."

"What's the dinner plan?" Ambrose asked me.

"We don't have one. In fact, we don't have a plan for anything that's going to happen over the next few days."

"Isn't that reckless?" he asked.

"Yes," Monk said.

"We're opening ourselves up to the unknown," I said. "It's called experiencing life."

"I close my door and lock it against the unknown and then hide in my bed where it can't find me," Ambrose said. "It's called protecting life."

"That's not living, that's hiding," I said. "We don't want to be locked down. We want the freedom and discovery that comes from simply waiting to see what happens. Not knowing what we're going to have for dinner is the first step."

"Does it have to be such a big first step?"

He turned to Monk for support, but his brother was curled up in a semifetal position on the couch, clutching the can of Lysol to his chest for comfort.

That's when I spotted a bunch of fast-food restaurants at the next exit.

"Have you ever had a drive-through meal before?" I asked Ambrose.

"No," Ambrose said.

"Then here comes another new experience," I said, and took the exit, pausing at the stop sign at the end of the off-ramp. There were lots of restaurants to choose from, so I picked Carl's Jr., the one with the fewest cars in the drive-through line.

I took a right, turning the motor home in a wide arc, and then made another hard right into the Carl's Jr. parking lot, clipping the curb and nearly sideswiping a parked Nissan, before sliding into the narrow drive-through lane, stopping just shy of the menu board.

"How does it work?" Ambrose asked.

"You pick what you want to eat from the menu and give your order to the cashier, who will communicate with you via a microphone. Then we drive up to the cashier's window, we pay him, then we go to the next window, where another person will give us our food in take-out containers. And then you drive off with it."

"People do this a lot?" Ambrose said.

"It's great when you want a quick snack on the go and don't have time to stop in a restaurant."

"I don't know why anyone would want to eat in their car," Monk said. "You have to eat from your lap, and food shouldn't be anywhere near that bodily zone."

"Why not?" I asked.

"Because the lap region is fraught with peril."

"You make it sound like there are land mines buried there," I said.

"Worse than that," Monk said. "It's like eating your food off a toilet seat."

"It's a moot point anyway," I said. "Since we're in a motor home, we can eat at the table."

"That's far more civilized," Monk said.

I drove up to the menu board so that the microphone was right outside my driver's-side window. Excuse me, the *port* side of the RV. The Monk brothers gathered behind my seat and peered out the open window at the menu selections.

"Welcome to Carl's Jr.," the cashier asked, his voice sounding scratchy over the bad speaker. "How can I help you today?"

"I'd like the Grilled Cheese Bacon Six Dollar Burger meal with a Coke," I said.

Ambrose furrowed his brow. "Why is it called Six Dollar Burger if it's $4.89?"

The cashier answered right away. "Because you are getting a Six Dollar Value for only $4.89."

"You should call it the $4.89 burger," Ambrose said, "and charge $4.89."

"It's better to charge $6," Monk said. "It's an even number."

"Good point," Ambrose said. "You should call it a Six Dollar Burger and charge $6."

"Would you like to order the Six Dollar Burger, sir?" the cashier asked.

"I can't understand your chicken choices," Monk said.

"How can I help you?" the cashier asked.

"You can explain to me why you only offer chicken strips in three- or five-piece quantities and not four or six and why you offer children chicken nuggets shaped like five-pointed stars in six- or nine-piece portions instead of a four- or six-pointed star in six- and ten-piece quantities."

There was a long pause before the cashier spoke again.

"How can I help you, sir?"

"Why does he keep saying that?" Monk asked me.

"He wants your order, Mr. Monk."

"Fine." Monk nodded, and then spoke in a deeper, more authoritative voice. "I *order* you not to produce chicken stars with an uneven number of points or serve them in odd-numbered quantities."

"I meant that he's waiting for you to order what you want to eat," I said.

"I can't decide," Monk said.

"I know what I want," Ambrose said, then leaned his head toward the open window, careful, though, to remain completely inside the motor home. "Hello, sir. My name is Ambrose Monk, and I would like to have the Six Dollar Burger and I'd like to pay $6 for it. I'd like the patty, the bacon, the cheese, the lettuce, and the bread all packaged separately. Thank you."

"I'll have the same thing," Monk said.

The cashier repeated our order, then added, "Do you really want your hamburgers served with all the ingredients packaged separately, or was that a joke?"

"The joke would be eating it with it all combined," Ambrose said.

"I don't see the humor," Monk said.

"Because you don't have a sense of humor," Ambrose said. "I do. A rather sophisticated sense, I might add, which is why I can appreciate the humorous aspects of the menu."

"There are jokes on the menu?"

"Just look at the Western Bacon Cheeseburger. It's described as a charbroiled all-beef patty, two strips of bacon, melted American cheese, two crispy onion rings, and tangy barbecue sauce on a toasted sesame seed bun. Nobody would ever eat that. It's a complex, subversive, satirical comment."

"A comment on what?" Monk asked.

"Gluttony and sloth," Ambrose said. "This Carl Jr. fellow has a wicked wit."

I drove forward to the cashier's window, and to my surprise and delight, Ambrose paid for our food, proving that being a penny-pinching tightwad didn't run in Monk's family. What didn't surprise me was that Ambrose insisted on paying six dollars for the six-dollar burgers, much to the dismay of the startled teenager manning the register. I told the cashier to consider it a tip for his patience.

We got our food in nearly a dozen bags, and I parked the RV in the lot so we could eat while the food was still warm.

The three of us sat at the table. The Monks stared at me incredulously while I ate my hamburger, and I stared at them with the same sentiment as they ate their hamburgers, the components of which were spread out over a dozen cardboard boxes.

Ambrose studied me as if I were performing some

strange and primitive ritual. "I don't know how it's even physically possible to eat a hamburger in your lap."

"Certainly not the way you do it," I said, motioning to all the boxes for their hamburgers.

"What other way is there?" he asked.

"Like this." I demonstrated by taking a big bite out of my hamburger, nearly squirting the lettuce and secret sauce from the other end.

Ambrose glanced at his brother. "I'm beginning to think that *you* are the one assisting *her*, not the other way around. How does she get along without you?"

Monk shrugged. "It's one of the few mysteries I haven't been able to solve."

14

Mr. Monk and the Trailer Park

The Sandy View Trailer Park was a few miles off the highway on a densely wooded bluff of pine and eucalyptus trees above a narrow strip of beach.

We drove in just before dark, which was a good thing, since the fifty or so RV spots were nestled amid the trees at the edge of a cliff. I didn't want to risk plowing into the water and power hookups, or grazing a tree, or going over the edge on my first visit to a trailer park.

There was a small gatehouse and store, built out of an odd mix of wood and neon that made it look like a log cabin that aspired to be a 7-Eleven, just past the gate. I ran in quickly, paid the rental fee, and got a Xeroxed map to our campsite from the clerk, a fat-cheeked, big-eyed guy in a checked flannel shirt, overalls, and a cap. He could have been a woodsy Satanist, but I didn't get a good look at him because I was in a hurry to get parked before the sun set.

I managed to park us in our spot without smashing

the picnic table or sideswiping the RV parked on our port side, an old Winnebago that even in the waning light looked as if it had seen a lot of road. Our neighbor's Winnebago was a class A, meaning it was one unit rather than a cab-over camper grafted onto a recognizable truck or van, and had a tattered, retractable awning extended over its campsite picnic table. The back end of the rig was wallpapered with bumper stickers from all the states, cities, and attractions that the owner had visited.

I hit the leveling control button on the dashboard. Our motor home shimmied gently as the vehicle hydraulically settled itself into a perfect balance on the uneven surface.

Monk and Ambrose clutched their seats during the process as if we were on a boat that was being violently tossed by stormy seas.

"Relax," I said. "The motor home is just leveling itself."

"It can do that?" Monk said, sharing a look of awe with his brother.

"Yes," I said, "it can."

"Amazing," Ambrose said.

I knew they'd like that.

"I don't understand why all vehicles aren't equipped with this sensible feature," Monk said.

"Why stop there?" Ambrose said. "They should install it on beds, chairs, desks, tables, bookcases, and file cabinets, too."

"And shoes," Monk said. "Then everyone would be level at all times on every surface."

"You're suggesting we wear hydraulic leveling shoes," I said. "Don't you think it would be cheaper, and far less cumbersome, to just rely on your own sense of equilibrium?"

"Mine, yes," he said. "Yours, no. Sadly, most people are seriously unbalanced."

"That's another reason why it's better to just stay at home," Ambrose said.

Once the motor home achieved its balance, I hopped out in a hurry, eager to hook us up to the electricity, freshwater, and sewer while I could still see what I was doing in more than just the dim glow of the lights from the neighboring Winnebago's windows.

Our RV had three holding tanks—one for freshwater, the other two, the gray and the black, for wastewater. The gray tank held whatever went down the sink and shower drains, and the black held whatever was flushed down the toilet. Neither of the wastewater tanks was even close to full yet, but I still didn't want to mix up their lines or accidentally open one of them all over our campsite.

The hookup, or shore power as the RV rental guy called it, was a metal box containing the electrical outlet and an adjacent faucet. We didn't really need the shore power or water—we had plenty of water in our holding tank and our batteries were charged—but there was no reason not to tap into those resources while we had the opportunity.

Monk had insisted on filling our holding tank with Fiji bottled water to start, which was a laborious task he did entirely on his own. But I made it clear that we wouldn't be able to repeat it on the road. So we compromised by installing a filter onto the hose that attached the RV to campsite faucets, but I'm sure that did little to make Monk feel secure. He considered tap water only slightly cleaner than urine.

I looked around for the sewer outlet and soon found a metal cap obscured by a clump of weeds at the edge of the campsite. The weeds were actually the sign that revealed the sewer's location. The RV rental guy told me to look for the weeds, which thrived on the fertilizing, sewer-line spillage.

Now that I knew where everything was, I could begin plugging our motor home into it all.

I opened up a compartment on the side of the RV and pulled out a long electrical cord, which I plugged into the shore power outlet. Next I took out the fresh-water hose line and attached it first to the RV's water valve and then to the campsite faucet, which I opened up. Power and water were now flowing freely into our motor home.

So far, so good.

Now I had to deal with the waste system.

I opened the compartment containing the wastewa-ter tanks and put on the pair of rubber gloves that I'd stowed there earlier. I screwed the wastewater hose to the Y fitting that served both tanks, which emptied through a common hose that I fed into the sewer outlet. I dragged the hose over to the sewer outlet and slid it open with my shoe, releasing a horrific odor. I held my breath and snaked the pipe inside. I hoped that Monk hadn't seen how I'd opened the outlet or he might de-mand that my shoes be incinerated.

I went back to the RV and opened the gray tank valve so the water from the sinks and shower could feed freely into the sewer. I wouldn't empty the black water tank for a couple days so that there would be enough liquid inside to flush out the solids. That's probably more de-tail than you want to know, so I'll stop right there. But I will say that it wasn't a task I was looking forward to, especially since I knew that I could expect no help what-soever from Monk when the time came to do it.

I was standing there, looking over everything, and go-ing through a mental checklist to make sure there was nothing that I'd overlooked, when I heard a man's voice behind me.

"Newbie?" His voice was ragged and had a slight Southern twang.

I turned and saw the man's gaunt face in the half-open window of the Winnebago. His weather-beaten skin was like a thin layer of fading paint, his hair a few strands of windblown straw. He looked like a scarecrow, brought to life by the translucent tube that was looped over his ears and stuck into his nostrils, feeding him with oxygen.

Whatever the disease was that had ravaged him had made it hard to peg his age. He could have been any-where between sixty and ninety years old. But his bright blue eyes flashed with vitality and a touch of mischief, so whatever his age, he was clearly young at heart.

"How did you guess?" I replied.

"I'm a keen observer of human nature. Plus you look terrified that you've made a mistake."

"Have I?"

He smiled. His teeth were yellowed and seemed to have too much space between them. I wondered whether that was a symptom of his disease or its treatment.

"You might want to turn on your propane. It will save you a trip outside if you want to cook a meal, heat your motor home, or have a hot shower. It can get very chilly here late at night and early in the morning."

I did as he suggested, and when I came back, I saw that Monk had come out with his level, which he pressed up against the RV at various points.

"It really is level," Monk said.

I smiled and noticed that our neighbor was smiling, too. I decided to make introductions.

"I'm Natalie Teeger, that fellow with the level is

Adrian Monk, and the man in the window staring at you is his brother, Ambrose."

"Glad to meet you, fellow wanderers. I'm Dub Clemens. How long have you been on the road?"

"Less than a day," I said, standing beneath his window. I could hear the hum of his oxygen device now. "We left San Francisco this morning."

"The successful end of the first day of a maiden voyage deserves proper recognition. Come aboard and we'll celebrate. I make the best martinis west of the Mississippi and east of it, too."

"Technically, that would be the entire nation," Ambrose said from his perch at the dinette window. "Minus Alaska and Hawaii, of course."

"By God, you're right," Dub said from his window, directly across from Ambrose. "I've got to get myself to Alaska and Hawaii so I can conquer their martini-meisters, too. So come aboard, sample the fruits of my decades of studious mixology, and tell me if I've got a chance at prevailing in those colder and tropical climes."

"We don't drink," Monk said.

"Speak for yourself," I said. "I'd love a martini, Dub. Let me just pop out my slide-outs and I'll be right over."

"I'll get the party started," he said, and disappeared inside.

I passed by Monk and went back into our motor home. He rushed in after me.

"That was obscene," Monk said, "and you aren't even drunk yet."

"What are you talking about?" I said, going to the control console mounted on the wall beside the door and squinting at the array of buttons.

"Your salacious remark about popping out," he said.

"I was referring to this," I said, and hit a button that

expanded the two slide-outs, the port-side dinette area and the starboard side of the aft master bedroom.

The slide-outs extended from the RV by a few feet on both sides, greatly enlarging the interior space. As soon as the dinette area began to move, Ambrose scrambled out of his seat and threw himself across the motor home to the safety of the galley.

"Does this vehicle ever stop moving?"

"Sorry about that, Ambrose. I'm enlarging the motor home to its full size," I said. "Now we have even more room to move around in."

"Are there any other surprises I should know about?" he asked.

"She's a lush," Monk said.

"Having one drink after a long day does not make me a lush," I said. "I am just being sociable."

"With a complete stranger," Ambrose added.

"That's how you make friends," I said. "Everyone is a stranger at first, even the people you eventually fall in love with."

"It's good that I'll be staying behind," Ambrose said. "I can keep a close eye on you and call for help if Mr. Clemens drugs your alcoholic beverages, pulls out an ax, and hacks you both to pieces."

"I doubt he's an ax murderer," I said, though for a moment I wondered whether his easy amiability hid any demonic intentions. I decided I was just being silly. None of the Satanists in *Race with the Devil* were as immediately friendly as Dub, nor were they as seriously ill as he obviously was, so I headed for the door. "Are you coming, Mr. Monk?"

"I'm not drinking anything," Monk said, following me. "I'll be your designated walker."

"It's not a long trip from his motor home to ours," I said. "I think I can handle it."

"We're on the edge of a cliff," Monk said.

"Good point," I said.

"I'll be keeping my eye on you both," Ambrose said.

We walked over to Dub's RV and knocked on the open door before entering.

"Come on in," Dub said, and we stepped inside.

Our RV was essentially a hotel suite on wheels, but his was an apartment. The linoleum was scuffed, the carpets were ragged and stained from use, the faux-leather couches were creased, and there were newspapers, magazines, and paperback books on almost every surface. But it wasn't unattractive or messy. The wear and tear and the clutter gave the motor home a lived-in quality that made it feel cozy and warm, a place where time had been spent and memories made.

But Monk grimaced, clearly put off that the place wasn't antiseptically clean. Although Monk had lived in his apartment for almost twenty years, it looked like a model home that had never actually been occupied. I found Monk's place cold and uncomfortable. Every time I tried to warm it up by hanging a photo taken of him, or by displaying a souvenir from one of our adventures, or by leaving something of my own around, like an afghan to curl up with on the couch on a foggy afternoon, he quickly got rid of whatever it was and put it in a cupboard.

The floor plan of Dub's RV was about the same as ours, except that the cockpit was fully integrated into the motor home. The creased, well-worn captain's chairs for the driver and passenger swiveled around to face the living area.

Dub was at the galley, emptying the contents of his silver mixing jug into the last of the four martini glasses he'd lined up on the counter in front of a frosty bottle of Bombay Sapphire Gin that he'd obvious kept stowed in his freezer. I wondered where the vermouth was.

He was not a well man. His skin was pale, and his sweatshirt and jeans were baggy, as if he'd shrunk a few sizes since buying them, and he wore shoes with Velcro straps so he didn't have to bother tying laces. The oxygen tube under his nose was attached to a long, clear line that pooled around his feet and snaked back into the rear bedroom, so he could roam around the entire RV without dragging the tank along with him.

I could see file boxes stacked between the bed and the wall and a laptop computer amid his rumpled sheets.

"Help yourself to some mixed nuts," Dub said, motioning to a bowl of nuts on the dinette table.

"We don't eat mixed nuts," Monk said.

"I do," I said, reaching for a handful.

"It's dangerous," Monk said.

"They're cashews and peanuts," I said. "Not nitro and glycerin."

"There are things that shouldn't be mixed," Monk said. "And by that I mean all things."

"You're an interesting fellow, Adrian," Dub said. "Where's your brother?"

"He can't make it," I said.

Dub looked out the open galley window and saw Ambrose looking right back at him from the window of our RV.

"Do you have a prior engagement?" Dub asked.

"Nope," Ambrose said.

"Feeling ill?"

"Nope."

"So why don't you join us?"

"I don't go out."

Dub nodded, as if he understood. "You're about to begin a love affair, my friend."

"I don't see how," Ambrose said, "or with whom."

"With that motor home you're in. You can be footloose and fancy free and yet you can sleep every night in your own bed and you never have to use a strange restroom. Wherever you go, you're always home."

"Is that why you travel in a motor home?" Monk asked.

"I'm a wanderer by nature, Adrian," Dub said, dropping a lemon peel in each of the martini glasses. "I've got lung cancer, and I barely have the energy to walk much farther than the length of this RV. But I'll be damned if I'm going to let it imprison me in a room until I die. That'd rot my insides faster than the cancer. So I hit the road. Besides, I still have one more story to write."

"I don't leave the house," Ambrose said. "Does that mean my insides are rotting?"

"Only you can answer that, my friend," Dub said. "But while you're at it, think about this: Depriving a man of his freedom by confining him to one place for a long period of time is the worst punishment that we, as a society, inflict on someone, short of taking their lives. Why do you think that is? And why do you think we have that in common with most civilized societies on earth?"

Dub picked up a tiny atomizer off the counter, sprayed something into the martini glass, and handed it to me.

"I saw that," Monk said.

"Saw what?"

"Don't play innocent with me. You spiked her drink," Monk said. "What did you put in there? LSD? Ecstasy? Rohypnol?"

"Vermouth," Dub said. "The ideal martini has three measures of gin to about one tablespoon of dry vermouth. But it's hard to get the balance quite right. It's more instinct than measurement, anyway. I used to put the vermouth in the glass first, then pour it out before adding the gin. But it was a tricky, imprecise procedure and a waste of good vermouth. The vermouth mist is a big improvement."

He handed me a martini.

"You are serious about your martinis," I said.

"H. L. Mencken, a titan in my field and a connoisseur of language, once said that the martini is almost as perfect as a sonnet. Since I can't write a decent sonnet, I applied myself to mastering the martini instead."

I took a sip. I'd been a bartender before Monk hired me as his assistant, and I'd made plenty of martinis in my time, but they tasted like rubbing alcohol compared to the exceptionally clean, dry, extra smooth drink that Dub made. It was the best martini I'd ever tasted and the last thing I ever expected to experience on my first night in a trailer park.

"It's incredible, Dub," I said.

He beamed with pleasure. "You want to take one of these over to Ambrose?"

"No, thank you," Ambrose said. "I don't indulge in spirits."

"You ever tried any?" Dub asked.

"I've had Hawaiian Punch when I needed to drown my sorrows," Ambrose said. "It gives me a headache."

"What do you drink when you want to celebrate?"

"Water," Ambrose said.

"The hard stuff," Dub said.

Ambrose shook his head. "Just bottled. I won't drink from the tap."

"You're a fascinating man." Dub turned and offered the glass to Monk. "Here you go, Adrian. Drink up."

"I don't think so," Monk said.

"You'll like it, Mr. Monk," I said. "It's crisp, dry, and strong. It tastes like cleanliness."

"Fiji water is as clean as a beverage can get," Monk said. "And it doesn't dull your faculties."

"What do you need your faculties for now?" I asked.

"To stay alive."

"We aren't in any danger," I said. "I don't see any axes around."

"He doesn't need one," Monk said. "He can use his gun."

"What gun?" I asked.

"The .357 Magnum under his bed," Monk said.

15

Mr. Monk and the First Night

I leaned to one side so I could peer into the bedroom and, sure enough, I saw the barrel of a gun poking out from under his bed.

"I'll call the police," Ambrose called out from our RV, a hint of panic in his voice. "As soon as I find the phone and put it back together."

It was in my purse, as you may recall, which was beside the driver's seat of our RV. But I didn't tell Ambrose that because I didn't feel the same sense of urgency that he did. Maybe it was the excellent martini or the smile on Dub's face. Whatever the reason, I felt relaxed and perfectly safe. I took another sip of my martini instead.

"The gun is not for you," Dub said.

"That's a relief," I said. "Saving it for devil worshippers?"

"I haven't run across any, but I don't think I'd shoot any of them if I did."

"You might if they ignited a ring of fire around your RV and started sacrificing goats."

Ambrose leaned his head out of the RV and shouted, "Where do you keep the rubber gloves, Adrian? I have to go into Natalie's underwear."

Dub gave me a look.

I flushed with embarrassment and took a big gulp of my martini. "Give me the gun, Dub. I may need to shoot myself before this trip is over."

"That's exactly why I have it," Dub said.

"You're going to shoot yourself?" Monk asked.

"That's the plan. When the day comes that I can't breathe, and I'm flopping around on the floor like a fish out of water, I'll pull the trigger and end my misery."

"That's going to make a big mess," Monk said, "and she's not going to appreciate that."

Adrian Monk, Mr. Sensitivity.

"I'm not going to be here," I said, and then immediately regretted the insensitivity of my own remark. "I mean, it's not that I don't care, Dub. I already like you so much that I can't bear to think about you dying."

"I don't like thinking about it myself," he said, "which is another reason I like to end the day with a martini. Or two. Or three."

"I wasn't talking about you, Natalie," Monk said. "I was referring to his girlfriend, a young Japanese woman in her early twenties, who is about five foot four, 120 pounds, and does all the driving."

Dub arched an eyebrow and sipped his drink. "How can you possibly suggest such a divine creature resides in this humble rolling abode with an old fart like me?"

"For starters, the strands of long black hair on the floor, the pair of traditional *tatami zori* sandals in the bathroom, and the bottle of lactase pills on the kitchen counter."

Dub smiled with amusement. I think he was very glad that he'd invited us over.

"You don't have to be a Japanese woman to have long black hair, wear *tatami zori* sandals, or be lactose intolerant."

"True, but most Japanese people of either sex have black hair. The length of that hair and the style and size of the sandals suggest the presence of a Japanese woman. The sandals also indicate the size of her feet, from which I can reasonably calculate her height and weight. It's an approximation confirmed, incidentally, by the distance between the driver's seat of the RV and the steering wheel, which is too tight to accommodate a man of your height, hence, it's clear that she also does the driving. Furthermore, difficulty digesting dairy products is a common affliction among ninety-five percent of the Japanese people."

"What makes you think this mythical Japanese goddess is in her twenties and not her sixties?" Dub asked.

"Her sunglasses are resting on the cup holder by the driver's seat. I can see from here that the lens doesn't have a prescription, which suggests that she has twenty-twenty eyesight, not something most people over thirty are likely to have. In addition, there's a tube of lipstick that's fallen between two of the couch cushions. It's the same color and brand favored by Natalie's daughter, who is in her late teens."

"A splendid demonstration of deductive reasoning," Dub said. "You must be a detective."

"As a matter of fact, I am."

"You are very observant, but you've made one significant error. Yuki isn't my girlfriend. She is my assistant."

"Everyone has one but me," Ambrose said.

I was so relaxed by my martini and caught up in Monk's performance that I'd entirely forgotten that

Ambrose was out there, eavesdropping on our conversation from the safety of our RV.

"I knew I wasn't capable of piloting this vessel on my own, so I asked Yuki, my neighbor back home in St. Louis, to join me on this last adventure," Dub said, then turned to Monk. "Speaking of which, she knows what I intend to do when my end comes, and she's fine with that."

"She must be a strong woman," Monk said.

"With a strong stomach," Ambrose added.

The Monk brothers, paragons of sensitivity.

"Where is she now?" I asked.

"We travel with her small motor scooter, and she scooted off an hour ago. My guess is that she's gone to the nearest town for some entertainment and a respite from my neediness."

"It's amazing how much you have in common with Mr. Monk and his brother."

"He's nothing like us at all," Monk said. "Look how he lives."

"I am looking, and for once it seems I'm more observant than you are. You and Dub are both traveling on the open road with your comely young female assistants at the wheel. Dub, like you, is a professional observer of human nature. And Dub, like Ambrose, is a writer who doesn't leave his house."

Dub looked out the window at Ambrose. "You're a fellow scribe? What do you write?"

"My specialty is instruction manuals," Ambrose said. "What's yours?"

"Investigative reporting, a profession that may die before I do, if it isn't dead already. I've already outlived all the newspapers I've worked for. I may be the last member of a soon-to-be-extinct species."

"What story are you chasing?" I asked.

"Chasing," Dub repeated, nodding appreciatively. "That's a very apropos, and yet ironic, choice of words. But I'm afraid the subject of my reporting is confidential for now. I wouldn't want to undercut my own scoop."

"Can you at least tell us where you're heading next?" I said. "Maybe we'll bump into you again on our travels."

"I have no idea, Natalie. I'm going wherever the story takes me," Dub said. "I just hope I finish it before the cancer finishes me."

We stayed for another hour or so, during which time Dub and I helped ourselves to the two orphaned martinis. I learned that Dub and Yuki had been on the road for three months but that he'd been researching his story for much longer than that.

Dub seemed less concerned that he was dying than he was frustrated about having to race his mortal clock to complete his reporting before his demise. And yet, I got the feeling that it was the race itself that was keeping him alive. I found myself wishing that the resolution of his story, whatever it was, remained just a bit out of his reach so that he might live a little longer striving for it.

While we talked, Monk silently busied himself separating the mixed nuts into individual bowls, which Dub had politely supplied without comment.

We left when my second martini glass was empty and Dub's energy was clearly beginning to flag. I thanked him for his hospitality, and when I got up to leave, I nearly tumbled to the floor, my legs floating out from under me. Luckily, Monk was there to catch me by the arm.

He helped me outside, and once we were in the cool night air, my legs seemed to regain their weight and my sense of gravity was restored.

I looked out at the moonlight, sparkling off the crashing surf below, and I could smell the salt water and the trees and the dirt under my feet. It was almost as bracing as Dub's martini.

"This trip was a great idea, Mr. Monk."

"I'm beginning to have my doubts."

"It's only the first day," I said.

"That's what worries me."

"Everything worries you."

"Not as much as it used to," he said, "until we went on this trip."

"That's because you're facing the unknown and the unplanned."

"I wish I'd known and I'd planned."

I wanted to take a walk before we returned to the motor home, and Monk reluctantly accompanied me so I wouldn't wander off a cliff or get kidnapped by, as he put it, "drug-crazed Gypsies."

I suppose that's no sillier than being afraid of lurking Satanists, but thanks to Dub's splendid martinis, I didn't have any cares at all.

There were RVs of all shapes and sizes in the park, some seemingly as large as aircraft carriers, others like pop-up tents on trailers. There was a communal, festive atmosphere in the park, with strangers mingling amid the various campsites, where families were barbecuing at their grills, or roasting marshmallows in their fire pits, or sitting on folding chairs, sipping beers, and looking at the stars. I almost started singing "Kumbaya."

The people in the park represented a broad cross section of ages, races, and socioeconomic classes, but with the exception of the Monk brothers, they shared a laid-back attitude and the same sort of easy amiability that Dub Clemens exemplified. Or maybe it was just me, feeling relaxed and a little high from the alcohol and fresh air, projecting what I was feeling on everyone I saw.

By the time we made the circuit of the park and got back to our motor home, I was so tired I could barely keep my eyes open. It seemed like a week had passed since Ambrose's birthday party, and it had been only one long, eventful day.

Ambrose was waiting for us, standing in the center of the motor home, his hands on his hips, as we came in. "Where have you been?"

"We took a walk," I said.

"Out there? In the dark? Are you insane?"

"You'd have the same reaction if we did it in the daylight," I said.

"That doesn't make it any less dangerous."

"I'm too tired to argue," I said.

"I'm exhausted, too," Ambrose said. "Worrying tires me out."

"So go to bed," I said, gesturing to the back room. "You have the master bedroom. Mr. Monk and I will be sleeping out here."

"We will?" Monk said.

"There's a folding sleeper inside the couch, and the dinette area converts into a bed," I said. "You can take the sofa bed, Mr. Monk, which is already made up with your sheets. I'll take the dinette."

"You intend to sleep on the surface where we eat our meals?" Ambrose said.

"I'm not going to be sleeping on the table. It folds away. Let me show you."

I went to the dinette and pulled a latch, and the table slid down so it was just below the level of the bench cushions. I lifted one of the seats and pulled out a set of cushions that fit like puzzle pieces over the table and between the benches, creating a sleeping surface roughly the size of a double bed. I lifted the opposite seat and took out my sleeping bag and pillow, which I dropped on my bed.

"Voilà," I said.

"So you intend to sleep on the surface where we eat our meals," Ambrose said.

"There's a sleeping bag and a big, thick cushion between me and the table."

"Also known as the surface where we eat our meals," Monk said.

"There are three beds in this motor home. I don't care who sleeps in which one. You decide."

"I have an idea," Monk said. "You can sleep in the driver's seat."

"I have an idea," I said. "*You* can sleep in the driver's seat."

"I'm not the driver," Monk said. "You are."

"Okay, then you can sleep in the passenger seat and I'll sleep in the sofa bed."

"Let's compromise," Monk said.

"Okay," I said.

"I'll sleep on the sofa bed," Monk said, "and you'll sleep in the driver's seat."

"How is that a compromise?"

"Because you won't be sleeping where we eat."

"Then I guess you'll be eating somewhere else." I rolled out my sleeping bag on the dinette-area bed, fluffed the pillow as a theatrical touch, and then headed for the aft stateroom, where my clothes and toiletries were stowed.

"Where are you going?" Ambrose called after me.

I stopped midway and turned around. "To the bathroom to change into my pajamas and brush my teeth."

"This bathroom?" Ambrose said.

"It's the only one we've got," I said.

Ambrose turned to Monk. "There's only *one*?"

"I thought you'd use the bathroom outside," Monk said to me.

"You thought wrong," I said. "But you're welcome to use it."

"I don't use public restrooms," he said.

"And I certainly don't," Ambrose said. "And if we all use this one, then it will become a public restroom."

"Then I guess you've got some problems to work out," I said. "Good luck with that."

I walked away.

16

Mr. Monk and the New Day

I brushed my teeth, used the toilet, and changed into sweats and a baggy T-shirt. When I emerged, Ambrose quickly shielded his eyes and looked at the floor.

"Ambrose, I'm not naked," I said.

"You're scantily clad," he said.

"I'm as clad as I was before," I said.

He kept his eyes shielded and his head down and barreled past me toward the bedroom. I unzipped my sleeping bag and climbed inside.

Monk reached under the sink and pulled out a bucket of cleaning supplies.

"What are you doing?"

"Cleaning up the bathroom so Ambrose can use it," Monk said.

"What do you think I did in there?"

Monk shivered. "I don't want to think about it."

He walked past me. I turned on my side, faced the wall, and closed my eyes, falling asleep almost instantly, which was truly a blessing. I slept peacefully through what I'm certain were two extensive cleanings of the bathroom and copious whining from the Monks.

I woke up totally rested and rejuvenated in the cuddly warmth of my sleeping bag at seven a.m. I rolled over and peered across the RV to the sofa bed. I saw Monk asleep on his back, his bedsheets tight and firm and up to his chin. I suspected that he was completely dressed, but there was no way to be sure without whipping off the sheets. I slipped my bare feet into my running shoes, grabbed my jacket, which was draped over the back of the driver's seat, and went outside.

It was sunny, the air crisp and chilly, redolent with the scents of sand and seaweed, pine and eucalyptus, bacon and eggs. I loved it.

I buried my hands in the pockets of my jacket and trudged down the winding trail to the beach. There was only one other person on the sand, and she was jogging barefoot toward me along the berm.

She wore a half top and shorts, her long black hair tied in a bun, which accentuated her slender neck. I knew her, even though I had never actually met her before. She stopped in front of me and was only slightly out of breath. If I'd run half the distance that she had at the same pace that she did I would have needed pulmonary resuscitation.

"Good morning, Yuki," I said.

"Same to you, Natalie," she replied. "I want to thank you and Mr. Monk for entertaining Dub last night."

"It was our pleasure. He's a wonderful host."

"Until last night, Dub was on a sharp downward spiral, physically and emotionally. I don't know what you two did, but he's himself again. Maybe now he'll stay that way until the end."

"Maybe that will be a long way off," I said.

"I hope you're right, but he'll be the one who decides when the time has come."

That reminded me of the gun under his bed. "Do you really think he'll shoot himself?"

"If he can't," she said, "I'll help him do it."

"You could go to prison for that."

"It wouldn't be the first time. The only reason I'm not there now is because he saved me. The least I can do is save him."

Her eyes welled up with tears, which she wiped away with the back of her hand, staring at me defiantly as she did so.

"You love him," I said.

"The same way you love Mr. Monk."

Her remark surprised me and, judging from the satisfied look on her face, she liked that.

"No offense, but you don't know anything about me and Mr. Monk."

"I know everything," she said with an enigmatic smile.

Before I could ask her what she meant by her remark, she ran past me and up the trail to the park, and I saw the elaborate snake tattoo that curled menacingly around her spine.

I suppose I could have chased after her, but I had the beach to myself and I didn't want to waste it. I walked slowly from one end of it to the other, enjoying the solitude and fortifying myself for the journey ahead with the Monk brothers.

Going back up the hill was a lot harder than the trip down, especially after my walk on the beach, and I was disappointed to see when I reached the top that Dub's RV was already gone and, with it, the meaning behind Yuki's enigmatic smile.

I trudged into our motor home to find both Monks up and busy. The dinette and couch beds were folded up, and Monk was scrubbing the tabletop with cleanser while Ambrose prepared waffles at the stove.

I showed my appreciation for their labors by using the public showers to clean up and get dressed. The water was freezing, there was sand on the concrete floors, and it smelled vaguely of coconut suntan lotion, but I found the experience refreshing, maybe because it was different, or perhaps because it reminded me of all the days I spent at the beach when I was growing up.

When I got back, breakfast was ready and waiting. I slid into the dinette across from the Monks and suddenly realized that I was ravenous. I devoured the waffles, which were terrific.

"Where to next?" Ambrose asked, bouncing excitedly in his seat like a child.

"You're in a jaunty mood today," I said.

"I met a beautiful woman. I don't meet many of them."

"Gee, thanks," I said, and saw his face fall. "I'm only teasing. You must be talking about Yuki."

"I told her that I wrote the owner's manual for her scooter," Ambrose said. "It's one of my raw, obscure early works."

"More obscure than your toaster oven manual?" Monk asked.

"*That* was a classic in the field," Ambrose said.

"There's a field for toaster oven manuals?"

"There's a field for everything, Adrian," Ambrose said, then directed his attention back to me. "Yuki kept her owner's manual in pristine condition and asked me to autograph it. Seeing that book again after so many years, and feeling the allure of the open road that I infused in every word, reminded me of my youth and put me in the mood for adventure."

"Then you shall have it," I said. "Today we're heading south on Highway 1 through Big Sur."

"When do we depart?" he asked.

"As soon as we finish breakfast," I said.

"Maybe we should head back north," Monk said.

"Why?" I asked.

"We blew through Santa Cruz and Monterey pretty fast. We might have missed something good."

"Like catching a murderer," I said.

"Hey, that would be fun," Monk said, turning to Ambrose. "Don't you think so?"

"Not really," he said.

"What happened to the united front we agreed to take?"

"That was before Yuki awakened my inner road warrior."

"You don't have one," Monk said.

"If Dub was right," Ambrose said, "we all do."

"And all it took to unleash yours was signing an owner's manual?" Monk said.

"It's more complex than that, Adrian. Yuki and her scooter owner's manual are powerful literary metaphors for the journey that awaits me and for my youth that has slipped away. If you were a writer like Dub and me, you'd see that."

"This isn't a story you're writing, Ambrose. It's life."

"Some would say that is exactly what life is—a story that we're continually writing for ourselves."

"You write owner's manuals," Monk said.

"And I own this." Ambrose tapped his chest with his thumb. "Maybe it's time I revised the manual."

I could have hugged him but there was a table between us. Instead I gave him a big smile.

"Happy birthday, Ambrose."

He cocked his head and looked at me curiously. "That was yesterday."

"It feels like today to me," I said.

I retracted the slide-outs and untethered the RV from the utility hookups in no time at all, but backing up out of our campsite took a good fifteen minutes because I relied on Monk to stand outside and guide me. It wasn't enough for him to keep me from hitting anything—he also wanted to be sure that I backed up in a perfectly straight line, and he used a tape measure to issue corrections to me.

"Three inches to the right," he yelled to me from behind the RV.

"How do I steer three inches?" I yelled back.

"I thought you knew how to drive."

"Steering isn't that precise. Besides, we're backing out of a parking space, not docking with the International Space Station. Am I going to hit the picnic table or not?"

"You aren't anywhere near it. But you're veering wildly off course."

"What's 'wildly off course' mean?"

"Three inches," he said. "Are you sure you're sober enough to drive?"

I was tempted to floor it and back the RV right over him, but I resisted the urge. Instead, I backed up slowly, giving him plenty of time to move out of the way and ignoring his protestations that I was "weaving crazily in all directions."

Monk stepped back into the motor home and insisted that I back out over again. I told him to forget it.

"You're being totally unreasonable," he said.

"What happened to the easygoing, more even Adrian Monk I knew back in San Francisco?"

"I'm relaxed," Monk said, "but I haven't lost my grip on reason."

"It doesn't matter whether I backed out in a straight line or not. All that counts is that I didn't hit anything."

"That's how it starts," Monk said.

"What starts?"

"Break one rule, and slowly but surely, no rules matter to you anymore. Before you know it, you're a sociopathic serial killer."

"Because I didn't back up in a perfectly straight line."

"And you're not even considering the impact your careless actions may have on others. Some child could come along, see those crooked tire tracks you left behind, and inexplicably feel compelled to shoplift candy bars from the campsite store, thus beginning his downward spiral and the total destruction of his life, perhaps culminating in murdering a woman on a beach in Santa Cruz."

Now I understood what this was all about: Leaving a murder behind unsolved in Santa Cruz had undermined Monk's sense of balance, and he was trying to restore it by obsessing over little things he could control.

The aggravation was a small price to pay in exchange for not sacrificing our road trip for a homicide investigation.

"Good point, Mr. Monk. I hadn't thought of the implications of my actions. So why don't you take our broom, go outside, and wipe away my tire tracks?"

Monk thought about that for a second, and then, without a word, grabbed our broom and went back outside. Ambrose looked at me.

"May I sit in the passenger seat today?"

"We don't have assigned seating, Ambrose. You can sit wherever you like."

Ambrose tentatively got into the seat and then

strapped on the seat belt with the careful solemnity of someone preparing to pilot a jet at the speed of sound. When he was done, he placed his hands on the dashboard and nodded at me.

"I'm ready," he said.

Monk returned a few minutes later and buckled himself into the seat in the dinette area, and then I drove us through the park to the road. Ambrose leaned back into his seat as if he was pinned against it by massive g-forces.

I stopped and checked the road for oncoming traffic. "I wasn't even going five miles per hour."

"I know, but it's still faster than I am used to moving. I'm preparing myself physically and psychologically for what's coming."

"But this isn't the first time you've been out of the house or in a car," I said as I pulled into the traffic and steered us onto the southbound freeway. "Mr. Monk told me you were in grade school together and that your mother dropped you off in her car."

"That was a very long time ago."

"I've always wondered: What made you go inside your house and not come out again? Was it a traumatic event of some kind?"

Ambrose shook his head. "I always felt panicky whenever I was outside. I like boundaries."

"Why?"

"There's too much going on outside, you can't keep track of all the details, all the people, all the things that are happening. Nothing stays the same, everything is always moving, there's danger everywhere, but you can't see it. It's like being caught up in a raging river. You get swept away and, before you know it, you're plunging over Niagara Falls to your doom."

Monk spoke up from his seat. "There's an order to

the universe that never changes and that establishes boundaries. If you follow that order, everything in life is manageable. It's only when you deviate from the natural order that things go awry. I see that order very clearly, and when something doesn't fit the way it's supposed to, I see that, too, which is why I am such a good detective."

I glanced back at Monk in the rearview mirror. I'd never heard him characterize his obsessive-compulsive disorder or his detecting skills in such a straightforward manner before. I had no idea he was so self-aware.

This trip was becoming as much of a revelation for me as it was intended to be for Ambrose.

"It's not that easy, Adrian," Ambrose said. "I don't have your skill, concentration, or emotional fortitude."

"But you managed to make it on the outside through most of your childhood," I said. "So what happened?"

"I caught the Hong Kong flu, and the school told me to stay home until I was healthy. They didn't want me infecting the other children. My mother didn't want me infecting the family, either, so she made me stay in the basement."

"You're kidding," I said.

"She was just being safe and sensible," Ambrose said.

"She should have let you stay in your own bed," I said, "where you felt comfortable, safe, and secure, not confined to the basement like you were some kind of leper."

"That's exactly what he was," Monk said.

"She was being prudent," Ambrose said.

"But not very loving," I said.

Whenever Julie got sick, I cared for her myself without worrying about my own health. All that mattered to me was making her feel better. It's part of being a parent. Of course, half the time I ended up catching the same cold or flu that she had, but I didn't see any need to mention that to the Monks.

"After I got over the flu, I realized I felt much, much better than I ever did before," Ambrose said. "So I decided I should just stay home for good. Mom agreed."

"What did the school think about that?"

"The administrators sent some people over who diagnosed me as agoraphobic. So I was educated at home by a teacher sent by the school district and by my mother. Those were happy times."

I glanced in the rearview mirror again at Monk, who had a sour look on his face. Apparently, he didn't agree with Ambrose's take on the past.

"Did your mother ever try to get you treatment?"

Ambrose shook his head. "No, but it all worked out for the best."

"I don't see how," Monk said.

"I am living more sensibly and safely than everybody else. I never get sick. I never get hurt. The world would be a safer place if everybody lived like me."

I didn't bother arguing with him because I knew that nothing I could say would cure him of his phobia. I was betting instead that what he'd see on our trip would make him begin to rethink his life of isolation.

Then again, if we didn't manage his trip very carefully, we could end up scaring him right back into his house. Taking him to the scene of a homicide on day one probably hadn't worked in our favor, not that it was our fault.

I would just have to try to steer clear of any trouble as best I could, which wouldn't be easy with Adrian Monk along for the ride.

17

Mr. Monk and the Gum

The high point, literally and figuratively, of our drive that day was when we crossed the Bixby Creek Bridge, an arched span that stretches 700 feet across a 260-foot-deep canyon on the jagged edge of the California coast.

The bridge is breathtaking and heart-stopping to look at, an architectural and engineering marvel of concrete and reinforced steel that seems to dare the forces of nature and gravity to knock it down.

My fear was that nature and gravity would team up to take that dare as I was driving over the bridge.

I imagined that the Big One would finally hit when we were halfway across or that some engineering flaw, hidden for eighty years, would suddenly express itself and the bridge would disintegrate as if it were made of sugar and we were a drop of water rolling across the top of it.

It was a tense few minutes. We all held our breath as

we crossed, and I don't think the Monk brothers started breathing again for another mile or two after that.

But then Ambrose startled me by letting out a victorious whoop, like a kid who'd just taken a ride on a roller coaster. I half expected him to ask me to turn around and drive over the bridge again.

"It feels good to be alive," he said.

"Yes, it does," Monk said.

"I'm not sure I ever noticed that before," Ambrose said. "Do you have to face death to feel grateful for living?"

"Of course not," I said. "I felt it this morning just walking on the beach. But sometimes, when you get caught up in the fast pace of daily life, you have to make a conscious effort to, if I may use a cliché, stop and smell the roses."

"And inhale an excessive amount of pollen, which could provoke a deadly sinus reaction that could cause you to drown in your own mucus," Monk said. "So for God's sake, don't stop and smell the roses."

"It's always nice to hear your cheerful point of view," I said.

"I wouldn't sniff a flower anyway," Ambrose said. "I might inhale a bee."

"And the good cheer continues," I said.

"To be absolutely honest, I should tell you that we weren't really in any danger on that bridge," Ambrose said. "It just felt that way."

"Good to know," I said. "But fear is often irrational. Knowing on an intellectual level that something is safe doesn't mean you will believe that it is. You, of all people, should understand that."

He scribbled something on a piece of paper and held it out for me to see. It was some sort of mathematical

equation. Anything more complex than two plus two
equals four is beyond my comprehension.

"What's this?" I asked.

"The equations that express the vertical and horizontal forces on the bridge and whether it can sustain
them," Ambrose said. "The supporting arch carries the
combined mass of all the concrete and the vehicular
traffic, which comes to a load of about 28,700 pounds
per foot."

"How do you know that?"

"I did some research on the Internet last night on our
probable route while you and Adrian were having cock-
tails with Dub Clemens," Ambrose said. "The ingenuity
of arch construction is that it actually shifts the load on
the bridge to the sides of the canyon that it's anchored
in. If we know the length and width of the span, and we
do, we can determine the horizontal and vertical force,
which I have, and from that we can determine the stress.
And if you know that the breaking point of concrete is
three thousand psi, which I do, you can easily calculate
the stress on the arch and the safety factor of the bridge."

"Oh yes, very easily," I said. "I'd do it myself if I wasn't
busy driving. So what have you come up with?"

He tapped the equation on the paper. "If SF is the
safety factor, FC is the breaking stress of concrete, and
F is the stress on the arch, the equation is SF equals FC
equals 3,000 equals 6.35 F472.4. Alas, the bridge can
support six times the weight it was designed to support,
which I find to be within acceptable limits. I wouldn't
have let you drive over it otherwise. But it was exhilarating nonetheless."

"Have you done this calculation for all the bridges
and overpasses we might drive over?"

"No, but I can," he said.

"Don't bother," I said. "Uncertainty is even more exhilarating."

"Uncertainty is ignorance," Monk said.

"Ignorance is bliss," I said.

"Only for the ignorant," he said. "Didn't we already have this argument yesterday? Didn't I win it?"

"Don't ask me," I said. "I'm blissfully ignorant."

I was also enjoying the scenery too much to continue arguing with him.

Big Sur is one of the most beautiful places in California, the combination of cliffs, coastline, and forests creating what Robert Louis Stevenson called the "greatest meeting of land and sea in the world," which is quite an observation coming from a guy who liked to hang around the forest of Fontainebleau in his youth and who traveled throughout the South Pacific later in life.

I mentioned that to Ambrose and figured the recommendation from a fellow scribe would convince him that we should spend a night or two at a campsite nestled in the dense forest, enjoying the solitude and the salty sea breezes wafting through the ancient redwoods.

But my suggestion was immediately, and vehemently, rejected by both of the Monks.

"If you've seen one tree, you've seen them all," Monk said.

"I don't like trees," Ambrose said. "They are swarming with ants, birds, snakes, squirrels, centipedes, lizards, termites, spiders, caterpillars, and sticky sap."

"Dogs frequently urinate on them, too," Monk said. "And if you get too close to a tree, an acorn or a pine cone or a branch or even the tree itself could fall on you. Even worse, a bird could defecate on you from above and you'd have to take your own life."

"Nature can be so dangerous," Ambrose said.

"That's why it should be avoided," Monk said. "The

other thing about nature is that it's not just dangerous, it's filthy. There is dirt everywhere, some of it wet."

"When Jack Kerouac wrote about Big Sur, he concluded that 'to be afraid of nature is to be afraid of yourself,'" I said, making another blatant attempt to play to Ambrose's literary sensibilities and sway him to my side.

"Kerouac was a beatnik hippie alcoholic who drank himself to death," Ambrose said.

"He probably made that insane observation while he was delirious with booze," Monk said.

"That would be the only explanation I can think of for saying something as crazy as that," Ambrose said. "Unless he was being deliberately provocative."

I dropped the argument because the Monks were right. It was a bad idea to park for a few days in Big Sur, but it wasn't any of their bizarre reasoning that convinced me.

Nature is something wonderful to see and experience, but that's hard to do from the confines of a motor home. We were probably already experiencing the best of Big Sur from that point of view. Stuck inside the RV, Ambrose wouldn't see much in a campsite besides the trunks of trees.

I realized that I had to start thinking about our trip exclusively from the perspective of what Ambrose could see, hear, touch, taste, and smell from within our RV.

That fact ruled out a lot of amazing places and attractions ahead of us, like the Hearst Castle and Disneyland, that would require him to get out of the RV to enjoy them.

It was going to make this trip a challenge, but that was always the case with anything involving the Monks.

As we drove down the coast, Ambrose watched the scenery go by in silent fascination, gradually relaxing enough to take his hands off the dashboard to consult the guidebooks for more information about what he was seeing.

Monk kept quiet, too, until we passed Morro Bay and the giant landmark rock in the water, which he loudly criticized as an "unconscionable monument to bird excrement" that was the "scourge of the California coastline."

"Imagine looking at that out your window every day," Monk said.

"It's a wonder that anyone lives in that town at all," Ambrose agreed.

We continued along Highway 1 as it curved inland, taking us past the college town of San Luis Obispo, which unofficially marked the midpoint between San Francisco and Los Angeles. It was also home to the California Polytechnic State University.

I took the Monks on a scenic drive through town, past the Mission San Luis Obispo de Tolosa, supposedly the inspiration for the ubiquitous red-tile roofs throughout the state, and then we meandered into downtown, where most of the quaint Spanish Revival storefronts had been occupied by national chains the way ugly hermit crabs move into pretty seashells.

I stopped at a downtown gas station to fill up the tank, stretch my legs, and, as a courtesy to the Monks, use the Chevron restroom instead of the one in our motor home.

The first thing I noticed when I came back to the RV from the restroom was that Monk was gone and Ambrose was sitting at the dinette table, looking out the window.

"Where's Mr. Monk?"

Ambrose gestured out the window. "He saw a scofflaw stick a piece of gum on a wall in the alley across the street, so he's gone after him to make a citizen's arrest."

I peered out the window and, sure enough, I saw Monk running into the alley between two shops.

"Unbelievable," I said.

I got into the driver's seat, drove the motor home into a parking spot, then jumped out and ran across the street to bring Monk back before he got into trouble.

I was approaching the mouth of the alley when Monk yelled at me, "Stay where you are!"

I didn't, of course.

I stepped forward and saw that the alley was actually a narrow walkway leading to the other side of the block.

Monk stood absolutely still in the center of the walkway, his back to me. He was obviously afraid to move, as if his foot were resting on a land mine and the slightest twitch would blow us both to bits.

But it wasn't what was under his feet that had made him freeze, or even the homeless person who was sleeping on the ground under a ratty Cal Poly logo blanket a few yards away from him.

It was what was on the walls.

There were gobs upon gobs, layer upon layer, of multicolored gum, spit from the mouths of thousands of people and stuck to both walls, from one end of the walkway to the other.

From a distance, it looked like two long, abstract expressionist murals, something Jackson Pollock might have done if he'd worked with bubble gum instead of dripping paint.

Up close, it was truly disgusting.

The gum was mostly stuck in simple globs, but some people tried to be creative with their moist contributions. They stretched their gum and looped it around other dried gobs like silly string. They formed gumballs into gooey graffiti, spelling out words, symbols, and names. They molded wads into Dentyne flowers, Juicy Fruit faces, Bazooka stick figures, and Doublemint snowmen.

The layers of gum were several inches thick. And there was more of it stuck to the pavement, without the same artistic flair, probably blobs that dripped from the walls or dropped accidentally from the mouths and hands of would-be artists.

I don't know whether people used the walkway as a toilet, or if years of dried sugar and drool smell just like urine. But the place reeked.

I walked up to Monk, careful not to step on any gum.

"I saw a man stick his gum on the wall. I ran over here to apprehend him," Monk said. "I didn't see what I was getting into until it was too late."

"Is that him?" I motioned to the vagrant sleeping on the ground.

Monk shook his head. "No, he got away."

"Okay, then let's go. There's nothing more you can do here."

"Someone needs to clean this place with a flame-thrower and then send the scorched bricks into outer space."

This was one time I actually agreed with him.

"It's not our problem," I said.

"It's the most disgusting thing I have ever seen in my life," he said. "If there is a hell on earth, we're standing in it."

I gently took his arm. "Let's go, Mr. Monk. We'll walk out of here together."

"I can't move."

"Yes, you can. We'll go very slowly."

"What if I step on something?"

"We'll watch our step."

"What if I lose my balance while I'm watching and I fall against one of those walls?"

"I won't let that happen."

He turned around slowly, and arm in arm we carefully negotiated a path among the dried gum on the ground toward the mouth of the alley where we came in.

Our heads were down, and we were so intent on what we were doing, we didn't see the three young people coming in until they tried to brush past us, nearly pushing us against the sticky wall.

Monk grabbed me for dear life and let out a frightened yelp.

The three of them—two girls and a guy—looked about the same age as my daughter. I pegged them as students, a brilliant deduction based on their age and the Cal Poly logo clothes they were wearing. They were chomping on gum, so I didn't have to be a detective to guess what they'd come here to do.

"Don't even think about it," Monk said to them.

"Huh?" the boy said.

"You are not sticking gum on that wall," Monk said.

"Chill, it's cool," he said.

"Not anymore. This is a crime scene," Monk said, "and you are contaminating it."

"Are you some kind of cop?" one of the girls asked.

"Yes," Monk said. "Now back out of here, slowly and carefully retracing your steps, and don't ever come back."

The kids shared a look.

"This guy is crazy," the other girl said. "He's scaring me."

"You should be scared," Monk said. "For your life."

That did it. The girls hurried out. The guy followed them, but he wasn't too pleased about it. He took a wad of gum out of his mouth and defiantly tossed it at the wall as he passed Monk.

"Call the police," Monk demanded.

"I'm not calling the cops on that kid."

We reached the sidewalk, and Monk took a deep breath, letting it out slowly, relieved to have escaped with his life.

That's when I noticed that the gift store on one side of the walkway entrance had a gumball machine in the window full of gum the size of golf balls. In fact, now that I was looking for it, I could see that several stores in the immediate vicinity were selling gum, even those shops that otherwise sold only clothes, soap, or jewelry.

"This entire alley is a crime scene," Monk said. "I'll secure it while you make the call."

"The gum has been on these walls for a very long time, Mr. Monk. I'm sure the authorities here know about it. The merchants here certainly do. The cops aren't going to come out here for that."

"They'll come for the murder," Monk said.

I felt a horrible, oppressive sense of dread. It was like a physical weight pressing down on my entire body.

"What murder?"

Monk gestured past me to the vagrant sleeping on the ground in the alley.

"His," he said.

18

Mr. Monk and the Murder

No matter where Monk went, he inevitably discovered a murder.

Statistically, it just didn't seem possible that one person could stumble across so many dead bodies. Any reasonable person would, if she knew how often this happened, keep herself and her loved ones as far away from him as possible.

I guess I wasn't as reasonable as I thought I was. I was still with him. But I wasn't happy that another corpse threatened to ruin our trip. And, irrationally, I blamed Monk for it.

"You're just desperate to find a murder to investigate. You weren't close to that homeless guy. How can you be sure he's dead? Maybe he's sleeping."

"It's the eternal rest, Natalie. And he's not homeless, either."

I looked back at the guy, and all I could see from

where we stood was the ratty Cal Poly blanket that covered most of his body.

"How do you know?"

"He's a young man. His hair is freshly cut, his fingernails are neatly trimmed, his skin is pale, and his leather sandals fit perfectly and are clean," Monk said. "None of that is what you'd expect to see with someone who lived on the streets."

"Maybe he's a homeless person who takes good care of himself," I said, knowing it was a stupid comment and hearing my desperate need for him to be wrong as a distinct whine that underscored my words like music.

"I know he's dead because he's wearing shorts, and his naked ankles are sticking out from under the blanket. I can see the purplish discoloration of his skin that indicates postmortem lividity, the pooling of the blood in the body that occurs once the heart stops pumping and gravity takes over. It also tells me that he was killed here."

I resigned myself to defeat and, since I'd left my purse and cell phone in the RV, went into the gift shop next door and used their phone to call 911.

I told the operator about the murder and gave her our names and Captain Stottlemeyer's contact information for the police so we could shortcut Monk and me being treated as suspects.

The uniformed police officers arrived first, followed by the paramedics, the medical examiner, the forensic team, and finally the lead detective. He was sandy haired and sunburned, wearing a polo shirt over faded jeans, a badge, and a gun clipped to his belt. He looked more like a tennis pro than a cop. He introduced himself as Detective Terry Donovan.

"I checked you two out with Captain Stottlemeyer in Frisco. He vouched for you, but here's the funny thing:

He didn't seem surprised at all that I was calling. It was almost like he was expecting it. What's with that?"

I shrugged. "I have no idea."

"So tell me what happened," Donovan said.

We did. Donovan looked at Monk incredulously.

"Let me get this straight. You chased a guy into an alley because you saw him stick gum on the wall?"

"I am a concerned, law-abiding citizen doing my civic duty," Monk said.

The medical examiner motioned to Donovan, who stepped aside to have a word with him out of our earshot. I looked back into the alley. The body was being taken away in a body bag and the forensic team was putting the Cal Poly blanket in a large, transparent evidence bag.

Donovan returned to us. "The ME says that the guy has been dead for several hours, maybe even since last night. His wallet is gone, and he was stabbed in the chest. Looks to me like we're dealing with a simple mugging gone tragically bad."

"Were there any defensive wounds on the victim?" Monk asked.

"Nope. I guess it happened too quick."

Monk rolled his shoulders and tipped his head from side to side. "What mugger brings along a vagrant's blanket to drape over the body?"

"Maybe the mugger was a homeless person who was sleeping in the alley and left his blanket behind when he ran off."

"He'd have to be crazy to do that," Monk said.

"Most of the homeless in this town are mentally ill, so that's not much of a stretch."

"I think it is. The victim was stabbed in the chest, which means he was facing his killer. There are no defensive wounds because the young man didn't see the knife and didn't think he was in any danger. That wouldn't be the case if he was that close to a homeless man," Monk said. "No, the killer wasn't a hobo. The killer brought the blanket to make the victim look like a sleeping vagrant and to delay the discovery of the body."

"That's one theory," Donovan said.

"It's what happened," Monk said.

"He's never wrong about murder," I said.

"Captain Stottlemeyer mentioned that," Donovan said. "Sorry, but I don't buy it."

Monk gestured to the walls covered with gum. "You need to get the DNA from all those pieces of gum."

"You've got to be kidding me. There's tens of thousands of wads there," he said. "It would take years, maybe even decades."

"Time well spent. Every one of those people has to be hunted down and prosecuted."

"The murder occurred hours ago, but that gum goes back years. We don't even know if the killer left a piece on the wall. It's not a practical use of our time and limited resources to test all that gum for DNA."

"So you're going to let them all get away with it?"

"This is Gumball Alley," Donovan said. "Putting gum on the wall is a local tradition."

"Do you also have alleys where people can spit tobacco, blow their noses, and urinate on the walls, too?"

It was a good thing that Monk didn't know that in the mid-1800s, bear-baiting shows, a blood sport in which a bear chained by one leg to a post fended off a pack of ravenous dogs, were regularly held in the park outside the Mission San Luis Obispo de Tolosa for the amusement of the locals.

"No, we've just got this," Donovan said. "It's community folk art. I've stuck a few pieces on the wall myself over the years."

"Ah, so that's it," Monk said.

"Now you understand," Donovan said.

"I do. You're only interested in covering up your own corruption. Surely there's at least one honest cop on your police force."

Donovan's casual demeanor abruptly evaporated, and his expression hardened. "We're done here. We'll be in contact if we need anything more. You are free to go."

Monk pointed at the alley. "That wall of gum is responsible for that man's death."

Donovan couldn't help himself—he had to ask: "How do you figure that?"

"It's a symbol of the rampant lawlessness that's allowed to exist in this town. It's a sign that says to everyone that anything goes here. The killer knew he could act with impunity."

"If this town disgusts you so much," Donovan said, "why don't you just get the hell out of here?"

"I intend to," Monk said. "Just as soon as I find the murderer."

"That's my job," Donovan said.

"You can't even keep those walls clean," Monk said. "How do you expect to catch a killer?"

I spoke up before Donovan did something rash, like chain Monk by the leg to a post and set a pack of dogs on him.

"We're leaving now," I said, taking Monk by the arm and leading him away. "Good luck with your investigation."

Monk came along with me, but he wasn't happy. "You expect me to walk away from this murder, too?"

"This one and every other one that you might come across on our trip."

"You think there will be more?"

"I hope not, but knowing you, it wouldn't surprise me."

"I have an obligation," Monk said.

"Yes, you do, to your brother and to me and to this road trip. You do not work for the San Luis Obispo Police Department."

"What about my obligation to the murder victim?"

"You don't have one," I said.

"I do now," he said. "What if this murder never gets solved?"

"It will," I said.

"If I investigate it," he said.

"Even if you don't."

"How can you be sure?"

"We'll check in with Detective Donovan after we get home from our vacation," I said.

"And if it's not solved, you'll bring me back here?"

"Sure," I lied.

"And to Santa Cruz, if that case isn't solved, either?"

"Of course," I lied again.

"Maybe we'd better hold on to the motor home for a while after the trip," Monk said. "We might need it."

We crossed the street and returned to our RV. I could see Ambrose staring at us wide-eyed through the window. We weren't doing a very good job making the outside world look enticing, a fact that he made very clear as soon as we stepped inside the motor home.

"I'm never going outside," he said.

"I know this looks bad," I said, "but what happened today is a fluke."

"Hardly. This is the second murder we've come across in two days. It's a wonder that you've survived as long as you have out there."

"It's really not as dangerous as it seems," I said.

"It's worse," Monk said.

I glared at him. "You're not helping."

"I want to," he said, "but you won't let me."

"That's not the help I am talking about," I said, gesturing to Ambrose. Monk looked at me blankly, not getting the message or willfully ignoring it. "Never mind. Buckle up."

I got into the driver's seat and hit the gas, not waiting for them to get settled. They were nearly knocked to the floor, but I didn't care.

We fled San Luis Obispo even faster than we'd escaped from Santa Cruz the day before. I needed to put miles between Monk and the investigation and to put emotional distance between Ambrose and another crime scene. I had to distract them both and I had to do it quickly.

We passed an enormous billboard for Pea Soup Andersen's restaurant and hotel, with its cartoon illustration of a fat chef holding a mallet and chisel over a pea, and I saw the answer to my problems.

Pea Soup Andersen's wasn't the answer. That was *where* it was located, just outside of Solvang, a mere fifty-six miles south and only a few miles off the highway.

Solvang was built by Danish settlers in the early 1900s to emulate the architectural style of their homeland. They didn't know they were creating California's first theme park, minus the roller coasters and Ferris wheels.

Ordinarily, I wouldn't have gone out of my way to see Solvang. The place struck me as a blatant tourist trap pretending to be something of genuine cultural and historical significance. Maybe it was once, but not anymore. To me, Solvang had a fake, Disneyfied look, born more out of animated cartoons than anything in Copenhagen, and that made the place feel like an enormous themed shopping center rather than an actual town.

But I figured all the windmills and the half-timbered

buildings, with their pointy gables, their flower boxes, their faux thatched roofs, and their nods to Hans Christian Andersen's fables, would still be a visual treat for Ambrose and something new for Monk to complain about.

I was right.

Ambrose was transfixed from the moment we drove into town and he saw the distinctive fairy-tale architecture, the cobblestone sidewalks, the gas streetlamps, the horse-drawn carriages, and the carved storks on almost every rooftop. It may have been superficial and phony, but it was as close to Denmark as Ambrose was likely to ever get.

Monk was adamantly against half-timbered structures, something I learned when we visited Germany a few years back, and he voiced his complaints once again, but I didn't listen to him, so I can spare you a repeat of his tiresome rant.

Ambrose opened the window, and almost immediately the rich aroma of fresh baked foods and sugary sweets wafted in from the many bakeries and candy shops that lined the streets. My stomach growled.

I found us a parking place in a lot right in the center of town, so even from the RV, Ambrose had plenty to look at. I volunteered to go out and bring Ambrose back a taste of the Danish delights. I insisted that Monk stay behind to keep his brother company. I was afraid that if I brought Monk with me, we'd inevitably stumble on something terrible, like the Little Mermaid with her throat slashed.

So I ventured out into the tourist-swollen streets alone, bombarded by opportunities to buy Danish food and souvenirs at every turn, and I did my consumer duty by giving my credit card a bruising.

I returned with lots of goodies, including an assortment of Danish pastries and some aebleskiver, puffed pancakes shaped like tennis balls that are ordinarily slathered with raspberry jam and powdered sugar. I got my aebleskiver the way they're supposed to be served as an example for the Monks, but I purchased theirs plain with the jam and sugar on the side.

We devoured the aebleskivers, then dug into the pastries. It wasn't a healthy lunch, more like one big dessert, but it certainly was sweet and tasty and, at least symbolically, got rid of the sour taste left in our mouths by our experience in San Luis Obispo.

After we ate, I gave Ambrose a little porcelain figurine of the Little Mermaid sunning herself on a rock and a key chain with tiny wooden clogs. Both of the tacky souvenirs were probably made in China, but that didn't matter to him. I bought them in Solvang, commemorating his visit to a place he'd never been to before, and that made them special. He told me he would cherish them.

Ambrose looked out the window and sighed. "It's like we're parked in a fairy tale. When I was a child, I used to dream of going to a place like this, but then it occurred to me that they didn't have running water or a decent sewage system and that their houses were firetraps made of mud and straw."

"Very true," Monk said. "It's fairy-tale squalor."

"I also worried about encountering a fire-breathing dragon, evil witch, or menacing troll, and then I didn't want to go anymore. I must say that this is an improvement on my dream."

"It's not often in life you can say that," I said.

"And I have you to thank for it," he said.

"I'm only the driver," I said and tipped my head toward Monk. "It's Mr. Monk who deserves your thanks. This trip was his idea."

Ambrose looked with warmth at his brother. "Thank you, Adrian."

Monk rolled his shoulders. He was more comfortable with corpses than he was with any show of emotion.

"You're welcome," he mumbled.

Apparently, Ambrose had forgiven us for drugging him and kidnapping him. Or maybe it was just the first signs of Stockholm syndrome. Either way, I saw it as progress.

19

Mr. Monk and the Big Step

Before we continued on with our journey, Monk and I sat side by side across the table from Ambrose, spread out the map of the western United States, and tried to figure out where to go next.

"We can avoid Los Angeles," Monk said, tapping the map with his index finger. "There is absolutely nothing to see there, and we didn't bring any gas masks."

"What would we need gas masks for?" Ambrose asked.

"The air down there is toxic," Monk said. "It's so dirty, you can actually see what you are breathing."

Ambrose shivered. "It's hard to believe such a place exists."

"It's even harder to believe that people live there of their own free will," he said. "But they don't live there for very long."

"They move?" Ambrose asked.

"They die," Monk replied. "Young."

I nudged Monk hard. He was diffusing all the goodwill and positive attitude our trip to Solvang, purchase of souvenirs, and massive consumption of sugar had won for us with Ambrose.

"We could continue south to Santa Barbara, a beautiful town, right on the water, and well worth seeing," I said. "After that, we could head east on the 126 toward Santa Clarita, transition to the Interstate 5 south, then on to the 14 and the 18 east toward Victorville until we hit I-15. From that point, we can decide whether we want to go to Las Vegas or the Grand Canyon."

Monk nodded. "I like that plan."

"Because it's a plan," I said. "Any plan would do."

"Plans are good," he said.

"But that doesn't mean we can't abandon our plan if something on the road catches our fancy or tugs us in a different direction."

"We don't have any fancies to be captured or tugged," Monk said. "We like plans."

"Where are we going to sleep tonight?" Ambrose asked, underscoring Monk's point.

I shrugged. "Anyplace that interests us, or wherever we happen to be when I get too tired to drive."

"Is that wise?" Ambrose asked.

"It's not like we have to rent a room somewhere. We are entirely self-sufficient."

"I am," Ambrose said, then looked at Monk. "But he's not."

"That's why I have an assistant," Monk said.

"Then it's settled," I said and got into the driver's seat. Five minutes later we were on our way out of Solvang and continuing on our journey.

The one-hour trip down to Santa Barbara on Highway 101 wasn't remarkable from a scenic point of view, so the Monks kept themselves amused singing "100 Cans of Lysol on the Shelf" until we got there.

I drove slowly down State Street toward the beach, giving the Monks plenty of opportunity to admire the charming town and its Spanish Mediterranean architecture, which was mandated by the city fathers so that every single building downtown seemed to be white with a red-tiled roof.

Monk appreciated the uniformity, and this was one of the rare instances when I did, too.

The whitewashed walls, the lush landscaping, the rows of palm trees, and all the little courtyards and fountains made Santa Barbara undeniably romantic and picturesque in a way that somehow felt authentic instead of merchandized.

Perhaps one reason for that was that many of the people who lived in Santa Barbara had a lot of money, so they weren't aggressively and blatantly trying to entice tourists to empty their wallets. The upscale attitude and rich sheen had a snooty downside, though. We got lots of nasty looks from people on the street as we drove by, as if we were riding in an overflowing garbage truck instead of an RV.

We drove down to Stearns Wharf, then south along Cabrillo Boulevard between the low-slung, five-star resorts and the long, beautiful beach, which was buffered from the street by a grassy park and a winding promenade filled with bike riders, roller skaters, and joggers, most of whom had impossibly perfect bodies. A strict body-fat-to-muscle requirement for anybody who wanted to exercise in public must have been in the city ordinances somewhere, too.

I would have liked to stay a while, strolling through the streets, visiting the galleries, and sampling wines from the Santa Ynez Valley. But that wouldn't have given Ambrose much to do, so we moved on.

As we headed back toward the freeway, we passed the zoo, and Ambrose spotted the giraffes through the trees. He shrieked excitedly like a child and pointed to them.

"Look! Giraffes! Can you see them?"

"Their necks are entirely out of proportion to their bodies," Monk said, squirming a bit in his seat. "It's just not right. Something should be done about that."

"I'll send a memo to God registering your complaint," I said. "It's time someone put him on notice about that."

My sarcasm was wasted on Monk because, as smart as he was, he couldn't discern it from straightforward speech. I'm sure that he took me seriously and wholeheartedly approved of what I said.

We were in and out of Santa Barbara in thirty minutes, which felt like I was cheating myself and the Monks, but that's the way it was.

We pressed inland for the next three and a half hours, stopping only for gas. We drove on the 126 through the fruit cup and nut bowl of Southern California. Citrus groves and fields of fruit, vegetables, and nuts lined both sides of the highway until we reached the housing-tract sprawl and big-box-store blight of Santa Clarita and Valencia.

As we headed south on I-5 to the 14 freeway, we passed the Magic Mountain amusement park, and Ambrose couldn't help gaping at the park's enormous roller coasters and water slides.

"I've ridden on some of those," Ambrose said.

"How could you have done that?" Monk said. "You've never left the house."

"I did it virtually," Ambrose said. "It's a lot safer and

much more sensible. All of life would be better if it could be done virtually."

"Only someone who has never experienced life would say that," I said.

From there, we headed into the high desert, exposing Ambrose to a landscape entirely different from any that he'd seen before.

But he wasn't able to appreciate it at first. He was too terrified and, to be honest, I was a little anxious myself. That's because we were traveling a two-lane stretch of blacktop known as Blood Alley that cut across the vast, empty desert scrub.

Blood Alley got its name because drivers in this desolate expanse tended to fall asleep at the wheel and drift into oncoming traffic. Or they attempted to pass the slower cars in front of them and misjudged how much open roadway they had to make their move before facing a head-on collision. Or they saw the seemingly endless stretch of road as their own personal racetrack, stomped the gas pedal to the floor, and lost control on one of the many sudden dips hidden by the heat sheen rippling off the asphalt.

The shoulders of the highway were lined with makeshift memorials, faded crosses, and piles of dried flowers, left to honor the foolish, the fatigued, and the innocent who traveled the road on their final journey to heaven or hell.

But after a while, the memorials disappeared, or perhaps were blown away by the dry desert winds, and then it was just us, the road, and miles of arid dirt, dotted with brittle brush and cactus. It was, in its own way, every bit as awe-inspiring as the California coastline.

The road was an undulating, uneven ribbon atop the sand, which made it feel as if we were a yacht riding the ocean swells instead of asphalt. Driving at a steady, reasonable speed, there was a certain rhythm to the swells that I found soothing. It was no wonder so many drivers nodded off.

The highway led into dreary, sun-baked Victorville, where the two-lane roadway widened into a boulevard lined with fast-food franchises and used-car dealerships, before it connected with the I-15, the primary artery between Southern California and Las Vegas.

Just a few miles northeast of Victorville on the I-15, civilization abruptly disappeared and within minutes there was nothing but hardscrabble desert and hills in every direction. Besides the cars on the highway, there were no signs of life. Even the massive power lines veered away, like giant metal giants marching off single file on a lonely path into the barren hills.

But with the desolation came four lanes, a higher speed limit—seventy miles per hour—and a sense of freedom, of possibility, of an entire world opening up in front of us just waiting to be explored. I found it extremely relaxing and, it seemed to me, so did Ambrose. His eyes sparkled.

"You like the desert?" I asked.

Ambrose nodded. "It's the first time that I've thought that stepping outdoors might not be so bad."

I pulled off the freeway at the next exit, which led to an overpass connecting two ends of a narrow road to nowhere.

"Where are we going?" Monk asked.

I ignored the question and drove along the rough, pothole-ridden road until we rounded a bend around the edge of one of the dry hills and the I-15 was out of our sight.

I stopped the RV and turned to Ambrose, who sat in the passenger seat.

"Here we are," I said. "Let's do it."

He looked at me. "Do what?"

I got up out of my seat, went over to the door, and opened it, letting in a blast of heavy, hot air that felt like a blanket, fresh from the dryer, had been thrown over me. I swept my hand out toward the desert.

"Try it," I said. "Take that step you were thinking about."

"I can't," he said, shrinking into his seat and tugging on his seat belt.

"You just said you wanted to."

"I had a fleeting interest," he said. "It fled."

"There's nobody out here but us. There are no distractions, no clutter, no noise, and no chaos of details to keep track of. You can see for a hundred miles. When have you ever been able to do that?"

Monk stared at me from the dinette area, and I gestured to him to come outside with me. He hesitated, then came to the door, motioning me over. I got close and Monk whispered.

"Are there any rattlesnakes, lizards, spiders, or red fire ants in the vicinity?"

"None," I whispered back. "Now get out here and set an example for your brother. This is an opportunity that might never come again."

I didn't give Monk a chance to argue. I grabbed him by the lapels and yanked him outside.

We walked a few feet away from the motor home and looked out into the distance, our backs to the door.

"This isn't going to work," Monk whispered.

"Be patient, Mr. Monk," I whispered back and then raised my voice. "It's amazing out here, Ambrose. It's like we are the only people on earth. Can you imagine what that feels like?"

"I've imagined it," Ambrose said.

I turned and saw him standing in the doorway of the

motor home, gripping the frame with both hands. Ambrose was holding on tight, but he was leaning ever so slightly forward.

It was as if we'd landed on the moon and our motor home was the landing module. He was gathering his courage to take that first small step for man and that giant leap for mankind.

Ambrose felt the pull. All he needed was someone to hold on to.

I looked at Monk and tipped my head toward his brother. For once, Monk got the unspoken message. He slowly approached Ambrose and held out his hand to him.

Ambrose took a deep breath, let go of the doorframe with one hand, and reached out to his brother.

Monk took his hand but didn't draw him near. He waited. Wincing, Ambrose stepped forward with one foot, lowering it carefully to the ground, and then waited to see what happened.

Nothing did.

But he remained standing, his body half inside the motor home and half outside of it.

It wasn't a comfortable position to be in, and the strain showed on his face. He had to make a decision. In or out?

Ambrose took another deep breath, closed his eyes, and let go of the motor home, planting both feet on the ground. Again he waited for something to happen.

But it already had—he was standing outside, of his own accord, for the first time in decades.

Ambrose opened his eyes, looked at me, and, still holding Monk's hand, took a step in my direction. And then another. And then another.

The Monk brothers stood there, hand in hand a few

feet from the motor home, looking out at me and the desert beyond.

Ambrose stood very stiffly and gripped Monk's hand so tightly that his knuckles were white, but after a long moment, he nodded, more to himself than to either of us.

"It's nice out here," he said.

"Yes," Monk said, "it is."

And he smiled.

20

Mr. Monk and the Peanuts

We were able to stand there for another five minutes
before Ambrose began to panic and made a hasty return to the confines of the motor home. But I considered
those few moments a great success, and I'm sure that
Monk did, too.

I picked up a rock, just like Neil Armstrong did, and
brought it back with me into the motor home as a souvenir of Ambrose's big step. I put it in the drawer with
his sand dollars, his key chain, and his figurine. Maybe if
he had these to look at when he got home he'd get swept
up in nostalgic wanderlust and maybe step outside for a
moment or two.

Since Ambrose seemed to like the desert so much,
and it was getting late in the day, I figured this would
be a good place to spend the night. I suggested that we
just stay where we were, but neither of the Monks felt
comfortable being out there on our own.

"What if we're attacked by hillbillies?" Monk whispered to me. "Or ravenous wolves? Nobody would ever know."

I didn't think we were in any danger from hillbillies or wild animals, but when he mentioned being attacked, I remembered that the first mistake the travelers in *Race with the Devil* made was camping off road. A remote area like this would be the perfect place for demon worshippers to picnic.

But I still thought we should stay in the desert, only somewhere a bit more populated. So I drove us back to the interstate and decided to pull into the first trailer park or campground that we came upon.

I didn't have to wait long. A few miles up the freeway, I saw a sign for Silver Spur, a trailer park with a mining camp theme out among the boulders and cactus.

The front office was a frontier-style wooden cabin with a hitching post and an empty water trough. Some rusty pickaxes, shovels, mine trolleys, and a couple of wooden wagon wheels were scattered around the property as decorative props. The camp didn't offer much in terms of amenities, just a laundry room, toilets, showers, and a small swimming pool with some weather-beaten furniture on the cracked concrete decking. But that was okay, all we really wanted was the solitude of the desert landscape, and there was plenty of that.

Almost all of the camping spots were taken, but they all had the same unobstructed view of the open desert, the barren hills, and, in the distance, the interchange where the I-15 and the I-40 met and then branched off in separate directions across the dry scrub plains.

We parked beside an old A-class that had a map of the United States on the back with nearly all of the states colored in with differing shades of red. My guess was that the red states were all places the RV's occupants had visited so far. Or perhaps they just wanted to remember which states voted for the McCain-Palin ticket in 2008.

Their window shades were drawn and there appeared to be nobody home. The garbage can beside their camper was overflowing with beer bottles, and there were cigarette stubs and bottle caps on top of the picnic table. I could see that we were going to get along great with our neighbors.

As I hooked us up to the utilities, my gaze kept drifting to the pool area in the center of the park. The pool itself wasn't very appealing, but the idea of floating in cool water in the middle of the warm desert was too enticing to ignore.

"I'm going swimming," I declared as I stepped back into the RV and went to the control panel. "Anyone want to join me?"

They both looked at me as if I'd suggested that we rob a liquor store together.

"Why would you want to do that?" Monk said.

"Because it's hot out," I said, and pushed the buttons to expand the slide-out sections of the motor home.

"Take a shower or have a Popsicle."

"I'd rather take a swim," I said.

"The only reason you need to swim is to save yourself from drowning."

"What about swimming for exercise or pleasure?"

"It's conceivable," Monk said, "if you have your own pool and no one else is allowed in it."

"Not everyone can afford that," I said. "So for me, it's a luxury when I have the chance to go in a swimming pool."

"Is it also a luxury to sprinkle your food with rat poison?" Monk asked.

"I don't see the connection," I said.

"I do," Ambrose said.

"You have no idea how many sweaty, filthy, diseased strangers have been in that pool. Or how many children have relieved themselves in there," Monk said. "You might as well take a dip in raw sewage."

To be honest, I wasn't surprised by Monk's reaction. When Monk and I were in Hawaii, he didn't want me swimming in the ocean because billions of fish relieve themselves in it. It was also why he doesn't eat fish, because they breathe water "thick with their own waste."

I ignored his protests, went into the bathroom, stripped off my clothes, and changed into my one-piece bathing suit and flip-flops. I slathered myself in suntan lotion, wrapped a towel around my waist, and when I stepped out again, the Monks had settled into the dinette with a bag of roasted peanuts, which they'd spilled out onto the tabletop and were busy shelling.

Both Monks quickly averted their gaze away from me and concentrated on shelling the nuts, though I was pretty sure Ambrose snuck a few glances as I went to the refrigerator to get myself a bottle of water, because when I looked back at him, his face was bright red.

"Save some room for dinner," I said.

"We aren't *eating* peanuts," Ambrose said, without looking up from his shelling. "We're *playing* peanuts."

"And I'm going to decimate you," Monk said.

The game was simple in concept but impossible to play, at least for me. You start by separating the nuts and their shells into two piles. The goal is to match as many of the nuts with the shells that they came from as you can. The person who matches the most nuts with their shells wins.

I've played the bizarre game with Monk half a dozen times. My lifetime high score is one, and that's only because Monk matched up everything else on the table and, out of pity, left a nut behind for me to put together.

Monk called it "the sport of the Gods" because it requires a level of such intense concentration that players reach a "transcendent state" that puts them in sync with the spatial dynamics of the universe.

Who knew a bag of roasted peanuts had such power?

I started for the door, but Monk spoke up.

"Wait a minute, Natalie. You're not carrying any soap or disinfectant cleanser with you."

"I'm swimming in the pool, not cleaning it."

"But you're not coming back in here dripping with sewage," Monk said. "This is where we live, eat, and sleep."

I sighed, went back to the bathroom, and got my clothes, a plastic bag for my suit, and all of my toiletries, as well as a can of Lysol cleanser just for show.

Monk nodded approvingly and then began shuffling the shells.

Once I was outside, I left the cleanser behind and headed for the pool. It was occupied by a deeply tanned, morbidly obese middle-aged man who stood in the shallow end, wearing a baseball cap and sunglasses and holding an enormous can of beer. He reminded me of a hippopotamus. A woman I assumed was his wife rested on a chaise lounge with a matching beer of her own. She had a beehive hairdo that must have been sprayed with a mist of quick-drying cement and wore a loud pink one-piece bathing suit with industrial-strength support that made her bust look like two ballistic missiles.

Two sunburned kids, a boy and a girl around ten years old, were doing cannonballs into the deep end while their parents sat together under the one working umbrella and read his-and-hers James Patterson paperbacks—he was reading Alex Cross and she was reading Women's Murder Club. A French poodle rested under the woman's chair and would probably have been reading something by James Patterson, too, if the author had written anything about dogs.

I smiled politely at everyone, put my stuff down on a chaise lounge, and stepped into the pool. It was luke-warm and smelled strongly of chlorine, but it was still a relief from the heat.

The Hippo made no secret of checking me out as I got into the water, and neither did Mr. Patterson. I swam from one end of the pool to the other, aware of their eyes on me.

I stopped for a moment in the deep end and saw that the two kids were standing on the edge of the pool look-ing at me, too. Even the dog had his eyes on me.

For a moment, I felt a cold shudder of fear . . . and recognition. I suddenly remembered a scene from *Race with the Devil* when the travelers stopped at a trailer park and everyone there, it later turned out, worshipped at the feet of Beelzebub.

I dunked myself underwater to clear my head and hide from their gaze. What was I thinking? Had I gone completely insane? I had to get a grip.

When I emerged I decided the kids were staring at me because they wanted me to get out of the deep end so they could do more cannonballs, and the guys were staring at me because they were guys, and the women were watching me because their men and children were. I had no idea what the dog's motivation was.

So I swam to the middle of the pool and floated on my back, swishing my arms and kicking my legs every so often to maintain my position. The kids got the deep end back and the Hippo had the shallow end to himself.

I closed my eyes and enjoyed the feeling of desert air on the top of me and the water underneath. My muscles unwound and my tensions melted away.

For the first time in more than twenty years, I was on

my own. My husband was dead, my daughter was off to college, and I was unmoored. I was no longer responsible to, or responsible for, anyone.

Well, that wasn't exactly true. I had Monk.

And I had come to accept the fact that he was more than just an employer to me, that no matter what happened, he would always be a part of my life.

But would he always *be* my life? Because that was what he was now, even more so since Julie had left for college.

There was a certain comfort in letting him become the center of my life.

And security.

Which made me wonder, was Monk the same thing to me that Ambrose's house was to him?

Was I sticking with Monk because it was what I wanted or because I was afraid to try something new?

My mind began to wander, and I must have dozed off, because when I opened my eyes again, it was dusk, and I was all alone in the pool.

Everybody was gone.

I stood up in the pool, stunned and disoriented. I didn't know it was humanly possible to float and sleep at the same time. And then I felt the hot sting all over the front of my body.

I'd burned myself from head to toe, but since I was wearing suntan lotion with an SPF of about 10,750, it wasn't as bad as it could have been.

I got out of the pool, grabbed my things, and went over to the bathrooms and showers. When I turned on the water in the little shower stall, three lizards scurried across the floor, startling me. I wondered what else was in the stall that I hadn't seen.

The water was cold and rough, as if it was spiked with sand. I couldn't do anything with my hair. All that time in the chlorinated water had made it look and feel like the end of a broom.

Monk ought to like that, I thought. He was big on brooms.

I got dressed, put my wet bathing suit in a plastic bag, and headed back to our motor home in the darkness, my path lit by the moon, a few park lights, and the flickering glow from flames in the campsite fire rings and barbecues. The air was thick with the aroma of grilled food.

The inside of the motor home was dark, the only illumination coming from the glow of park lights outside the dinette window. The Monk brothers were still at the table where I'd left them hours before. Their attention was completely focused on the task in front of them. Their hands moved rapidly over the table, yet somehow they managed to never touch each other. It was like they were hypnotized, performing their task with speed and efficiency while consciously unaware that they were doing it.

I closed the door hard, the sound startling them both so much that they flung their shells into the air. They looked at each other, and then at me, and then outside, as if they had no idea how they'd ended up where they were sitting.

"How did it become night?" Ambrose asked.

"I believe it has something to do with the sun setting," I said.

"We must have really gotten into the game," Monk said.

"It's been great," Ambrose said.

Monk nodded and referred to a notepad beside him. "Up until this match, we were tied, six to six. Shall we call this one a draw?"

"It feels like the right thing to do," Ambrose said.

"Six and twelve are nice, even numbers. It's good to end up even."

"It's the best," Monk said.

We'd all become lost in our pursuits, each of us emerging from them with the sense that we'd achieved some kind of balance within ourselves and with the world around us. I did it floating in a swimming pool in the desert. They did it with a bag of peanuts.

I guess it doesn't matter how you achieve balance as long as it happens now and then.

21

Mr. Monk and the Weird Sisters

Ambrose prepared spaghetti and meatballs for us for dinner. He made sure that each noodle was the same length, and laid them out individually on our plates so they wouldn't get tangled up. And then he served us each two perfectly round meatballs in a zesty tomato sauce on the side. He didn't put them on top of the noodles because he took the *and* in spaghetti *and* meatballs very seriously. His interpretation was that they were meant to be served together, but separately.

After dinner, we had our leftover Danish pastries for dessert and watched a *SpongeBob SquarePants* marathon on TV. The Monks thought the cartoon was hilarious, but I didn't think it was funny at all. I found everything about the show aggressively irritating.

"How can you dislike it?" Monk said, barely able to breathe, he was laughing so hard. "SpongeBob is square. And so are his pants!"

That got Ambrose giggling so hard I thought he'd

throw up. When he finally got hold of himself, he said, "And he lives in a pineapple!"

"Under the sea!" Monk said, and they erupted into laughter all over again.

"Yes," I said. "I know."

"But there are no pineapples in the ocean!" Monk choked out, and still more hilarity ensued.

I was glad they were both so happy. I occupied myself reading the guidebooks about the places we might visit and putting skin cream on my sunburn.

Bedtime involved the same awkwardness as the night before. The only change this time was that I didn't sleep through it when Monk and Ambrose cleaned the bathroom. I probably could have slept if it wasn't for our neighbors, who were playing hip-hop loud enough to wake Tupac Shakur.

The songs were pounded into my head. In every one of them, the women were referred to as "bitches" and "hos"—and they were always eager to party and do the guys in a variety of ways.

And that, my friends, is the cleaned-up, PC version.

I couldn't understand what any woman would find appealing about songs that cheer men on to degrade them, verbally and physically. What was even more shocking was that half of the songs were sung by women.

It made me feel old. Why? Because my parents thought the same thing about the music I used to listen to.

But this stuff was far more explicit and crude than the hardest-edged music of my day.

Then again, my parents probably consoled themselves with the same rationalization, too.

Monk came out of the bathroom, peeling off his cleaning gloves, and stood beside my bed, where I was cozy in my sleeping bag.

"You have got to tell them to turn down their music," Monk said.

"I'm in bed. Why don't you do it?"

"Because you're down with those dudes. You speak their funky jive. I don't."

"You sound fluent to me," I said, rolling over and showing him my back.

"Fine, then I guess we'll just have to try and sleep through it," he said, and headed back to the bathroom.

I knew he was right. If they were going to listen to one of us, it would be me.

I got out of the sleeping bag, put on my flip-flops, and wrapped a jacket around myself, even though it was still very warm outside. I wasn't naked, but I didn't want to confront a bunch of partying guys in a T-shirt and sweats.

I trudged over to the RV, which was practically shaking from the vibration of their subwoofers, and had my fist up to bang on the door when I saw the pair of mud-caked, tar-stained boots on the front step.

The boots must have been a size fourteen, and I didn't want to meet the drunken, tattooed, neo-Nazi, devil-worshipping, ex-convict monster who fit into them, at least not on my own.

I scampered back to our RV, where Monk was waiting for me at the door.

"The noise hasn't stopped," Monk said. "Are you sure they understood you?"

"I didn't talk to them."

"Why not?"

"Because I need backup," I said. "The guys in there are huge and possibly Satanists."

"How do you know?"

"Haven't you heard the music they are listening to?" Ambrose said, stepping up behind Monk. "They must be Satanists. Or worse."

Monk dismissed the idea with a wave of his hand. "I hear kids on the street listening to that kind of music right outside my door every day."

"And you wonder why I don't go outside," Ambrose said.

Monk turned back to me. "Did you see any of them?"

"No, but I saw their boots."

"That's all? You are being ridiculous. I'll go with you, but you'll have to do the talking. I'm not very street anymore."

As if he ever was. He stepped outside and we went over to the RV. I pounded on the door, while Monk regarded the boots.

"How bad can they be if they are considerate enough to leave their dirty shoes outside?" Monk said.

Someone turned down the music, and I heard footsteps coming to the door. I took a deep breath and prepared to face one of Satan's minions.

"We're about to find out," I said, taking a step back.

The door opened to reveal a little old lady with white hair wearing a flowered dress and furry slippers.

"Hello," she said with a sweet smile. "Can I help you?"

I didn't see how she could be in the same camper with that music unless she had her hearing aids turned off. So I spoke loudly.

"Um, yes, we are in the RV next door and your son is playing his music awfully loud. Could you please ask him to turn it down so we can sleep?"

She smiled. "There's no need to yell, dear. My son can't hear you no matter how high you raise your voice. He's out on the road, jamming gears on an eighteen-wheeler like his dad used to, from the Mississippi to the Pacific. But we'll be glad to turn the music down a notch."

Another woman appeared behind the white-haired lady. She was also old, but her hair was dark black and tied in a ponytail that tumbled all the way down the back of her denim shirt to the waist of her faded jeans.

"Don't stand there yapping with the door open, Bessie. You're letting in all the mosquitoes," she said.

"There are mosquitoes?" Monk said, whirling around as if there might be a big one standing right behind him, holding an ax.

"Come on in," Bessie said. "Have some milk and cookies."

Monk practically leaped into the motor home, mostly to escape the mosquitoes. It certainly wasn't for the milk, which scared him even more than blood-sucking insects.

I went in out of curiosity. I wanted to learn more about two old ladies who listened to hard-core hip-hop.

But once inside, I realized I had it wrong. There were *three* old ladies.

The third woman had her hair in a bun, wore a hand-knitted sweater and polyester slacks, and had two jangling charm bracelets around her thin, age-spotted wrists. She sat at the table, which was cluttered with cards dealt for bridge, a plate piled high with brownies, another plate covered with cookies, and lots of beer cans.

I didn't see any milk.

The décor was generic motor home, but with a big glass display case built in to their impressive entertainment center. The case was jammed full with stuffed animals, spoons, rocks, postcards, seashells, mugs, dolls, banners, poker chips, and other stuff I assumed were souvenirs of their travels.

"Get out a couple of glasses, Mabel, we've got guests," the ponytailed lady said. "I'm Gertie Zarkin, and these are my sisters, Bessie and Mabel. Sorry we disturbed you with our music, but aren't you going to bed awfully early? The night is young and so are you."

"We've had a long day on the road," I said. "We started out near Carmel this morning and even stopped for a bit in San Luis Obispo and Solvang."

"That is a long day," Mabel said.

"I can't believe that was your music we were hearing," Monk said.

"What do you expect us to listen to?" Gertie said. "Artie Shaw? Perry Como? Neil Diamond?"

"I don't know, but you're too old and sensible to be listening to songs about dancing, drug abuse, and relentless fornication."

"We may be too old to do as much of that as we used to," Gertie said, "but that doesn't mean we don't enjoy what we can get, even if now it's mostly hearing about it instead of doing it."

"Thinking young keeps you young," Mabel said, taking out two glasses from the cupboard and setting them on the table. "You have to change with the times or you get stuck."

"It's also why we hit the road in a motor home rather than sit around on our porches knitting socks," Gertie said. "It's not old age that kills you. It's the sitting around on your fat ass doing nothing. You start to rust."

"I have to admit, though, that I'm a little old-school," Bessie said. "I still love Snoop Dogg."

"I'm old-school, too," Monk said. "But I prefer Marmaduke."

"She's talking about Snoop Dogg," I said. "Not Snoopy."

"Snoopy *is* a dog," Monk said.

"They're not the same thing," I said.

Bessie went to the refrigerator. "What can we offer you? Milk? Juice? Beer? Tequila?"

"Ensure?" Gertie added.

"Do you have any Fiji bottled water?" Monk asked.

"Only water we have is out of the tap," Bessie said.

Monk shivered. "Nothing for me, thanks."

"I'm fine, too," I said.

"Maybe I can tempt you with these instead." Bessie lifted the plate of brownies up to us. They looked and smelled heavenly. "Help yourselves."

"Thank you," I said, immediately reaching for one.

"I wouldn't," Monk whispered to me. "They might be laced with marijuana."

"They aren't laced with pot," Bessie said. There was certainly nothing wrong with her hearing. "They're *loaded* with it."

"You aren't serious," Monk said.

"I still use the recipe that I got in Amsterdam forty years ago," she said. "It's world-famous and packs a wallop."

"Possession of marijuana is illegal," Monk said.

"Not if it's for medicinal purposes," Bessie said. "We all have legitimate prescriptions."

"Pot is great for my arthritis," Mabel said.

"You know what they say—a spoonful of sugar helps the medicine go down," Bessie said. "So does a lot of chocolate."

I put the brownie back. "No, thank you."

Bessie winked. "I understand, honey. You don't want to get high in front of your father."

"I'm not her father," Monk said, wandering over to their display case. "I'm her boss."

"And you travel together in a motor home?" Gertie said. "I'm surprised you're so liberal when it comes to nookie but not when it's about a little weed."

"We are not intimately involved," Monk said.

"We're taking Mr. Monk's brother on a road trip for his birthday," I said. "I'm their driver."

"What's your profession?" Mabel asked Monk.

"I'm a consultant to the San Francisco Police Department," Monk said. "I investigate homicides."

"Sounds exciting," Mabel said. "Are you investigating one now?"

"I should be investigating two, one in Santa Cruz and one in San Luis Obispo"—Monk glared at me—"but she won't let me."

"I thought you were the boss," Bessie said.

"Not when we are on vacation," I said. "How long have you three been on the road?"

"For a few years now," Gertie said. "We're wandering aimlessly but with the general intention of hitting the forty-eight contiguous U.S. states."

"But we're in no hurry. We spent too much of our lives in a rush to get somewhere, to achieve something," Bessie said. "Now it's nice just to take each day as it comes."

"And do it together," Mabel said.

"At our age, we aren't rushing to reach the end of our journey," Bessie said. "It's a destination that doesn't seem as far away as it used to."

"Or as far away as we'd like it to be," Gertie said.

"But we keep ourselves active," Bessie said. "We're just relaxed about it. Does that make sense?"

"It does to me," I said. I hoped I had their zest for life and willingness to keep up with popular culture when I was their age.

Monk gestured to the display case. "Are these souvenirs from your trips?"

"We pick up something everywhere we go," Mabel said. "We just got that Golden Gate Bridge salt shaker in San Francisco last week."

"Sometimes we need to be reminded where we've been," Bessie said. "Anything that gooses the memory is good at our age."

"The pot helps, too," Mabel said.

"So does getting laid," Gertie said. "Keeps all the neurons firing."

Monk looked at his watch. "Oh my, we're late. We really have to go."

"Late for what?" Gertie asked.

"Flossing," Monk said. "I don't want that tartar building up. That's how you lose your teeth."

"Don't I know it." Mabel plucked out her dentures and showed them to us.

Monk reared back as if she had a tarantula in her hand instead of a set of teeth.

"Where are you going next?" I asked.

"Out the door," Monk said, slipping past me.

"I meant them, Mr. Monk," I said.

"Yosemite by way of the California Gold Country," Gertie said. "Then on to Reno."

"So you're making a loop through California," I said.

"It's a big state—it's hard to get it all in otherwise," Mabel said. "What's your next destination?"

Monk waved to me from the door. "Our motor home. Let's go, Natalie. We don't want to get gingivitis."

"You can start flossing without me, Mr. Monk. I'll catch up," I said, and I turned back to the ladies as he hurried away. "We haven't decided where we're going yet. I suppose it'll either be Las Vegas or the Grand Canyon."

"You could do both," Mabel said, picking up a brownie and wrapping it in a napkin.

"Mabel is our navigator," Bessie said.

"Go to the Grand Canyon, and then you can double back to Kingman and head northwest through Las Vegas," Mabel said. "You could even squeeze in Yosemite and Sacramento on your way back to San Francisco."

"Sounds like a good plan," I said. "Enjoy your trip."

"You, too," Mabel said, and handed me the brownie. "A treat for later. It will help you sleep."

"Thanks," I said and started to go out the door. I paused when I saw the boots and turned back to them. "May I ask you a stupid question?"

"Of course, honey," Bessie said.

"Who wears the big boots?"

The women shared a smile.

"We picked them up on our travels," Mabel said. "We use them for protection."

"I don't understand," I said.

"We're three vulnerable little old ladies on the road," Gertie said. "But nobody is going to mess with us if they think it means messing with him."

They laughed. So did I.

"A drunken, tattooed, neo-Nazi, devil-worshipping, ex-convict monster," I said. They looked at me. "Sometimes my imagination runs wild."

"Why leave all the fun to your imagination?" Gertie said with a wink.

I waved good night to them, unwrapped my brownie, and took a bite out of it as I strolled back to our trailer.

It turned out that Mabel was right about the brownie. I fell asleep while Monk and Ambrose were still in their first hour of flossing.

22

Mr. Monk and the Duel

Monk shook me awake at two a.m. wearing yellow dish gloves and shining a flashlight in my face.

"What's the emergency?" I asked.

"You're a drunk and a junkie."

"What are you talking about?"

"You boozed it up yesterday, and what did it lead to?" He held open his hand to show me some crumbs on his yellow rubber palm. "*This*. I found these in your jacket pocket. There are more of them outside."

"You went through my pockets?"

"Do you know what these are?"

"Crumbs," I said and put my face back into my warm pillow. He shook me again.

"There's marijuana in these crumbs," Monk said.

"Is that why you are wearing gloves?" I mumbled into my pillow.

"I don't want to get high," he said.

"You can't get high from holding crumbs from marijuana brownies."

"So now you're a drug expert?" Monk said. "I'm here to scare you straight, sister."

I rolled over and looked at him. "Sister?"

"This is how it starts. First booze and weed, and then one morning you wake up and you're one of those women in the songs we heard tonight."

"I'm Lil' Kim?"

Monk shook me again. "Wake up and smell the random drug test."

"You want me to pee in a cup?"

"Hell, no," he said.

"So what sort of random drug test did you have in mind?"

He looked at me for a long moment. "Count backward in twos from 2,888,222."

"I had one bite, Mr. Monk, and threw the rest away," I said.

"I'll get you started. Two million, eight hundred eighty-eight thousand, two hundred twenty."

"If you don't believe me, you can dig through the trash. It's still wrapped in the napkin."

"You go get it," he said.

"The only place I'm going is back to sleep." I closed my eyes and rolled on my side.

"What if some chipmunk gets his paws on it during the night?"

"Good night, Mr. Monk."

"He could eat it and become deranged."

"Go to bed," I said.

He leaned over me and aimed his flashlight in my face. "If we wake up tomorrow and find out that some child has been attacked by a pothead chipmunk, you will have to live with that guilt for the rest of your life."

I snatched the flashlight from his hand, turned it off, and shoved it into my sleeping bag.

"Go. To. Bed."

He stood there for a long moment.

"Are you going to give me back my flashlight?"

"No," I said.

"But it's dark," he said.

"That's because it's night."

"How am I supposed to get back to my bed?"

"Keep walking until you hit something," I said. "That's your bed."

"What if I have to get up in the middle of the night?"

"You already have," I said. "So now you'll just have to suffer until morning."

"Is that your best shot? Don't make me laugh. I suffer all the time, day in and day out, year after miserable year, so bring it on, lady. No one suffers like I do. No one. I can do it in my sleep."

"Good," I said. "Then you have no problem."

I'd trumped him and he knew it. He stood there staring at me for a long moment, trying to figure a way out of it. There wasn't one, but I couldn't sleep with him hovering over me.

"If you don't move in four seconds," I said, "I am taking off my top."

Monk scampered back to the safety of his bed. I could feel him glowering at me in the darkness, but I could sleep through that.

"You're mean when you're stoned," he said.

Bessie, Gertie, and Mabel departed in their motor home for the Gold Country before I got up and, as far as I know, nobody was mauled by any deranged animals during the night.

We had Wheat Chex cereal for breakfast. Without

milk, of course. Ambrose seemed chipper, but Monk spent the entire meal silent and scowling at me.

"What's wrong, Adrian?" Ambrose asked.

"Nothing," Monk said.

"Then why do you have that look on your face?"

"I slept badly," he said.

"I think it was that music," Ambrose said. "It was very disturbing."

"So were the harridans who were listening to it," Monk said. "They are the Weird Sisters."

I was impressed by Monk's allusion to Shakespeare's *Macbeth*. And, apparently, so was Ambrose.

"Double, double, toil and trouble," Ambrose said. "I'm glad I didn't meet them."

"Don't listen to Mr. Monk," I said. "I thought they were sweet and inspiring."

"Of course you did," Monk said.

I don't know why Monk didn't out me at that moment as a drunken junkie to his brother and I didn't care. I had nothing to apologize for. But Monk did. He'd invaded my privacy by going through my pockets, and I wasn't letting that slide.

After breakfast, I got up and took my first shower in the motor home. I was quick, but I knew Monk would still spend an hour decontaminating the area before he used it. I put on some skin cream for my sunburn, got dressed, and stepped out.

Monk was waiting for me. Ambrose was washing dishes, his back to us. Monk leaned in and whispered to me.

"I didn't tell Ambrose about your disgraceful behavior last night because it would have crushed him. He idolizes you."

"And you don't?"

"I thought I knew you," Monk said.

"Having a martini one night and a bite of a brownie the next doesn't make me a bad person."

"Two martinis and a hashish brownie," Monk said.

"Nor does it make me a drunk or a drug addict," I said. "I'm an adult on vacation and I am taking it easy. I haven't done anything wrong or irresponsible, and I don't appreciate you treating me like I have. And you have no business going through my personal belongings."

"You're right. I am being totally unreasonable. So how do you plan to relax tonight? Smoke some crack? Snort some coke? Maybe hold up a liquor store?"

"If this is how you are going to behave, then we're turning around and going home. We'll be back in San Francisco tonight. Is that what you want?"

Monk glanced over at his brother, who was happily washing dishes.

"He went outside yesterday," Monk said. "Who knows what might happen today?"

"That's up to you, Mr. Monk. Do we go on or do we go back?"

He sighed and looked back at me. "We go on."

"Will you ease up on me?"

"Will you give me back my flashlight?" Monk said. "I can't sleep in the dark without it."

"Deal," I said.

We took the I-40 east toward the Grand Canyon. I figured we could easily make it there in a day, so I decided we could afford a little detour onto Route 66 once we crossed the Arizona border at Needles.

Much of the original Route 66, celebrated as the Mother Road and America's Main Street, was bypassed or paved over by the interstate, but there were still original patches, like the 120-mile stretch between Oatman and Seligman, decaying under the baking sun, weeds poking through the cracks in the dusty, faded asphalt.

We got off the interstate and picked up Route 66 in Oatman, an old gold rush town that was still much like it was in the 1800s, with wood-plank sidewalks, false-front buildings, and burros wandering wild up and down the street.

Oatman reminded me a lot of Trouble, a gold rush town in central California that Monk and I had spent some time in on a case not too long ago.

Ambrose was fascinated, leaning forward in his seat.

"It's like we've driven through a time warp into the Old West," Ambrose said. "Back to a time when there was no adequate sanitation."

"Don't over-romanticize it," I said.

"Why do they leave this place standing?" Monk asked.

"So people can experience what it was like back then," I said.

"Why would anyone want to experience pestilence and death?" Monk said.

"I prefer Solvang," Ambrose said.

"This is more authentic," I said.

"Authenticity is overrated," Monk said, "and frequently disgusting."

We drove through the center of town, then followed the road up into the hills, past the abandoned gold mine that had once supported Oatman.

I didn't mention to the Monks that this stretch of road was known as Bloody 66, even back in the 1940s and early 1950s before the mountain route was bypassed entirely by the interstate. I tore the page about it out of the guidebook, too, just to be safe.

This particular section of Route 66 got its bloody appellation from its narrow, corkscrew path up into the dark mountains and down again. Some cars would die struggling up the grade, others on the way down when the brakes failed on the hairpin curves and they went over the edge. In the latter case, it wasn't just the cars that died, but also the people in them.

I wasn't concerned. I figured modern engines were stronger than those old ones, and I intended to be very slow and careful going around the curves. It would be the vehicular equivalent of a pleasant stroll through a winding path.

I was wrong.

The crumbling road into the Black Mountains twisted along a jagged hillside that took us around one blind corner after another as we crept up. There were no guardrails and I could see the rusted, charred wreckage of cars in the ravine below, lying in the dry weeds like the bleached bones of dead animals.

"Are those cars down there?" Ambrose asked.

"I don't know," I said. "I'm paying attention to the road."

I sat erect, my body stiff with concentration, my back damp with sweat. As scary as the drive uphill was, I was sure the one down would be even worse, with blind switchbacks along the edges of sheer cliffs. I cursed myself for not catching Route 66 on the flats outside Kingman instead of taking it through the mountains.

"Why are we going this way?" Monk asked, as if he was reading my mind.

"It's a piece of history," I said, trying to justify it to myself as well as to him. "It's the last remaining stretch of the original Route 66."

"Did it ever occur to you that there's a reason that they bypassed it with the interstate?"

"Yes," I said. "But there are some interesting places worth seeing before they are gone forever."

"This isn't one of them," Monk said.

The deep, bellowing wail of a horn startled me. I reflexively yanked the wheel, and the motor home nearly scraped the serrated, rocky face of the mountainside.

"What the hell was that?" I said.

I looked into my side-view mirror and saw a huge brown tanker truck behind us, belching smoke. I hadn't noticed the truck before, but then again, all of my concentration had been focused on what was ahead, not behind. The massive grille was caked with mud and the tinted windshield was spattered with dead bugs that left so much goop that I wondered if he'd actually hit a few birds.

"There should be a law against something that filthy on the road," Monk said, looking over Ambrose's shoulder at the reflection in the passenger-side mirror.

The truck honked again. And again.

"What does he want?" Ambrose said.

"I think he wants us to go faster," I said. "Or let him pass."

I glanced again in the mirror.

The truck looked like it had emerged from one of those ravines, clawing its way up through the arid desert and the rusted wreckage, to get back onto the Bloody 66 again, to belch and roar and chew the asphalt and whatever roadkill it could get.

What did that make us?

I was letting my imagination run away with me, and I needed to focus on the road.

It's just a truck, I told myself.

"Is it legal to pass on this road?" Ambrose asked.

"Not here. There's a solid yellow line dividing the lanes on both sides," Monk replied. "If the line is broken up, like dashes, that means you can pass."

The truck was tailgating us now, the unseen driver

leaning on his horn so it made one long, furious shriek, like an Indian war cry.

"I think you should let him pass," Ambrose said.

"It's illegal," Monk said.

"There's no one here," Ambrose said. "What difference does it make?"

"The law is the law, whether there's anyone around to enforce it or not," Monk said. "You have to self-police or civilization crumbles and the world descends into anarchy."

I didn't see any traffic ahead of us, so I steered the motor home to the right, lowered my window, and waved the truck forward.

"What are you doing?" Monk asked.

"Letting him pass."

"Didn't you hear a word I just said?"

"Nope," I lied.

The truck moved into the left lane and charged up beside us, still honking, the engine roaring. I turned to look at the driver, and at the same instant, he swerved at us.

I yanked the wheel hard to the right and the motor home scraped against the rocky face of the mountain, shearing off the passenger-side mirror.

"See?" Monk said. "Anarchy."

"That was fast," Ambrose said.

"The son of a bitch did it on purpose," I said.

"Of course he did," Monk said, "because you told him it was all right."

"I did not!"

"You did the moment you waved him forward," Monk said. "You declared that civilization doesn't exist on this road."

The tanker portion of the truck was passing us now. Whatever was in that tank, it was deadly. I could see the faded word "FLAMMABLE" beneath the layer of muck and I was pretty sure I also saw a skull and crossbones.

"Get his license plate," Monk said. "We'll have him cited by the police for reckless driving."

That's when the truck cut in front of us. I slammed on the brakes, barely avoiding being sideswiped by his enormous, jagged bumper. The truck disappeared over the crest of the hill as we skidded to a stop.

"Bastard!" I yelled, punching the dash with my fist. Ambrose and Monk looked at me. "Well, he is. Did you get his license plate number?"

"His plate was covered with mud," Monk said. "I couldn't even see what state it was from."

"He must be in a big hurry to get wherever he's going," Ambrose said.

"He's a bastard," I said.

"The bastard certainly isn't a very responsible driver," Ambrose said. The profanity didn't roll easily off his tongue, but he seemed to like the sensation anyway.

I pressed on the gas, but with our momentum lost, it was a grind getting our motor home moving up the hill again. It took us a few minutes to reach the crest and the ruins of a gas station and trading post that was once made of stacked stone. The faded sign and the vintage pumps were still there, and some piles of rock, but that was it.

The truck was gone. That was a relief. I'd half expected him to be waiting for us to continue whatever game he was playing, like the truck in *Duel*, the classic TV movie that started Steven Spielberg's career. In that one, the truck was like a shark and poor Dennis Weaver in his tiny Dodge Dart was the chum.

I'd been afraid that our trip would mirror *Race with*

the Devil when it was really *Duel* I should have been worried about.

I took a moment to catch my breath, and then we started downhill, the road twisting in one tight curve after another. I was going slowly, trying not to ride the brakes, rolling at an easy clip that almost made the curves fun.

Until I came out of a tight turn and was headed right into the back of the truck, which was parked in the center of the lane directly in front of us.

I screamed, stomped on the brakes, and wrenched the wheel to the left all at once. The rear of the motor home fishtailed to the right, and we came to a screeching, rubber-peeling stop just inches from the edge of the cliff, sending over a small avalanche of loose rocks into the dry brush below.

The motor home rocked slightly from side to side and settled, blocking both lanes of the roadway. I looked past Ambrose out the passenger window and saw the truck speeding away down the hill.

Ambrose looked at me, his face white with terror. "The bastard."

23

Mr. Monk on the Mother Road

Monk got out and directed me as I backed up so the rear of the RV wouldn't scrape against the rocks. He got back inside and I drove slowly, and warily, around the curves until we finally spilled out of the Black Mountains and onto the open road.

We didn't see any sign of the truck.

It was long gone.

Monk wanted to go into Kingman and file a report with the local sheriff, but I didn't see the point.

What information did we have to give them?

Even if we *could* track down the driver, what evidence did we have against him that would prove any of our accusations?

All we could do was push on and try to put the experience behind us.

Monk reluctantly agreed with me. We wouldn't let some truck driver's road rage, or the superficial damage to the motor home, ruin our trip.

We didn't spend any time in Kingman except to gas up and get some cold drinks. The same could be said for most of the people who showed up there.

The city didn't offer natural beauty, historical interest, or even kitsch appeal. It had always been a place that existed to serve the needs of travelers who found themselves stuck midway between where they'd been and where they wanted to go. Back in the 1800s, it was a way station for the railroad and, long before that, a watering hole for weary Indians loping across the dry Hualapai Valley. It was also the gateway to what remained of the original Route 66 before it was consumed again by I-40 east of Seligman.

When the interstate bypassed Route 66, it left the roadside towns that had once thrived on the cross-country traffic to waste away, becoming space-age ghost towns.

And that's exactly what I wanted to see, the ruins of those diners, motels, and gas stations. There was something eerily beautiful about them, at least in the pictures that I'd seen in books, and a glimpse into a not-so-distant, desperately hopeful, and ridiculously enthusiastic past.

I thought Ambrose might be intrigued by it, too. And he was. Monk, on the other hand, found it all very frustrating. He saw the deserted, decrepit buildings, the rusting gas pumps, the broken windows, the faded signs, and the weed-choked parking lots of Hackberry, Valentine, Truxton, and Peach Springs as "messes" that somebody needed to clean up.

Time would do that. It already was in its slow, inexorable way. It wouldn't be long until the desert reclaimed it all and left the scraps for archaeologists to find someday.

In fact, it felt like we were driving through a post-apocalyptic wasteland, looking at what was left of humankind after some horrible event in the 1960s had wiped out everyone but us.

But it wasn't just us.

He was there, too.

At first he was just a speck in my side-view mirror. But then I saw the belch of smoke and I knew.

He's baaaack.

The theme from *Jaws* played in my head, the two-note progression and the deep, driving horn that signaled the relentless approach of evil.

I pressed on the gas pedal. The motor home surged forward. Monk and Ambrose noticed the sudden acceleration.

"What is it?" Monk asked.

I glanced at my mirror. The truck was closing in fast. *Daaaa-dum. Daaaa-dum.*

Monk scrambled up behind my seat and looked in the mirror.

"It's him," he said.

"You better sit down and buckle up, Mr. Monk. We could be in for more trouble."

"What does the bastard want from us?" Ambrose asked.

"This could just be his idea of fun," I said.

"We should call the police," Monk said as he buckled up on the couch.

"Out here? In the middle of nowhere?" I said. "Even if we could get a signal, which I doubt, what could they do for us? How quickly could they get out here? We're on our own."

I was pushing eighty miles per hour, but the truck was still closing in even faster, narrowing the distance between us. When he was close enough for us to see the glint of sunlight off his grille, he leaned on the horn for a good, long roar.

And then he rammed us.

The RV jerked forward, and I floored it. The speedometer inched up to ninety.

The truck rammed us again. I swerved, nearly losing control of the motor home. And that's when he hit us again.

I struggled to control the vehicle.

Monk unbuckled his seat belt.

"What are you doing?" I said, risking a glance over my shoulder. "Sit down."

But Monk wasn't listening. He was making his way to the galley.

I couldn't risk taking my eyes off the road, so I shouted orders to Ambrose.

"Tell me what Mr. Monk is doing," I said.

The truck rammed us again.

"He's falling," Ambrose said.

I swerved, the RV weaving as I struggled to regain control of the car and stay on the road.

"He's crawling to the galley," Ambrose said.

I could see a long curve coming, the ruins of an old diner alongside it. If the truck rammed us at the right moment, he could flip us and send us rolling into the building.

"He's pulling himself up and taking the fire extinguisher off the wall," Ambrose said.

I was holding our speed at a hundred miles per hour. I could see in the side-view mirror that the truck was tailgating us, closing the distance between us again as we neared the curve.

He was going to ram us again.

"Adrian is staggering to the bedroom," Ambrose said. "He's bouncing off the walls."

We closed in on the curve. The big rig surged forward, I heard the hiss of the fire extinguisher, and I braced myself for an impact that didn't come. I looked in the mirror and saw the blast of white foam covering the truck's grille.

The big rig weaved wildly, whipping from one side of the roadway to the other, as the driver fought for control. I let my foot off the gas and pumped the brakes, slowing us down as we hit the long curve.

I held the steering wheel tight and took the turn as wide as I could and then veered into the lane for oncoming traffic as I came out of it. Luckily, there was no one coming in our direction.

And there was no one following us, either.

When we came out of the curve, I looked in the mirror again and saw the nasty big rig far behind us, receding in the background.

Monk emerged from the aft stateroom, replaced the fire extinguisher in its wall mount, and then sat down at the dinette to catch his breath.

"What did you do?" I asked.

"I opened the back window, waited until he got real close, and sprayed his grille with the fire extinguisher."

Ambrose smiled. "In other words, Adrian smothered the bastard's engine by clogging the air intake."

"That will teach him to mess with us," I said.

"With me," Monk said.

"With you," I agreed.

"And my security deposit," he added.

With the truck disabled, Monk thought we had a chance to have the driver apprehended. So when we rolled into Seligman, which was still relatively bustling thanks to being within sight of the I-40, I stopped outside the Snow Cap Drive-In and called 911 on my cell while Monk went out to inspect the damage to the RV.

I told the operator what had happened to us, and roughly where on the road we'd crippled the truck. She

said they'd send a deputy to take a look and asked us to
wait at the hamburger stand to fill out a report. It might
be some time, she said.

Having another encounter with a law enforcement officer made me nervous. With Monk's luck, the cop would
either mention an unsolved murder that he was working
on or he'd be called to a homicide scene while we were
talking with him and he'd invite us along. But we didn't
have much choice. Even if the truck was gone, we needed
to file a police report if we had any hope of my insurance
covering a portion of the damage.

"You want to come out and stretch your legs with
me?" I asked Ambrose.

"I can stretch them just fine in here," he said.

I opened the door and faced the Snow Cap.

The hamburger stand looked the same today as it had
fifty years ago when the owner built the place out of
scrap wood he collected while working on the railroad.
The raw, ramshackle, improvised style of the building
gave the diner its quirky charm.

A billboard ran across the entire front edge of the flat
roofline and offered malts, creamy root beers, shakes,
burgers, tacos, and "dead chicken" in big letters to catch
the eye of passing motorists. Colorful drawings of the
offerings adorned the white walls around the picture
windows and neon-rimmed illustrations of soft-serve
ice-cream cones were mounted like turrets on each corner of the roof.

A corner of the parking lot was cluttered with all
kinds of nostalgic scrap, from phone booths and vintage
gas pumps, to road signs and a small collection of an-
tique cars, one of which was a white 1936 Chevy deco-
rated like the exterior of the restaurant and festooned
with flowers and flags.

It was my kind of place.

I turned back to Ambrose. "How would you like an ice-cold, creamy root beer?"

"That would be nice," he said.

I went outside and found Monk standing behind the RV, his arms crossed, a grimace on his face. I followed his gaze. The back end was dented, but it wasn't nearly as bad as I thought it would be. The bumper had taken the brunt of it, redirecting the force to the sides of the vehicle, so there were also dents on the port and starboard of the RV.

"Look at the bright side," I said. "The damage is equally distributed around the entire vehicle."

"That's true," Monk said. "There is that."

It also meant that the cost of fixing the motor home would be a whole lot higher than if just the rear was smashed, but I knew that was less important to him than the symmetry.

"I reported the incident to the authorities. We're supposed to wait here until a deputy shows up," I said. "I'm going to get root beers for Ambrose and me. Do you want anything?"

"A wipe, please," he said.

I took one out of my purse and gave it to him. He wiped his hands, sighed contentedly, and handed it back to me. For him, disinfecting his hands was relaxing and refreshing.

To each his own.

I dropped the wipe in a trash can and went over to the door of the Snow Cap. The door had two doorknobs, one on each side. It was odd and silly but it was symmetry that Monk would appreciate.

As soon as I entered, the man behind the counter aimed a mustard bottle at me and squirted it. I jerked back as a stream of mustard shot in my direction. It took me a second to realize it was just yellow string.

The mustachioed man, deeply tanned and wearing a Snow Cap T-shirt, laughed uproariously at his prank, which I'm sure he repeated a hundred times a day.

"Welcome to the Snow Cap!"

"Thanks," I said.

The chaotic interior was plastered with a dizzying and overlapping array of Route 66 memorabilia, license plates, old advertising placards, thousands of postcards, law enforcement agency patches, street signs, photographs, stickers, napkins, and anything else that could be glued, taped, stuck, stapled, or tacked on a wall. It was like I'd stepped into the home of an obsessed hoarder who also sold hamburgers and shakes from amid the clutter.

There was no way I could let Monk ever step inside the place.

I turned back to the counter. "Two creamy root beers, please."

He filled two cups with draft root beer and let the frothy head spill over the sides.

"Would you like straws with that?"

"Yes, please," I said.

He dropped a handful of hay on the counter and laughed again. I slid a few bucks his way. He gave me my change, two drinking straws, and a squirt of red string from a fake ketchup bottle. I couldn't blame the guy for getting his kicks where he could. If I was stuck living in Seligman, I'd go a little batty, too.

I brought the root beers out to the RV. I went up to the door and handed Ambrose his. He stood inside and took a long sip from the cup.

"That is very, very tasty," he said, a line of froth above his upper lip.

"Lick your lips," I said.

He did and it made him smile.

"This is a fun drink," he said. "I don't think I've ever had a fun drink before."

I strolled down the street with mine, sipping it as I went. I stopped at a gift shop full of cheap souvenirs and bought Ambrose a postcard of the Snow Cap.

When I emerged, a Sheriff's Department patrol car was cruising up behind our RV. The deputy, wearing reflective sunglasses, a wide-brimmed Stetson-style hat, and a sharply starched uniform, was introducing himself to Monk as I approached.

"Howdy, ma'am," he said. "I'm Deputy Ford. I was just telling Mr. Monk here that we sent a car out to take a look-see. Unfortunately, if there was a disabled big rig out there before, he's gone now."

"You could put out an APB," Monk said. "Set up roadblocks. Get a few helicopters up looking for him."

The deputy scratched his cheek. "I understand you're upset about the damage to your vehicle, but the situation just doesn't merit that kind of response. It's not like he robbed a bank."

"He's a reckless driver," Monk said.

"And a bastard," Ambrose spoke out from the open window above us. "A reckless bastard."

"That may be, sir," the deputy said, "but he's gone."

"He could get somebody killed," Monk said.

The deputy nodded. "But he hasn't yet."

"So you're going to wait until he does?"

"This is a big country out here, Mr. Monk, lots of places for him to get off the beaten path, including the Hualapai Indian Reservation, and wait things out. And in case you didn't notice, there's a big interstate over there. He could be anywhere by now. I'm afraid the best I can do for you is take down your report."

So I invited Deputy Ford to join us in the motor

home. He sat at the dinette table with us and listened to our story, taking notes and asking questions. When he was done, he gave us his card and wrote the report number down on the back of it so we could give the information to our insurance company.

"We'll keep our eyes open for any trucks that match the description of the one that allegedly hit you," the deputy said, getting up from his seat.

I got up, too, and led him to the door. I wanted to get the deputy out before he had a chance to mention any murders and suck Monk into an investigation.

"There's nothing alleged about it," Monk said.

The deputy stopped and turned around. "I'm sure if we find the truck driver, he's going to have his own side of the story to tell. He could say, for instance, that Ms. Teeger here was the reckless driver and he was the injured party. This is your first time behind the wheel of a recreational vehicle, isn't it, ma'am?"

Before I could answer, Ambrose spoke up in my defense. "I resent the implication. That story is ridiculous!"

"It may be," the deputy said. "That's why I referred to your charges as allegations. Without seeing the incident myself, and without the benefit of independent, objective witnesses, I can't really say what happened and what didn't. That's for a judge to decide."

"Good point," I said. "Thank you for your time."

But Ambrose wasn't willing to let it go. "But the truck driver has no logical or rational defense. She'd have to be drunk or on drugs to smash up our motor home like this, and you can see that she's not."

Monk stiffened, and I could almost hear his pulse rate jack up with fear. I could have slapped him for looking so guilty. I had a martini two nights back and a bite of a marijuana brownie—that didn't make me a drunk or a druggie. There was nothing for him, or me, to feel guilty about. But I could see how that might be hard to explain to a cop, especially if Monk did the explaining.

"I can't say that with certainty," the deputy said.

"She'll take a Breathalyzer test right now if you want," Ambrose said. "And then you can."

"That isn't necessary," the deputy said.

"Or a drug test," Ambrose added. "She'll do both, right now, and put this shameful allegation to rest before it can be made."

Monk let out a squeak. I spoke up quickly.

"Deputy Ford said it wasn't necessary. He was trying to make a point, and I appreciate it." I practically shoved the deputy out the door. I didn't believe there was enough marijuana in my system to even show on a drug test, but I sure as hell didn't want to take the chance that I was wrong. "Thank you again for filing a report."

"My pleasure, ma'am," he said. "You drive safely now, and have a nice trip."

He tipped his hat to me and headed back to his car. I sighed with relief. Monk came up behind me.

"You're lucky I vacuumed the floors," Monk said, "so it was clean in here for our unexpected guest."

"I don't think he cared about our floors," I said.

"He would have if he'd spotted your crumbs," Monk said, then whispered, "I hope you're happy. Now I'm as guilty as you are."

"Let's get out of here," I said and closed the door. That's when I remembered something. I picked up my purse off the counter and gave Ambrose the postcard of the Snow Cap Drive-In that I'd bought for him at the gift shop.

"For your collection of souvenirs," I said. "Thank you for defending my honor."

"It's the least I can do." He looked at the postcard of the Snow Cap fondly and then out the window at the real thing one last time. "Do you think we can get another root beer for the road?"

"Sure," I said.

"Ask them to make it real frothy."

24

Mr. Monk and the Grand Canyon

As we took the I-40 east, the arid landscape became steadily greener until we found ourselves an hour later driving through corridors of ponderosa pines and Douglas firs where the Kaibab National Forest and Coconino National Forest met at Williams, the last town bypassed by Route 66 and the gateway to the Grand Canyon.

We stayed in Williams only long enough to gas up, and then we took the sixty-mile drive north on Highway 64 to the rim of the Grand Canyon.

"The air smells different here," Ambrose said, rolling down the window and taking a deep breath.

"That's because we're somewhere else," I said.

"I've never smelled different air before. I've always smelled the same air. The light is different here, too."

"That's because we're in a different part of the country, at a different elevation, in a different landscape than the San Francisco Bay Area."

"It's jarring," he said.

"It's also a different time," I said.

"What do you mean?"

"You didn't feel it?" I said. "We're an hour ahead."

"Ahead?"

"When we crossed into Arizona, we entered the mountain time zone. We are one hour ahead of the West Coast."

Ambrose looked over his shoulder at Monk. "We've traveled forward in time."

"Yes and no," Monk said.

"Is it or is it not an hour into the future compared to San Francisco?"

"It is," Monk said, "but—"

Ambrose interrupted him. "For decades, I have been living in my house and in the past. Now I'm on the road, living in the future. This is truly amazing."

"You think that's cool," I said. "Wait until you see the Grand Canyon."

"Nothing can top this," he said.

He was wrong.

Our spot in the parking area faced a grassy promenade that was crowded with tourists along the south rim of the Grand Canyon, a mile-deep gorge carved into the earth over the course of seventeen million years by the flow of the Colorado River. Or, if you believe creationist theory, it was formed by the global floodwaters that sent Noah sailing off on his ark with all those animals. All that mattered to us, though, was that the canyon was there and Ambrose didn't have to step outside the comfort of his ark to see it. We had a clear view.

And as soon as Ambrose saw it, he pressed his face and the palms of his hands against the window. For several long moments, he couldn't speak. Tears welled up in his eyes and rolled down his cheeks. He looked at his brother beside him.

"Do you see that, Adrian?"

Monk nodded. "I do."

"I can't find words to describe it," Ambrose said, wiping the tears from his eyes. "The color, the light, the shapes, the immensity of it all."

"The problem is that the layers of exposed strata aren't the same thickness and everything is all craggy and uneven," Monk said. "The canyon wall should be smooth. The canyon should be straight."

"Not everything has to be smooth and straight, Mr. Monk," I said.

"It should be," Monk said.

I pointed out the window. "What could be more magnificent, awe-inspiring, and beautiful than that?"

"That," Monk said, and pointed outside, too, "if it was even, smooth, and straight."

"You honestly can't see the magnificence, the grandeur, in all that spectacular imperfection?"

Monk shook his head. "No, I can't."

"I can," Ambrose said.

Monk looked at him and cocked his head. "You *can*?"

"What I see is not just the canyon itself but the tremendous forces and the millennia that shaped it."

"You can see that?"

"You can, too, Adrian, if you try."

"Maybe if I squint," Monk said and squinted.

"I don't think it's a matter of narrowing your view," I said, "but of expanding it."

"I can't see across the millennia, Natalie."

"You can if you look out there, Mr. Monk. The lowest exposed layer of rock, the Vishnu Schist, is two billion years old."

Monk gave me a look. "I didn't realize you were an expert in geology."

"It's just a fact I picked up in the guidebook."

"Perhaps I might have been able to as well, but someone tore out one of the pages and I couldn't read on after that."

I looked away to hide my guilt. "I'm going outside. Would anyone like to join me?"

Monk actually took a step back. "I'm afraid of heights."

"You don't have to walk up to the edge," I said.

"This is as close as I want to get," he said.

"Me, too," Ambrose said. "But I'd like to open the window. I don't want a layer of glass between me and what I am seeing. I want to know that it's real."

I slid open the window and stepped out of his way so he'd have it all to himself.

Ambrose leaned forward, not quite sticking his face out, but putting it where the glass had been. He took a deep breath and reached his hand out tentatively into the air.

"My God," he said. "It is."

I took a walk along the rim, stopping at several overlooks, but after a while I became numb to the view. It seemed to flatten out and lose its power. I think it was just too much work for my mind to try to wrap itself around the scale of what I was seeing, and it simply gave up in exhaustion.

But there were other pleasures. The air was crisp and clean in a way that it wasn't back home, and I felt like I was getting twice as much oxygen as usual. Perhaps it was merely the difference in the air that I was appreciating, just like Ambrose.

I'd had a chance to appreciate a lot of differences in

my life, but Ambrose hadn't. Not a lot changes when your environment is rigidly controlled and you're the only one in it.

Writers like to say that the best drama and comedy come out of conflict. Without conflict, you have no story. The same could apply to life. Without conflict, and without the contrast and changes that it brings, life loses its energy, the spark that keeps the engine running.

I couldn't see how Ambrose had lived without it. And maybe that was what he was beginning to see, too.

That was certainly what spurred Dub Clemens and the Weird Sisters on their journeys. They took to the road in a fervent, perhaps even desperate, belief that the constant stimulation of new experiences would keep them alive. It didn't have to be something as monumental as seeing the Grand Canyon. It could be something as simple as tasting the froth of a creamy root beer on your lips in a place that you've never been before.

I was struck once again by what a wonderful idea this trip had been and marveled that it was Adrian Monk, a man who dislikes change more than anyone, who'd come up with it.

I went back to the RV and, as I neared it, I saw the Monk brothers looking out the window, Ambrose in wide-eyed wonderment and Monk squinting with disapproval.

At that moment, all the aggravation of the last two and a half days—the arguments, the crime scenes, the run-ins with the crazy trucker—seemed completely worth it.

And I realized something else.

I wasn't afraid of motor homes or Satanists anymore.

We remained in the parking lot for several hours, until a forest ranger came along and told us that we'd overstayed our welcome.

So we left and found a KOA campground near a stretch of Highway 64 that was being widened and repaved. I would have preferred a quieter, more rustic locale closer to the canyon, but the best campsites on our budget were already full, the slots reserved months in advance.

But the place we found wasn't so bad. It was outside of Red Lake, midway between the Grand Canyon and Williams, and had a nice-size pool, a clubhouse that looked like a log cabin, a playground for kids, and even one for dogs. I parked in front of the general store, paid for our spot, and returned to the RV.

"What does KOA stand for?" Ambrose asked as I got in.

"Kampgrounds of America," I said and steered us to our spot, a flat concrete pad that was shaded by a couple of trees but was only fifty yards from the freeway. We had our own picnic table, a basic BBQ grill, and a hookup that included cable TV and free wireless Internet.

"*Campground* is spelled with a *C*," Monk said.

"Maybe the founder's name was *Kamp* with a *K* and the place is named after him," I said.

"That's no excuse," Monk said.

"Maybe Mr. Kamp was trying to be humorous," Ambrose said. "Like people who spell *easy* with just the letters *E* and *Z* or spell *right R-I-T-E* or *quick Q-W-I-K*."

"I don't see what's humorous about bad spelling," Monk said. "It encourages illiteracy and sloppiness."

"Or they're saying it would make much more sense to spell *right* and *quick* the way they actually sound," I said.

"We can't just change the spelling of things willy-nilly," Monk said. "It's not up to us."

"Who is it up to, then?" I asked,

"A higher authority," Monk said.

"Like who?"

"*Whom*," Monk corrected. "See? That's what happens when you start spelling *camp* with a *K*. The next thing to go is grammar."

I went outside to hook up our lines. While I was doing that, an enormous motor home the size of a Greyhound bus pulled into the spot next to us. An epic depiction of the westward migration of settlers inching across Monument Valley, eagles soaring overhead, wrapped around the motor home. The array of satellite dishes and radio antennas on top of the RV was so elaborate it looked like the conning tower of an aircraft carrier.

As I stood there watching, the motor home steadied itself and, once it had secure footing, began to unpack, expand, and push out like one of those huge robots in *Transformers*, changing from an RV into an entire house, including a veranda, which unfolded from the passenger side and revealed sliding glass doors. There was even a first-floor garage—a section underneath the rear stateroom opened up and a ramp slid out with a MINI Cooper convertible on it.

The front door of the RV swung open and an African-American man in his thirties hopped out in a Tommy Bahama silk shirt and cargo shorts, took a deep breath, and let it out slowly. I half expected him to plant a flag and claim possession of the land in the name of his king, which was probably himself.

"God, I love camping," he said.

At first I thought he was talking to me, and I was about to answer him, when a blond woman stepped out behind him. She had perfect cheekbones, perfect hair, perfect breasts, perfect skin, and perfect legs. I wondered whether she was real or another *Transformer*. She might have been a toaster before they parked.

"Me, too, sweetie," she said. "I'm going to get us some T-bones."

"You do that," he said. "I'll get us set up."

She practically skipped off to the MINI Cooper.

"There's more?" I asked.

"Excuse me?" he asked, noticing me for the first time.

"This motor home isn't done unfolding itself into stately Wayne Manor? I mean, what's left to do? Push out the hot tub?"

"That's inside," he said.

"Oh, right," I said. "Ours, too."

His perfect woman drove off in the convertible and the garage closed. It was amazing.

"I take it you're unfamiliar with the Windermere Superlative 6000," he said.

"I've never run across one," I said.

"I'm not surprised. There are only a few dozen in the U.S. It's imported from Germany. It's got all the basic creature comforts, indoors and out."

He took a key fob from his pocket, aimed it at the RV, and hit a button. Awnings unfurled on all sides of the vehicle and, at the same time, a cargo door opened up and a grilling island with a gas barbecue, a minirefrigerator, and granite countertops slid out. If those were his basic creature comforts, I was living like a savage.

"You're really roughing it," I said.

"I like to commune with nature, but that doesn't mean I've got to be uncomfortable while I do it. But this RV hasn't got it all. There's one big thing missing."

"The helipad," I said.

"You'd think with all of this innovation they could come up with a way for the RV to hook itself up to the utilities and empty the toilet tanks so I don't have to."

"Yours doesn't do that?" I said. "Mine does."

He glanced at our scratched and dented rental. "How does it work?"

"I do the hookups while the guys inside laze around. What you need is a butler."

He waved off the suggestion. "The whole point of getting this was so just the two of us could get away from it all."

It looked to me like he'd brought it all with him, and then some.

"After we grill our T-bones, we're going to sit outside and watch *Avatar* on the big screen," he said. "In 3-D. You and your two friends are welcome to join us. We'll have fresh, hot popcorn and ice-cold soft drinks."

"You're just inviting us so we won't complain about the noise," I said.

"You see right through me," he said. "Plus it's much more fun to watch a movie with an audience."

"That's very kind of you," I said, "but we didn't bring our 3-D glasses."

"We've got plenty," he said.

If there was one thing I'd noticed about RVers on our trip, it was that they were a very friendly bunch who liked to party. We'd yet to meet a neighbor who hadn't invited us to socialize with them. I suppose that's nice if you're an outgoing sort, a people person, but it could be a real pain if you wanted some privacy. Or were someone like Monk.

I turned back to the motor home just as Monk hurried out the door.

"I saw you talking to our neighbor," he said. "Am I too late?"

"For what?"

"To stop you from accepting another invitation to sin."

"Sin?"

"You know what I am talking about."

"No, I don't," I said.

"We can't afford to have any more trouble, Natalie. The law is watching us now."

"They are?"

"You have to resist temptation. So, what did he offer you? Alcohol? Drugs? Sex?"

"A movie and popcorn."

"That's all?"

"The movie is in 3-D," I said.

Ambrose came to the door, eyes wide with excitement. "Really? Am I invited?"

"You both are," I said.

Monk narrowed his eyes with suspicion. "What's it rated?"

"Triple X. Did I say 3-D? I meant 36-D."

"Aha," he said.

"I was teasing. It's PG-13. We can watch it if we're accompanied by an adult." I turned to Ambrose. "So I hope you will accompany us."

"I've never seen a 3-D movie before," Ambrose said. "Do you think I'll be able to see it from the window?"

"Sure you can. It's the best way to do it. It will be like going to a drive-in movie."

"I've never been to a drive-in," Ambrose said.

"When I was growing up, I went to a lot of drive-ins with my parents and my friends. That was in the dark ages before HBO, DVRs, DVDs, and digital downloads, when going to the movies was like a party, especially at a drive-in on a warm summer night, when everyone waited outside their cars and milled around, waiting for the sun to go down, the smell of hot dogs and mustard and fresh buttered popcorn in the air. God, I miss that smell."

What I remembered most about the drive-in, besides

the time that I got terrified by *Race with the Devil*, was the excitement and novelty of seeing movies in our pajamas and sleeping bags in the way-back of our station wagon.

I also remembered a different kind of excitement and novelty that I experienced at the drive-in when I was a teenager. That was fun, too, but it was definitely a sin, and not one any of us, with the possible exception of our hosts, would be experiencing tonight.

"You're going to love it, Ambrose," I said.

"I can't wait," he said.

Neither could I.

25

Mr. Monk at the Drive-in

I couldn't resist changing into my sweats and T-shirt and bringing my sleeping bag outside with me to see the movie. Monk was adamantly against it and stopped me at the door.

"Are you insane?" he asked.

"There's nothing dangerous or immoral about what I'm doing."

"It's both," he said.

"I don't see how."

"You're going outside half naked and bringing your bed with you."

"I'm not half naked. I'm fully dressed."

"In your pajamas. That's half the clothes you should be wearing, so you are halfway to naked."

"That's not the same as half naked."

"It has two meanings," he said.

"No, it doesn't. Besides, I'll be covered up in my sleeping bag, so that kills your immoral objection. What's the dangerous part?"

"There's no way you can sit outside in a sleeping bag and not get dirt on it."

"So?"

"Where are you going to sleep tonight?"

"In our motor home in my sleeping bag."

"But your sleeping bag will be dirty."

"There might be some dirt on the outside," I said. "But not the inside."

"Dirty is dirty, inside or out. It's unsanitary. I don't see the point of all this, anyway. You're not planning on sleeping outside, are you?"

"No," I said.

"Then why are you bringing your sleeping bag outside with you?"

"It's for sentimental reasons, Mr. Monk. This is how I watched drive-in movies when I was a child."

"But you aren't a child anymore. You grew out of it."

"Sometimes I wish I didn't," I said, and went outside. He followed me.

Our neighbors were waiting, and we formally introduced ourselves. They were Rodney and Kim Newton from Kentucky. He was in the advertising business. She was a professional hand model.

The Newtons had arranged a bunch of high-end outdoor furniture in a semicircle in front of a huge flat screen mounted on the side of their RV. They had movie theater–style bags of fresh popcorn waiting and even bottles of ice-cold root beer. They handed us each a pair of 3-D glasses in sealed plastic bags and told us to make ourselves at home.

Monk took that as an invitation to rearrange the seats in a straight line while I passed along a bag of popcorn, a bottle of root beer, and a set of 3-D glasses to Ambrose, who'd followed my lead and was in his pajamas and bathrobe.

We settled in for the movie, which was in full surround sound, thanks to strategically placed speakers and subwoofers in and around the RV. It was the best-looking and -sounding drive-in movie I'd ever seen.

I curled up in my sleeping bag with my popcorn and root beer, and I was in heaven, all snuggly and warm and content, wowed by the movie, the communal experience, and a sense of excitement and novelty that I hadn't felt in thirty years.

I glanced back at Ambrose, who was watching the movie in rapt attention, a goofy smile on his face. I was reexperiencing the childhood I'd lost, and he was experiencing the childhood he'd never had.

I looked over at Monk, whom I expected to find scowling at my sleeping bag, which was draped over the edge of the chair onto the dirt like a mermaid's tail. But his attention was distracted by something in the distance. He got up to look at it.

I craned my neck to see what had distracted Monk. But I couldn't see past the motor home from my seat, so I reluctantly got up out of my sleeping bag, put on my flip-flops, and chased after him.

Monk was drawn toward a bunch of people holding candles at the far corner of the grounds, where a cluster of identical motor homes was arranged together to create a camp within the camp and where someone was massacring "Stairway to Heaven" on a harmonica.

But none of the people here were wearing horns, or masks, or long capes. These were all men wearing overalls or T-shirts and jeans. Some were wearing bright orange reflective vests over their clothes so no cars would hit them. I brilliantly deduced, without any help from Monk, that they were road workers.

As we got closer, I could see they were gathered in front of an RV where a shrine of candles, bouquets, and buckets of Kentucky Fried Chicken had been created on the steps around a pair of well-worn, tar-covered work boots, a construction hard hat, and a framed photograph of a big, barrel-chested man with a broad smile. Not what I'd call a Satanic altar.

"What is this?" Monk asked.

"It's a memorial service," I said.

A man near us turned, clearly having overheard us. He was deeply tanned, and his clothes were covered in a fine layer of dirt and tar, but I could still read the name on his patch: Lenny.

"It's for a buddy of ours. PJ Starks. We all worked together laying down highway."

Score one for my brilliant deductive abilities.

"What happened to him?" I asked.

Lenny shrugged. "He got high two nights ago and wandered barefoot out onto the dark highway. Ended up as roadkill. A hit-and-run in the middle of the night. We found him when we went out to work in the morning."

Monk leaned over and whispered to me, "Let that be a warning to you about your love of the evil weed."

I ignored the comment. "What are the buckets of fried chicken for?"

"It was PJ's favorite meal. He'd eat a bucket by himself for a light snack. Two with fixin's if it was a meal."

Monk leaned close to me again and whispered, "He wouldn't have lived much longer anyway."

I elbowed him hard. Monk let out a little yelp. "We're sorry for your loss."

Lenny nodded. "Those are going to be hard boots to fill."

We turned to head back to the Newtons' motor home when we saw that the Newtons were standing right behind us, close enough to have overheard the conversation.

"Please excuse us for intruding," Rodney said, "but whenever you're done here, you're welcome to wander over to our RV. We're watching *Avatar* outside and we've got an endless supply of popcorn. We'd be pleased to have you join us and take your mind off your troubles."

One of the other men spoke up. "Are you the guy in the Windermere Superlative?"

"Yes, sir," Rodney said. "That's us."

"That rig is so cool. PJ would have loved it," the man said and started to blubber.

"You bet your ass we'll be there," said Lenny. "Because PJ would've been the first person at your door to welcome you to camp, a bucket of chicken in each arm, a big grin on his face."

"Just so he could get a peek inside your rig," another man said.

"And then he never would've left," yet another man said. "You'd have had to adopt him!"

All the construction workers shared a hearty, knowing laugh at the memory of their friend. The warm, spirited laughter seemed to end the memorial service on an upbeat note. We moved to the Newtons' RV en masse, the construction workers dragging lawn chairs and benches along with them.

Despite all the extra seating, Monk and I decided to give up our chairs and watch the movie from inside our motor home with Ambrose instead.

It was actually much better that way. I folded down the dinette, made the bed, and curled up in my sleeping bag between Ambrose and Monk. They were so entranced by the movie, I don't think they even noticed that my shoulders were against them both.

Or how happy and safe I felt.

I was in the way-back of my dad's station wagon once again, watching a movie at the drive-in with my friends.

We left for Las Vegas early the next morning, but not before saying good-bye to the Newtons, who let us keep our 3-D glasses as mementos of our night at the Grand Canyon.

We certainly could have stayed at the Grand Canyon another day or two, but Ambrose felt he'd seen as much as he could from the RV, and he was probably right about that. Besides, he liked the ritual we'd established of going somewhere new each day. And Monk liked rituals, so everybody was happy.

We headed west on I-40, back to Kingman, but since we weren't on Route 66 this time, we weren't covering exactly the same ground again, so it was new to Ambrose.

In Kingman, we gassed up again and took Highway 93 northwest into Las Vegas. The road took us through some craggy mountains and then, much to Ambrose's delight, down to the Colorado River and the Hoover Dam, which we had to cross to reach Nevada on the other side, but not before our RV was inspected by Homeland Security and bomb-sniffing dogs.

Once again, Monk reminded me how lucky I was that he'd thoroughly vacuumed the motor home, removing any trace of marijuana.

As I drove slowly across the dam, Ambrose recited facts about the structure from memory.

"The dam weighs 6,600,000 tons, contains 4,360,000 cubic yards of concrete, and is 726.4 feet tall from the foundation to the roadway we're on," Ambrose said. "There's enough concrete in this dam to pave a highway, sixteen feet wide, from San Francisco to New York, which is 2,906 miles—2,582 miles if you were able to travel in a straight line instead of utilizing existing highways. But you know what the most amazing fact of all is?"

"Those are all even numbers," Monk said.

"Then it must be a very good dam," I said.

"It's my favorite dam," Ambrose said.

"You have favorite dams?" I asked.

"Who doesn't?" he replied.

It was a good thing we'd taken the trip when we did, because driving over the Hoover Dam wasn't going to be possible for much longer. Soon all the vehicular traffic was going to be diverted downriver to the nearly completed Hoover Dam Bypass, an arched bridge that was a breathtaking 820 feet above the river and 1,900 feet across. It was a sight to see in its own right, even uncompleted. The bridge looked similar to the one in Big Sur, but this one was higher, longer, and even more audacious, which was fitting for a structure that would be a companion piece to the Hoover Dam.

The drive into Las Vegas wasn't remarkable, but as the skyline came into view, I was struck by how often and radically the city changed, particularly the Strip, where the construction never seemed to stop. New resorts were constantly being built while old hotels were continuously being remodeled and expanded. Even the street itself was continuously in flux, with new medians, pedestrian overpasses, and traffic-flow schemes.

It had been only a few years since I'd last visited and even longer since I'd lived and worked there as a blackjack dealer, but it was as if the old city had been razed and a new one was built in the interim. Caesars Palace alone had more face-lifts and additions than a Marin County trophy wife.

The Strip is pretty spectacular at night, with all those

lights flashing, pirate ships battling, video screens blazing, and volcanoes erupting against the dark desert skies.

But during the day, it was bleak and tawdry.

The resort towers looked gaudy and overwrought in the sunlight, their massive scale and exaggerated architectural flourishes a blatant cry for attention, like a streetwalker in a halter top, fishnet stockings, and high heels trying desperately to catch a man's eye.

But Ambrose was transfixed, seemingly as awed by the preposterous re-creations of the New York skyline and the Venice canals as he'd been by the Grand Canyon.

Monk directed Ambrose's attention to the Paris Vegas Resort, with its replicas of the Arc de Triomphe, the Paris Opera House, and the Louvre beneath the footings of its half-scale Eiffel Tower.

"I've been to Paris, France, and saw all of that," Monk said. "They have a magnificent sewer system, too."

"The sewer of sewers," Ambrose agreed. "Did they re-create that here, too?"

"Of course not," I said.

"I don't see why they didn't," Monk said. "It's a much more important historical achievement than a tower."

"Because nobody wants to gamble, eat, sleep, or shop in a sewer," I said. "Would you?"

"No, but they could have re-created it for educational purposes. If it wasn't for the sewer system, Paris wouldn't be known as the City of Light. It would be known as the City of Filth."

"The Las Vegas Strip isn't about education, Mr. Monk. It's about thrills and spectacles, come-ons and distractions, fantasy and illusion, entertainment and seduction, anything to get you to lose your self-control, to spend and gamble without thinking."

"I don't see how re-creating the Venice canals does that," Ambrose said.

"Think of the resorts as enormous fishing lures, and you're the fat, happy bass. All they want to do is attract your attention and get you to come inside. And it's hard to resist spending money on something once you're in a casino."

"They won't get me," Ambrose said.

"Or me," Monk said. "But they will probably get her."

I couldn't argue with that.

The only resort on the Strip that welcomed RVs was the iconic T-Rex, with its three hotel towers, designed to look as if they were made of enormous blocks of carved stone, rising over the misty rain forests and spewing volcanoes of prehistoric earth, where monstrous animatronic dinosaurs roamed, battling one another and tumbling into rivers of molten lava from eight to eleven p.m. every weeknight.

The adjacent T-Rex RV Park had a magnificent view of the dinosaur show and the Strip, which Ambrose would surely appreciate once the sun went down.

I left the Monks in the motor home and went into the rocky grotto of the T-Rex lobby, famous for its lights disguised as stalactites, to check us into the RV park.

I thought it was smart of the T-Rex folks to make campers go into the casino to register for a camping spot rather than erect an office outside for check-in. It gave the resort an opportunity to use the grandeur and spectacle of the lobby and main casino to lure campers into gambling or shopping.

It certainly worked with me, as Monk had accurately predicted. To be honest, I didn't fight it much. There's no point in going to Vegas if you don't gamble just a little bit.

So I took a moment to try my luck at one of the slot machines that ringed the edge of the steaming pools of Dinosaur Grotto, where you could lose a buck a pull while watching a very lifelike brontosaurus chew on leaves.

I lost twenty bucks, so I gave up and went over to the blackjack table, where I bought another twenty dollars' worth of chips.

I figured that I had more control over the odds playing blackjack or, at least, the illusion of it. I played a couple of hands, won another twenty bucks, and decided to stop while I was ahead.

In Vegas, breaking even is a win.

I went to the cashier's cage and cashed in everything but one five-dollar chip to take back to Ambrose as a souvenir.

When I got back to the RV, Monk and Ambrose were passing the time with another rousing game of peanuts. I set the five-dollar chip down on the table in front of Ambrose.

"What's this?" he asked.

"Since you'll never gamble, I made a sacrifice and gambled for you. I won that. It's a five-dollar chip from the T-Rex casino."

He picked it up and examined it. "I assume people gamble more readily with token currency instead of cash because it doesn't feel real."

"It also makes it easier for a dealer to keep track of how much money is in play on the table since each denomination is a different color," I said. "But the chips also make great souvenirs. Every casino has their own chips."

"In essence, their own currency," Ambrose said. "These casinos are like countries unto themselves. But what country would ever have created coinage with a snarling Tyrannosaurus rex head as its emblem?"

"Bedrock," I said. Monk and Ambrose both looked blankly at me. "You know, 'a place right out of history'? Where the Flintstones lived? Fred and Barney? Pebbles and Bamm-Bamm?" I got more blank stares. "Never mind."

"Thank you for getting me that chip, Natalie. It was very thoughtful. I've never owned genuine token currency before, unless you count the money in a Monopoly game."

"Should I add the chip to your collection?"

"Please," Ambrose said.

Monk cocked his head. "His collection?"

I opened the drawer in the galley and took out the seashells, the clog key chain, the Little Mermaid figurine, the desert rock, the Snow Cap postcard, and the 3-D glasses I'd collected and placed them all on the table.

"His souvenirs," I said.

Ambrose looked at the items with pleasure, holding them up, one by one, as if they were precious jewels. "I never appreciated souvenirs until now."

"That's because until now you've never gone anywhere or done anything," Monk said.

"That's not true, Mr. Monk," I said. "Ambrose has lots of souvenirs."

"I do?" Ambrose said.

"Souvenirs are tangible things that remind you of the experiences, events, and relationships that make you who you are," I said. "There are some things you don't want to forget, even for a moment."

Monk rolled his shoulders and tipped his head from side to side, as if I was revealing the answer to some great mystery, and that struck me as very odd.

Surely Monk knew what a souvenir was. After all, he'd brought an unused street sweeper's broom back from Paris to remember his trip by (though he reverently kept it wrapped in plastic in his closet).

"You don't just pick them up on trips," I said. "You could say a wedding ring is a kind of souvenir. Or all of those newspapers you've saved for your dad since the day that he abandoned you."

"They reminded me of him," Ambrose said, almost apologetically. "They still do."

"There's nothing wrong with that, Ambrose. It just means that you have feelings."

Ambrose shook his head. "It's not just the newspapers. My whole house is a souvenir. And I live in it. What does that make me?"

"The same as me," I said.

"I'm nothing like you, Natalie. You're outgoing, youthful, adventurous, attractive. You've been married, you've had a child. You've traveled the world and had dozens of jobs," Ambrose said. "I am none of those things. I have done none of those things. We are nothing alike."

I slid onto the bench seat beside Ambrose and took his hand in mine.

"There's no practical reason for me to keep my house. I live alone. Julie is gone. It's too big for me, and the mortgage is more than I can afford. But I bought that house with Mitch. The last night we ever spent together was in that house. I raised our daughter under that roof. Besides Julie, it's the only thing I have left that Mitch and I shared. I will *never* let go of that house. So my house is a souvenir that I live in, just like you do."

Ambrose nodded. "At least you can walk out the door."

I picked up the rock and put it in his hand. "So can you."

"What is this rock for?"

"That is my souvenir of the day Ambrose Monk stepped outside for the first time in thirty years. But you can keep it for me."

I gave him a kiss on the cheek. Ambrose blushed and picked up the casino chip.

"You know what this is?" he said. "My souvenir of this moment."

I smiled and looked across the table at Monk, who'd remained uncharacteristically silent during the conversation, to see his reaction.

I recognized the expression on his face, but it made absolutely no sense in the context of where we were, what we'd said, and what we were doing.

"You've just solved a murder," I said.

"No," Monk said. "I've solved three."

26

Mr. Monk Goes to Yosemite

"But you haven't been investigating any murders," I said as we drove out of Las Vegas a few minutes later, leaving the city and our deposit on the camping spot behind. "I made sure of that."

"Apparently I was and I didn't know it."

I could keep Monk from the crime scenes, and from interviewing suspects and examining clues, but I couldn't stop him from thinking.

"I don't understand why we couldn't spend the night in Las Vegas," Ambrose said. "I wanted to see the dinosaurs fight and fall in the lava. I've never seen that before."

"We can come back," Monk said. "The dinosaurs aren't going anywhere. The murderers are."

"Ah, *murderers*, as in more than one," I said. "And since you insisted we make a beeline for Yosemite, which is seven hours away, I'm guessing you're talking about those three old ladies we met outside of Victorville."

"I didn't say that," Monk said.

"You didn't have to," I said. "I'm not in your league as a detective, but that deduction was easy, even for me. I just find it hard to believe that they're capable of killing anyone."

"Who have they killed?" Ambrose asked.

"The woman on the beach in Santa Cruz, the student in the alley in San Luis Obispo, and the construction worker at the Grand Canyon," Monk replied. "And probably more."

"But the Zarkin sisters couldn't have killed all three of those people. The timing is all wrong," I said. "The women would have had to have been in two states at once, and that's impossible. What evidence do you have that they've killed anyone?"

"None at all," Monk said.

"So why are we leaving Las Vegas," Ambrose said, "depriving me of seeing the city by night, and rushing to Yosemite?"

"To get the evidence that I don't have and to stop the Weird Sisters before they kill anyone else."

"Why don't we just call the police and let them handle it?" Ambrose asked.

I had the answer to that question.

"Because the only cop who'd believe Mr. Monk, without any evidence or explanation, that three old ladies are traveling the country killing people is Captain Stottlemeyer, who doesn't have jurisdiction in Santa Cruz, San Luis Obispo, the Grand Canyon, or Yosemite National Park."

"That doesn't mean we shouldn't call him," Monk said.

"To what end?" I asked.

"So he can marshal the forces in preparation."

"For what?" Ambrose asked.

"The arrest," Monk said. "Those harridans are killers, and I'm going to take them down."

I dutifully called Captain Stottlemeyer and put him on the speaker. He told Monk the same thing that I had, but that he would go ahead and make a fool out of himself anyway and alert the authorities in Santa Cruz, San Luis Obispo, and Arizona of Monk's suspicions.

"It's not a suspicion," Monk said. "It's a fact."

"That you can't prove," Stottlemeyer said.

"Yet," Monk said.

"That's a big stumbling block when it comes to getting cops to arrest people, particularly three old ladies," Stottlemeyer said, and then pointed out that there was no guarantee the women would actually be in Yosemite. They could have changed their plans.

So Monk gave Stottlemeyer the names of the Zarkin sisters and the license plate number of their RV so the captain could try and track their movements through credit card use, traffic citations, and any other applicable databases.

"You memorized their license plate number?" Stottlemeyer said. "Was this before or after you suspected them of being killers?"

"Before," Monk said.

"Then why did you memorize it?" Stottlemeyer asked.

"Because I saw it," Monk said.

"You don't have to memorize every license plate that you see."

"It's instinctive and automatic," Monk said. "You have no control over it."

"Oh, really? I couldn't tell you my license plate number," Stottlemeyer said.

Monk recited it to him. "That's for your police department sedan. Would you like to know the license plate number of your personal car?"

"No," Stottlemeyer said.

Monk told him anyway, then informed him of which states the women had visited, a fact he'd gleaned from the diagram of the United States on the back of their motor home.

"I'm betting you'll find unsolved murders in all of those states," Monk said.

"Of course I will, Monk," Stottlemeyer said. "Every state has unsolved murders. That's a given. What's not is that these old ladies are responsible for any of them."

"They make marijuana brownies," Monk said. "And they eat them while listening to funky music."

"What does that have to do with anything?" I asked.

"That's how it starts," Monk said. "One day you're a drug fiend eating marijuana brownies and the next day you're an ax murderer. It's the logical conclusion."

Stottlemeyer got off the phone to make his other calls and we continued with our journey.

We spent the next six hours plodding north on Highway 95 across the bleak and dry Pahute Mesa before hitting Highway 6 at Tonopah, a sun-bleached and eerily vacant old mining town, and heading west.

It was while I was filling the tank at a gas station in Lee Vining, the last town before the fifty-mile drive and ten-thousand-foot climb up Tioga Pass and into Yosemite, that Stottlemeyer called me back to notify us that the Zarkin sisters had arrived in the park that afternoon. Their license plate number was registered by the park rangers when they signed up for a camping space.

I got the name of the campgrounds and asked the captain whether he'd alerted the park police about the women.

"And what would I tell them, exactly?" he said. "I

know Monk, they don't. They have no reason to believe
his story or keep an eye on three senior citizens in a motor home."

"But you do," I said.

"That's why I'm calling you from my car. I'm on my
way. But it's at least a four-hour drive from San Francisco to Yosemite. Do you think you can keep Monk
from charging anybody with murder before I get there?"

"Nope," I said.

"I didn't think so. You could puncture the tires of
your RV and spend the night wherever you are."

"I could, but if Mr. Monk is right, and they are murderers, what's to stop them from killing another person
tonight?"

He sighed. "Be careful."

I promised him that I would be and I got us back on
the road.

I'm sure Ambrose would have been astonished by
Yosemite, with its incredible views of waterfalls spilling
over massive granite cliffs into forests of giant sequoias
and black oaks. But by the time we got there, it was too
dark for us to see any of it. All we saw was the narrow,
winding strip of asphalt in front of us, my headlights
barely piercing the depths of the pitch-black night created by the dense forest. I felt like I was on the bottom of the Pacific Ocean driving through the Mariana
Trench.

But I managed to find my way to the campground,
nestled deep in the woods on a rise above a river. I registered us with the loopy park attendant who stood in the
window of the small trailer that served as the front gate.

The attendant looked like Smokey the Bear, only
with more hair, and had a drowsy grin on his face, as if
he was amused but couldn't muster the energy to laugh.

As we drove in, I spotted the Zarkins' distinct motor

home, with the map of the United States on the back, parked to my left, at one end of the camp and overlooking the river.

"Look who else is here," Monk said, and gestured out the passenger window. On the opposite side of the park, also at the edge of the rise, was Dub Clemens' motor home, which I recognized from the collage of faded and peeling bumper stickers from all the places he'd been.

"I take it that it's not a coincidence that they're both here," Ambrose said.

"Nope," Monk said.

"You don't seem surprised."

"I'm not," Monk said. "And I'm sure that none of them are surprised to see us here, either."

That's when I remembered my encounter with Yuki, Dub's assistant, on the beach. I told her that she didn't know anything about us. Her reply, and her enigmatic smile, was unsettling then and even more so now:

I know everything.

I got us parked, facing the river, in a spot smack between the Zarkins and Dub.

There was no shore power or utilities for us to plug into. We would be self-sufficient, which wasn't exactly a hardship. We had food, water, and everything else we needed except, perhaps, a way to contact the outside world. There was no cellular service in the park.

As soon as the motor home leveled itself, Monk got up and headed for the door. I blocked his path.

"Where are you going?"

"To expose the harridans, of course," Monk said.

"Wait a minute," I said. "You can't just march over to their motor home, knock on the door, and accuse them of being serial killers."

"Why not?"

"Because they might shoot you in the face."

"I don't think so," Monk said. "They'd never make it out of the park."

"They could kill you in some other, more insidious way," Ambrose said.

"Better me than someone else," Monk said. "That way I won't feel the guilt."

"You won't feel anything," I said.

"This is a very bad idea," Ambrose said. "They could kill us all."

"We're talking about three old ladies," Monk said.

"Who you say are serial killers," Ambrose said.

"Their victims didn't know those wicked old crones were killers until they killed them," Monk said. "We do. We are prepared. If they make a move on us, we can take them."

"I could live without getting into a brawl with three old ladies," I said.

"Trust me, Natalie, it won't come to that." Monk moved past me and walked out the door. "Let's go. Justice can't be delayed."

Which really meant, of course, that he couldn't possibly wait another second to face the killers and dazzle them with his brilliance. But I couldn't really blame him, even if it was a stupid thing for him to do.

That's because Monk's summation was the one moment in his life when the world was in perfect balance, everything fit, and he was in complete control. There was no way he could deny himself that balance, not when it was so close. Nor could I.

"Lock the door, Ambrose," I said, and dutifully followed my boss.

27

Mr. Monk Finds His Balance

Despite my many misgivings about what we were about to do, I had to admire the confidence and sense of purpose in the way Monk marched across the park to the Zarkins' motor home. He was in utter command of himself and, it seemed, the world around him.

He reminded me of a scene in *Patton* where the general storms outside into the open during an air raid and doesn't take cover, not even when machine gun bullets are raking the ground all around him. Patton just stands there, angry and defiant and immortal, shooting at the planes with his pistol.

What Patton did was insane, but there was something admirable and heroic about his lunacy. That night, I could say the same about Adrian Monk. And I was following him into the open field, without cover, just like the good soldier that I was.

When I saw the huge, mud-caked boots again on the steps of the Zarkins' motor home, I could vividly picture the big man who'd worn them. He wasn't a drunken, tattooed, neo-Nazi, devil-worshipping, ex-convict monster. He was a man with a broad smile on his face and two buckets of Kentucky Fried Chicken in his arms. Now I wanted to confront those old hags as badly as Monk did.

I looked at Monk. He looked at me.

"Let's take 'em down," I said.

Monk nodded and pounded on the door. Bessie opened it with the same sweet smile on her face that she'd had the first time she'd greeted us.

"Why, hello there. What a delight to see you both again," she said. "Won't you come in?"

I hesitated, but Monk bounded right in. "Sorry for arriving earlier than you expected."

Gertie and Mabel were standing in the galley. Gertie was glaring at us, her arms crossed. Mabel seemed dazed, unwilling to look either one of us in the eye. But Bessie was all smiles.

"I'm afraid we're fresh out of brownies to offer you," Bessie said.

"You didn't even save some for your son?" Monk said. "Or is he still having engine troubles with his truck?"

That's when I remembered that Bessie had mentioned her son when we'd first met: *He's out on the road, jamming gears on an eighteen-wheeler like his dad used to.*

That's how they could be in two places at once. The old ladies did the killings in California while Bessie's son murdered the construction worker in Arizona . . . and then tried to kill us on Route 66.

"My God," I said. "You're a family of murderers."

"And they collect souvenirs from their kills," Monk said, motioning to the display case. "Bessie's son brought the boots out to them in Victorville to add to their collection, which, as you can see, includes sand dollars from Santa Cruz and gumballs from San Luis Obispo."

"Aren't you the clever one," Bessie said.

"He's not clever," Gertie said. "He's just irritating."

I walked up to the display case. There were dozens of knickknacks in there. If each one represented a kill, then these little old ladies and their son were responsible for a shocking number of murders all across the country.

"This is how you stay young, by killing people?" I said.

"It's thrilling," Bessie said. "The adrenaline keeps your heart pumping and your nerves firing."

"There are other ways you can get that without killing people," I said.

"Spoken like someone who has never done it," Gertie said. "Nothing packs the same wallop."

"I killed a man once," I said. "In self-defense. I didn't enjoy it."

"Like sex, the first time is never much fun," Gertie said. "But it gets much better with practice."

"How many years have you been doing this?"

Mabel shrugged. "I've lost track. But when you get to be our age, you start forgetting lots of things."

"You remembered enough to have a guilty conscience," Monk said. "And that's what led you to make your big mistake. When we told you where we'd been, and that I was homicide consultant to the San Francisco police, you wrongly assumed that we stopped by to say hello because were onto your murder spree and wanted to engage you in a cunning game of cat and mouse."

Now it all made sense to me. They'd misinterpreted everything we'd said that night, reading hidden meanings into our words that existed only in their minds.

"So when I told you we were going to the Grand

Canyon, you thought we knew what Bessie's son was doing, too," I said. "That's why you sent him to kill us."

"But you did," Mabel said. "You knew all about him."

"No, we didn't," I said.

"You mean you *guessed* that he was a drunken, tattooed, neo-Nazi ex-convict?" Bessie said.

Wow, I thought, *I am good.*

"So you're saying that he's not a devil worshipper, too?" I said.

"Of course not," Mabel said. "Shame on you."

"Now you're just trying to piss us off," Gertie said.

They may not have been devil worshippers, but these women and their lovely son were worse than any of the bad guys in *Race with the Devil*.

It wouldn't have surprised me one bit if they had a cauldron in the back of their motor home and black, pointy hats.

"Sending him after us was your big mistake," Monk said. "I would never have stopped wondering why that trucker was so intent on killing us or how he knew where we were going to be. I would have figured it out. I always do. But, to be fair, I might not have put everything together so soon if we hadn't heard about the barefoot construction worker getting killed in a hit-and-run."

"And saw his other pair of boots," I added.

"This all makes for a nice campfire story to scare the kiddies with," Gertie said, "but that's all it is. You can't prove anything."

"We can prove enough," Monk said. "And I know how we can prove the rest."

"Good luck with that," Gertie said, and showed us to the door.

"Your days of killing are over," Monk said. "Tomorrow you're retiring to prison. Sweet dreams."

Monk walked out and I followed, backing out, so I

could keep my eyes on the old hags in case one of them decided to come after us with a meat cleaver.

Gertie slammed the door behind us.

"That felt good," Monk said as we walked away.

"I'm glad you enjoyed it, but I'm not sure what you accomplished besides letting them know that we are onto them."

"They already knew that," Monk said, "or thought they did."

"Now they can start covering their tracks."

"They could have started yesterday, but they didn't. They thought their son would do that for them. And they can't do much about that now."

"They can ditch those souvenirs," I said.

"They won't. They mean too much to them. Besides, tossing them out here wouldn't do them much good. All we have to do now is keep our eye on them until Captain Stottlemeyer gets here in a few hours."

"I'm not sure we can wait that long," I said.

"They know they are finished," Monk said. "They are resigned to their fate."

"They don't strike me as people who resign," I said. "They strike me as people who kill."

"Those days are over now," Monk said. "Weren't you paying attention to the conversation?"

"What did you mean when you said you didn't have all the proof but you knew where we could get the rest?"

"I'll show you," he said.

Monk led me past our motor home, waving at Ambrose in the window to let him know that everything was fine, and continued on to Dub's RV.

Yuki opened the door as we approached.

"You're just in time. Dub has just finished preparing our martinis," she said, then smiled at Monk. "And one refreshing glass of Fiji bottled water for you."

We stepped in, and Dub stood up to greet us from the captain's chair he'd been sitting in, the oxygen tank at his side. "Greetings, my friends. What news do you have from the road?"

He barely got the words out before he lapsed into a brutal coughing jag that doubled him over. Yuki put her arm around his shoulder and lowered him back into his seat, gently stroking his back and comforting him until he caught his breath again.

Monk crouched in front of him and looked him in the eye. "I've got the ending to the story that you've been chasing. It's all over, Dub."

"Oh, thank God." He wheezed, his eyes bright despite his deathly pallor.

"I'm lost," I said.

"Dub is a reporter," Monk said.

"Yes, I know that," I said.

"The story he's been investigating is a string of unsolved killings across the country," Monk said. "He believed that they were connected and although he couldn't convince anybody that he was right, he has been doggedly following the trail for years. But it wasn't until the last week that he'd finally zeroed in on the killer and was only a few days behind."

"How did you figure that out?" I asked.

"His bumper stickers," Monk said. "They are from the same states that are colored red on the back of the Zarkin motor home."

"Dub knew he was on the right track when he saw that the famous detective Adrian Monk was on the same trail, too," Yuki said.

So Dub had made the same mistaken assumption that the old women had. They all thought Monk was on the case. The only people who didn't think so were Monk and me.

I looked at Dub. "Why didn't you tell us what you were doing two days ago?"

Yuki put her hand on Dub's, signaling him to relax and that she would answer my question.

"Dub wanted to find the killer himself. It was going to be his last, big story. The evidence is all there." She gestured to the file boxes in his bedroom, and I saw the gun beneath his bed. "Dub knew he was getting close, but he was afraid he'd die before he found him. If that happened, I was to take all the evidence to you. But it didn't. Dub got his man."

"He's here." Dub started coughing again. Each cough was deep and sharp, stabbing him in the chest like a butcher knife.

"*They're* here," Monk said. "It's not just one killer. It's four. Three old women traveling in a motor home and one of their sons, who drives a big rig."

Dub's eyes went wide. "No, no. *He's* here."

I felt a sudden chill.

"The truck," I said. "Are you saying that it's here, in the camp?"

"It's parked back in the trees," Yuki said, "at the far end of the grounds. He arrived a few hours ago."

I had a bad, bad feeling about this.

"Stay here," I said, and went for the door.

"Where are you going?" Monk asked.

"There's got to be a phone or a radio in the front office," I said. "I'm calling the park rangers."

I ran out of Dub's trailer and across the dark campgrounds to the small trailer at the front gate. I peered in the window. The attendant was asleep at his desk, his face in an empty cake pan.

I opened the trailer door, rushed inside, and tried to shake him awake. But he was out cold.

That's when I saw the chocolate crumbs on the plate

and understood why he'd had that silly grin on his face before.

He was high.

From the brownies the Zarkins had given him.

I looked for his radio, knowing with dread what I'd discover when I found it.

The radio was on a shelf above the desk.

And my worst fears were confirmed. It was dead, the wires ripped from the back of the unit.

There was only one reason they'd drug the attendant and disable the only means of communication out of the camp.

They didn't want us to be able to call for help.

And that could mean only one thing.

I bolted from the cabin and was running back across the grounds to Dub's RV when I heard the diesel growl of the engine and saw the headlights flash on, like a monster awakening and opening its eyes.

I looked over my shoulder just as the truck burst out of the trees in an explosion of leaves and dirt.

And it was coming for me.

I dove out of the way, and the truck rumbled past, so close I could smell the hot rubber on the tires. But instead of coming back around, the truck kept on going, horn bellowing with rage, hell-bent on snaring its prey.

Our motor home.

I scrambled back to my feet, yelling Ambrose's name and running toward our RV, but my cries were drowned out by the wail of the truck's horn and the roar of its engine.

Ambrose heard it, too. He stood in the open doorway of our motor home, terrified of what was coming, but more terrified of stepping out.

"Jump!" I screamed, still running. "Jump!"

But I knew that Ambrose couldn't and wouldn't, and

that the truck would smash into the motor home, obliterating it and sending the pieces into the river below.

I kept on running and screaming even though I knew it was futile, that there was no way I could stop the nightmare that was unfolding in front of me.

The truck charged ahead, only seconds away from impact, when there were three earsplitting gunshots in rapid succession.

A tire blew, the windshield shattered, and the truck veered away from our motor home and kept on going like a runaway train, broadsiding the Zarkins' RV and blasting through it like it was made of Styrofoam, the momentum propelling both vehicles into the river below.

I turned and saw Monk standing outside Dub's trailer in a firing stance, backlit by the light in the window, the smoking .357 Magnum still aimed in his hands.

He could've been Dirty Harry, if Harry wasn't dirty.

Monk slowly relaxed his stance and rolled his shoulders before dropping the gun. He held his hands out to me as I approached him.

"I need a wipe," he said.

No, he definitely wasn't Dirty Harry.

He was Clean Adrian.

28

Mr. Monk Goes Home

Captain Stottlemeyer and Lieutenant Devlin arrived just as the four body bags were being carried up from the river to the morgue wagons. The campground was illuminated by portable lights that drew thousands of bugs that were bedeviling the police officers, forest rangers, and forensic investigators who were everywhere.

I sat in our motor home with Ambrose and Monk, but I would rather have been with Dub and Yuki, sipping my third martini. After what I'd been through, I needed something stronger than Fiji water.

Stottlemeyer and Devlin approached our RV, stopped for a moment to take note of the forensics team that was photographing the dents and scrapes and taking samples, and then came inside.

"Hello, Captain," Monk said. "Thanks for coming all this way."

"I see I arrived late for the party," Stottlemeyer said, and then introduced Lieutenant Devlin to Ambrose and vice versa. "It looks like a tornado touched down here."

"I'm really, really sorry about the mess," Monk said. "I wanted to help clean up, but they wouldn't let me."

"Next time, you might want to wait until some cops are around before you confront a murderer," Stottlemeyer said, "especially if there is more than one of them."

"You think there will be a next time?" Devlin asked.

"Without question," Stottlemeyer said.

"C'mon, Captain," Devlin said. "This is just a freak occurrence. What are the odds that Monk will stumble across another killer during a vacation?"

"In Monk's case, I'd reverse the question," I said. "What are the odds of him *not* stumbling across a killer on his vacation. It happened before in Napa, Hawaii, Germany, and France."

"And you still went on vacation with him?" Devlin said.

"It could happen going to the grocery store with him," Stottlemeyer said.

"It has," I said.

"But the fact remains, Monk, that you stopped a family of serial killers that has been murdering people for years, across the United States, without anybody noticing," Stottlemeyer said. "That's a hell of a thing you did."

Monk shook his head. "You're congratulating the wrong man. Dub Clemens is the hero. He realized what was going on long before anyone else and didn't give up. He's accumulated the evidence that will bring closure to a lot of grieving families nationwide."

Stottlemeyer nodded. "We're going to go talk to the authorities, see what we can do to smooth things out so you can go on your way again tomorrow."

"Thanks, Captain, we appreciate that," I said. "Do you like martinis?"

"Love 'em," he said.

"Go introduce yourself to Dub Clemens before you go," I said. "You won't be sorry."

"I'll do that," he said and walked out with Devlin.

Monk turned to Ambrose. "I'm sorry for ruining the trip."

"Are you kidding? I'm proud of you, Adrian. The captain was right. You did a wonderful thing here tonight. Two wonderful things."

"What was the second?" Monk asked.

"You saved me," Ambrose said.

We spent three more days on the road and managed to visit Lake Tahoe and Sacramento without coming across any more corpses or deranged killers. That was a real achievement for Monk.

We returned to Tewksbury late in the day, backing the motor home into Ambrose's driveway and getting as close to the house as we could get without parking in the living room.

Much to our surprise, Ambrose made it from the motor home to his front door without too much drama, though he practically dove into the house as if it was a life raft.

Over the next half hour, we brought in all of Ambrose's belongings that we'd packed into the motor home. The last thing I brought inside was a shopping bag containing his collection of souvenirs, which had expanded a bit over the last few days.

He took the bag from us and smiled. "Thank you for the best birthday present I've ever had. I can honestly say that it's an experience that has changed my life."

"I've been dreading the end of this trip," Monk said.

"Really?" I said. "You enjoyed it that much?"

"No, I'm afraid what the damage to the motor home is going to cost me when we return it," Monk said. "You might have to take a significant pay cut."

"Don't worry about it," Ambrose said. "You can just leave it here."

"Abandoning it and running away is a nice thought," Monk said, "but eventually, the rental company is going to want it back and will come looking for it."

"No, they won't," Ambrose said. "While you were unloading the RV, I called the rental company and agreed to buy it from them. They are bringing over the papers for me to sign tomorrow."

Monk and I were totally dumbfounded.

"Why did you do that?" Monk said.

"I'm keeping it as a souvenir," Ambrose said.

"That's an expensive keepsake," I said.

"I've been saving my money for years," Ambrose said. "It's about time I spent it on something."

"You're just going to leave it parked in the driveway like that, all dented and scratched up, as a memento?" Monk said. "What will the neighbors say?"

"I'm going to fix it up like new," Ambrose said. "So it will be in perfect shape for my next road trip."

I felt a pang of anxiety. It was one thing to take Ambrose on the road as a special occasion, but I certainly didn't want to make a habit of it.

My misgivings must have shown on my face, because Ambrose looked at me and smiled.

"Don't worry, Natalie, I don't expect you to be my driver," he said. "Or you, either, Adrian, though you are both welcome to join us."

"Us?" I said.

Ambrose's smile widened. "I've made other arrangements. I spoke to Yuki before we left Yosemite. When Dub passes, Yuki is coming to work for me."

"You've hired an assistant?" Monk said. "What do you need one for?"

"The same reason you do," Ambrose said. "So I can have a life."

I couldn't resist the opportunity that comment gave me to tease Monk. "Is that what I have done for you, Mr. Monk?"

"On the contrary," Monk said, turning and heading for my car, "it's what I have done for you."

I gave Ambrose a good-bye kiss on the cheek and hurried after Monk. "I had a life."

"You were a single mother working in a dive bar being groped by perverts and being vomited on by drunks," he said. "I saved you."

"You were afraid to leave the house because you didn't think that you could carry enough disinfectant wipes with you, that you'd run out, become infected with bubonic plague, and die 'a miserable, drooling death.' I saved you."

We stopped at my car.

"Okay," Monk said, "let's call it a draw."

"So you're saying that we saved each other."

He shrugged. "If that's what makes you happy."

"It certainly does," I said.

Don't miss another exciting book
in the *Monk* series

MR. MONK ON THE COUCH

Available in hardcover in June 2011 from Obsidian.

There is never a day off from death.

I was sitting at my kitchen table in my bathrobe and slippers, eating a cream cheese–slathered bagel for breakfast and reading the massive Sunday editions of the *San Francisco Chronicle* and the *New York Times* when I got a phone call from Captain Leland Stottlemeyer of the San Francisco Police Department, notifying me of a homicide.

I'm not a cop, but I'm on call 24/7 for the police department anyway. That's because I'm the personal assistant, driver, secretary, shopper, and all-around beast of burden for Adrian Monk, the brilliant detective and the SFPD's only paid consultant (though he isn't paid nearly enough for one person, let alone two, if you ask me).

I'd received well over a hundred such calls from Captain Stottlemeyer over the years, so starting my day with a corpse was as routine for me as a breakfast bagel.

There was a time when seeing the dead really bothered me. It wasn't so much the bloodshed as it was my firsthand knowledge of the grief and lasting heartache the victim's loved ones would soon experience. Each murder reminded me of what it felt like when I learned that my husband had been shot down over Kosovo.

I also felt like an intruder, not on the death, but on the crime scene.

I didn't belong there. I was extraneous, irrelevant, a tourist.

Even worse, I was unskilled, untrained, unofficial, and uninterested.

I was useless to anyone but Adrian Monk, and even then my duties were minimal. My job was to make sure nothing distracted him (and he could be distracted by something as innocuous as a stain on someone's tie or the creak of a loose floorboard) and to supply him with disinfectant wipes (which he needed constantly).

But as time went on, and I got caught up in the investigations, all of that changed.

I learned how to read a crime scene, how to process evidence, and how to question witnesses and suspects.

I also picked up some deductive skills and crime-solving instincts of my own, enough that I not only felt comfortable at a crime scene, but entitled to share my thoughts on a case if I had any and expect them to be taken seriously.

I wasn't just a reluctant observer anymore.

I began to *like* participating at crime scenes.

I looked forward to the puzzle, to the challenge of solving a crime, and the satisfaction of learning the solution, something Monk always discovered, even when it seemed like an impossible feat.

But the biggest change in my attitude toward homicide was more recent and profound, arising out of my experiences on Monk's last few big cases.

I'd begun to think of myself as a pretty good detective in my own right, not that I'd shared that opinion with anyone else yet. I'd barely admitted it to myself.

Being a detective was certainly not something I'd ever aspired to or a field that I had any interest in (beyond my childhood desire to be one of *Charlie's Angels*, but that had more to do with their clothes, their independence and their sassy attitudes). Becoming interested in detecting myself evolved slowly and unconsciously out of my relationship with Monk and, to a lesser degree, with Captain Stottlemeyer and his former lieutenant, Randy Disher, who'd recently left the department to become the police chief in Summit, New Jersey.

But it had happened, and now I was eager to somehow put myself to the test, which I knew wouldn't be easy, or perhaps even possible, with Adrian Monk around. His powers of observation and deduction are as astounding as they are irritating, so much so that he often solves cases within minutes of arriving at a crime scene. It didn't leave much room for anyone else to shine, much less a novice like me.

Monk has an uncanny ability to spot the slightest thing—whether it's an object, behavior or event—that's uneven, odd, lopsided, or out of place, and when it comes to homicide investigation, that's usually the piece that solves the crime.

He's able to spot that telling detail because he obsesses over little things that are invisible to most of us. We don't see them because they are ridiculously mundane or irrelevant, except when they are not, which is any time there's a dead body involved.

It's a personality quirk that works great for Monk when it comes to solving crimes but not so well when it comes to functioning in normal society.

That's mostly where I came in. I facilitated his interaction with others and with his environment.

In other words, I tried to keep people from driving him crazy and vice versa while, at the same time, trying to hold on to my own sanity.

But it wasn't enough for me anymore just to stand there, straightening things and handing out wipes.

After getting Stottlemeyer's call that Sunday morning, I quickly dressed in a T-shirt, a v-neck pull-over and jeans, hurried out of my little Victorian house in the Noe Valley area of the city and drove north to Pine Street, where Adrian Monk lived in an even-numbered, second-floor apartment that measured exactly eight hundred square feet in an art deco building with four floors.

When I arrived, he was in the kitchen, in the middle of his Sunday morning ritual of cleaning his cleaning supplies.

There was a time, not so long ago, when I found it odd to see him spraying a can of Lysol with a can of Lysol, but not anymore.

It's amazing what you can become accustomed to.

Monk was wearing a white apron and yellow rubber dish gloves and was happily humming one of his favorite songs: Tommy Tutone's 1982 annoying hit, "867-5309," aka "Jenny." He liked the song because the phone number adds up to thirty-eight, an even number, and it was released in an even-numbered year, and it hit #4, also an even number, on the Billboard charts.

"Just give me a moment to finish up," Monk said, buffing the can of Lysol until it gleamed.

"It's Sunday morning, I'm double-parked out front and there's a bunch of cops and crime scene investigators waiting on us who've locked down an entire block in the Marina District. But there's no hurry."

My sarcasm was wasted on Monk, who didn't understand it and wouldn't have cared even if he did. I knew that but it didn't stop me from indulging myself anyway.

"When was the last time you cleaned your cleaning supplies?" he asked.

"Um, let me think." I looked at my feet as I pretended to ponder the question; then after a long moment, I raised my head. "Never."

"You've *never* cleaned your cleansers?"

"They're cleansers, Mr. Monk. How much cleaner can they get?"

"Do you clean your vacuum?"

"I empty the bag."

"That's not the same thing," he said. "Do you clean your broom?"

"When my broom gets dirty, I throw it out and buy a new one."

I thought he'd appreciate that. But he didn't.

"It gets dirty every time you sweep."

"I'm talking about when it gets really dirty."

"That is when it gets really dirty. When was the last time you threw out a broom?"

I had to think about that for a moment. He grimaced and looked up to the heavens. "Oh, dear God. She has to think about it."

"A year or two," I said.

Monk marched over to his huge utility closet and took out one of his many brooms, the brush wrapped in plastic. He held it out to me. "I want you to have this."

"I have a broom," I said.

"Cleaning your home with filthy equipment is like washing your hands with dung. It's a miracle you're still alive." He thrust the broom out at me again. "In the name of all that's holy, take the broom."

I took it just to shut him up. "Thank you. Can we go now?"

He put his cleansers in a rubber box, placed it on a shelf in his utility closet, then took off his apron and neatly folded it.

"Promise me that you'll throw out your old broom the instant you get home."

"I'll throw it out."

"In an incinerator," he said.

"I don't have an incinerator."

"You, of all people, should get one." He went down the hall and got his coat.

I followed him. "*You* don't have one."

"Because I'm careful to keep myself and my belongings free from dirt and disease," he said and held the front door open for me. "You wallow in it."

I walked past him outside. "Then I must have a terrific immune system."

"You're being selfish," Monk said, closing the door and locking it behind him. "You aren't considering the danger your filthy conduct poses to the people around you."

"You mean yourself."

"Of course I do," he said, as we walked side by side to my car.

"You don't think *that's* selfish?"

"I represent all of humanity," Monk said.

"How do you know?"

"Because there are only two of us in this conversation," Monk said. "And humanity wouldn't pick the filthy one."

Obsessive.
Compulsive.
Detective.

MONK

The mystery series starring the brilliant, beloved,
and slightly off-beat sleuth from the
USA Network's hit show!

by Lee Goldberg

Available wherever books are sold or at
penguin.com

OM0011